WITH THESE HANDS

KRISTY ROLAND

WITH THESE HANDS

Written and published by Kristy Roland

ISBN-13: 9781495985713
ISBN-10: 1495985717

To my husband and children:

Thank you.

Author's Notes:

If you are familiar with the Atlanta area and surrounding counties in Georgia, you will notice that I have taken great liberties in describing these areas. It was done in an intentional manner to fit the story as needed. All representations in police procedures may have been altered for the story.

Power is of two kinds. One is obtained by fear of punishment and the other by acts of love. Power based on love is a thousand times more effective and permanent than the one derived from fear of punishment.

Mahatma Gandhi

Part One

Chapter One

People become who they need to be in order to adapt. Everyone carries with them a sense of duplicity to use at their own game in life. Creating a persona was only as difficult as the lies he couldn't keep up with. Although he was one person, well aware of his actions, his duplicity was strong when he put the effort into the plan. People around him fell into the illusion without failing him. His mother always said he had charm.

As far as duplicity... his daughter created her own.

"We'll miss you, Mama," Joni said, and jumped into the back seat of the Cadillac.

"Don't forget your seatbelt," Roslyn hollered from the front porch of their two-story brick house.

Lyle Chaskey didn't give a second thought to his wife.

"I really won't miss her," Joni said. Guess that made two of them.

"Don't be disrespectful so close to home," he warned with a smile.

"Daddy, do you think it's better to be honest even if it hurts her feelings, or lie and be safe?" Such a smart girl for only ten years old.

They were out of their subdivision when he gave her another life lesson. "It doesn't matter. You have to create your own rules and stick to them."

"What's that mean?"

"Always go with your intuition."

"Right," she said. "Where are we going, Daddy?" Joni climbed over the front seat and quickly snapped the seatbelt in place. According to Roslyn, Joni wasn't allowed to sit in the front seat, but Lyle wouldn't tell. Every Sunday was their special time together, and he looked forward to being with her. As a family they went to church together, ate lunch some place nice, then he and Joni would take off somewhere. Their map was folded away in the Cadillac's glove box, and she pulled it out and asked again, "Where are we going, Daddy?"

"It's not where we're going that matters, it's how you feel when you get there."

He looked over at his daughter, her crooked blonde pigtails, map in hand, an eager look on her face because the map was her responsibility for every one of their little expeditions. Atlanta was circled on the map because that was always their focal point. It was the only city circled on the map. "We're going south of Atlanta." Minutes later, they were out of Kennesaw and traveling south on Interstate 75. Pointing at the map, he said, "Down here."

"Then just follow the fat red line."

Her eyes widened as they passed through the city, just like they did every Sunday except the city was getting ready for the summer Olympics, and Joni was mesmerized. Thankfully, the road construction was over. She giggled at some billboard signs, and then they had a fifteen-minute conversation about how people got into the Olympics.

"You have to find something you really love and be the best at it."

"I'm Amanda's best friend."

"Then you should get a gold medal."

"And when I grow up, I'm going to get a gold medal in all the Olympics. I'm good at running and playing chase. And cooking with Mama." Joni folded the worn map into a small square that showed the southern parts of Atlanta.

"How's school going?" Lyle asked.

She sighed. "Amanda gets mad because this other girl wants to be my friend, but when I play with Amanda, I always have to act like I know what she's talking about."

2

Learning to be who she needed to be. Even from a young age, a person had to make decisions, and Joni was great at being adaptable. Talk about duplicity. His kid could have won the Olympics for being adaptable. People never held up to the expectations Lyle set for them. His mother let him down his entire life. Joni was the exception. She surprised him every day, and still, he had so much to teach her.

Lyle reached under his seat and pulled out a gift for his daughter. When she saw the little blue elephant beanie baby, she nearly jumped out of her seat. "Thank you, Daddy. I wanted this one so bad."

Joni hugged that thing the whole drive to Fayetteville, which took less than an hour. The easiest towns were the ones with small populations, and even though he knew Fayette County was highly populated, it was still full of hidden places. Like trying to find the perfect hiding place when he was a kid. Sure, he was always found, but wasn't it the thrill of being so clever that mattered?

Starr's Mill was an old corn mill on the south side of Fayette County that had been built in a bend off of Whitewater Creek. Lyle turned down the small road and made his way to what looked like a red barn next to a small waterfall.

The air was hot and sticky, smelled of pine needles and algae water. The beanie baby was sticking out of Joni's back pocket as she ran to the creek to catch a frog she spotted. She carefully watched the water, but when her attempts at catching it failed, she ran toward the mill. As he kept a close eye on her, he surveyed the land. A two-lane highway ran along the east side, a stretch of woods along the north. A few houses were spread out and the place sat behind a small church. He wondered how quiet it was out here at night and followed Joni to the other side of the mill. She was too close to the water, but he let her be. Sometimes people had to figure things out on their own. A few people were in the water fishing and Lyle didn't want to draw attention to

3

himself or his daughter. When Joni became tangled in some nearby thorn bushes and began to cry, he said, "You got yourself in there. How are you going to get out?" She struggled against the vines until her hair tangled in the sticks.

"Ouch, Daddy, help me."

Scratches covered her thin legs, and Lyle moved branches out of her way and grabbed at the vines to free her. Once he lifted her out, she wiped her eyes. The scratches weren't deep, but blood had surfaced to the skin. Roslyn wasn't going to like this.

"I'm okay."

Lyle knelt down in front of her. "You know better than to cry. You take the pain you cause for yourself. Didn't you see all those thorns?" Joni lowered her head. "Come on." She held his hand as they walked along a small path through the woods, all the while so he could scope out the area. Tall pine trees covered most of the land. He scraped the toe of his boot across the pine needles, exposed dry red clay.

"I like this place," Joni said. Lyle liked it too. And the more he saw of it, the more his body itched with need.

By the time they'd made it back to where they started, sweat dripped down Lyle's back and Joni was again too close to the water. "My frog, Daddy, look." Before he could tell her to be careful, he saw that undeniable slip in her footing and she fell into the shallow water. She went under, but he yanked her up within seconds, put her back on her feet as her clothes dripped water.

Joni coughed and pulled the elephant from her pocket. "He's ruined."

"I'll get you another one."

"You're good at saving people," she said and coughed again. The words were a lie. Since he had on an undershirt, he pulled off his plaid button up and used it to dry his daughter.

"You're all dirty."

"Mama's gonna be mad." She squeezed water out of the elephant, ringing its neck in the process.

Lyle touched his nose to Joni's. "I don't care. We won't go home until you're dry. That way, she won't have anything to yell at us about."

***

That's not what Roslyn yelled about. When they stepped through the front door she said, "Do you know what time it is?" and Lyle didn't want to explain to her it didn't matter. He was spending time with Joni. "She has school tomorrow, Lyle."

"It's okay," Joni said.

"And you're filthy." Then she spotted his gift. "You bought her another beanie baby?"

"She deserved it."

"That sassy mouth doesn't deserve another toy."

"Drop it, Roslyn." Lyle pulled off his shoes and set them in the closet.

"You should hear how she talks to me."

"Any different from the way you talk to me?"

Roslyn bit her tongue, turned to Joni, and pointed upstairs. "Start the water. I'll be there in a second."

Joni didn't budge. "I'm ten years old. I can bathe myself."

Roslyn felt Joni's ponytail. "Your hair is disgusting."

"You're disgusting."

Roslyn snatched the elephant away and said to him, "Are you going to let her talk to me like that?"

"Do as your mother said." Joni lowered her head and marched her way upstairs, pounding her feet on each step she took. Roslyn gave him a look, and Lyle said, "Cut it out, Joni." By now, she was at the top of the stairs and didn't bother to turn around to look at them. He knew getting her in the bath would be a problem. She was probably already in her room writing in

5

a notebook about how the good time she had with her father was ruined by her evil mother.

Let her write, Lyle thought. It was easier to ask for Joni's forgiveness than to have Roslyn pissed at him all night.

***

The insomnia wouldn't let his mind rest. He waited until his wife and daughter were sound asleep, and slipped outside. The house was in a small, no-named subdivision and sat on a few acres with the nearest neighbor a football field away. The house was nice, and they'd been there since before Joni was born, and Lyle liked the seclusion yet close enough to be at an arm's reach of all the things he needed.

A detached garage was to the left of the house and every time he looked at the place, his hands itched with something Lyle couldn't describe. He got in the Cadillac and drove three miles to Kennesaw State University, where he scoped out the nearby townhouses and apartments. As soon as he saw two college girls walking, his heart sped up, and he gripped the steering wheel.

They were perfect. And drunk. One was blonde, the other brunette. Both dressed liked they'd gone out, and as his eyes followed them down the sidewalk, he couldn't help but notice where they were going. He rubbed his sweaty palms on his jeans and ignored his erection. It wasn't time. These things took preparation and he couldn't screw it up by rushing. He'd never see those two girls again, but they were nice to look at.

The desire to hurt came to him with such electricity, like a thousand bees stinging his brain at once. He drove down Ponce de Leon a few times until he found what he was looking for. Long legs stretched out of her short skirt and when she climbed inside his car, he could see straight to her tonsils.

"We gonna do this in the car? If you want the ass, it's extra." Whores in Atlanta were cheap. Sleazy motels even cheaper.

He wanted to tell her she'd do whatever he wanted, but the whole point was to control himself, so he let her say what she wanted until he had his fill. If she didn't know how to stay in line, she'd find herself face down in a ditch because no one cared about the whores.

Lyle paid cash for the room and wondered how many men she'd screwed tonight.

"Name's Mimi." She stood next to the bed looking bored, waiting for him to tell her what he wanted. "What's a handsome guy like you doing like this?" He unzipped his pants, sat down on the bed, and pretended to be smitten by her comment. "The quiet type," she said.

"How about you be the quiet type and get to work?"

Mimi knelt down between his knees, and it took every ounce of control to keep things easy, just get a fill, go home. "Is that how you like it?" she said, pulling her mouth away. Lyle leaned his head back and imagined the young college girls he'd seen walking earlier. Thought about the blonde and brunette taking turns on him. Roslyn wasn't into it like that. She used to be, but then she changed and now it was dirty. She was no longer a part of his fantasy, but his wife served her purpose.

"I think you're ready," the whore said.

Lyle looked down at her. "No, I'm not." He pushed her head back down.

"Hey." She jerked herself free. "You need to chill out, okay? You want it rough? Pay extra."

If Mimi was getting paid, how can she have rules? The only rules Lyle played by were his own. She wasn't going to expect him to pay and then tell him how he was going to get it. After getting back to work on him, he grabbed her hair and pushed himself down her throat until she fought him. The more she fought against him, the easier it was to shut down his brain. Switch it off. Click. Like a switch.

7

Lyle let her go long enough to put on a condom, and his brain only registered the part about her saying how sore her jaw would be. That wasn't the only thing that would be sore.

He made her bend over the bed and he held her down as he shoved himself into her, pulled out and shoved where she didn't want it. The more she fought, the more it turned him on.

"You stupid fucker," she said, and he shoved her face down into the mattress. She was such a useless waste of life. No worries on his part, because who was she going to tell? The police? The thought made Lyle push harder, her sounds muffled in the blanket.

When he finished, he shoved her to the floor and didn't look at her as she cursed him. "Shut up," he said, but she went on and on until he threw a twenty her way.

"What? The price was thirty, but after what you just did, it's fifty."

"You weren't that good." Lyle went to flush the condom and when he came back, the bitch had a gun aimed at him. "Whoa." He held up his hands, played nice. "Look, I'm sorry. Here." He opened up his wallet and handed her a wad of cash. "Sorry. I got carried away."

"Damn straight."

As soon as she reached for the money, he pulled the gun away and punched her in the face. She crumpled to the floor and Lyle picked up all his cash and left the hotel.

Chapter Two

The urge to hunt intensified. He worked his normal shift at the logistics center where he managed the inbound department, but before he went home, he drove through Kennesaw State again but knew the chances of seeing the two girls from last night were slim. Puzzle pieces had to match up perfectly in order to play the game.

By the time he'd gotten home, Roslyn was bitching about him being late and how she expected better. He sat at the table and shoveled food into his mouth in an attempt to act like he cared. Sometimes he cared, but right now he had other things on his mind and even as Joni asked him questions about lions and tigers and bears, he only gave her half-assed answers as his mind wondered.

Later, while Roslyn did the dishes, she said, "I swear, Lyle, I think sometimes your brain needs a jump start, like it's missing the connections."

"Why are you still mad about me being late?"

"Where were you?"

Lyle wanted to punch her, but he kept his voice soft. While he rubbed her back, he said, "I took you in when nobody wanted you. Nobody. I gave you a house. Clothes. Everything you ever wanted. You only work when you want to. I don't ask much from you, so stop asking so much of me. Just be a mother, okay?" He spun her around and stared at her for a long moment, and was so close to asking her if her life was better on the streets fucking people for money.

She said, "I hate it when you act like this."

"Like what?"

"Like you don't do a damn thing wrong. Sometimes you're a totally different person."

"Am I not a good husband to you?" *Control*, he told himself. Even though he could make Roslyn stop her bitching in a split second, he at least attempted to make her see things his way first.

"I swear I think I could put a bullet in my head and you wouldn't even notice."

Lyle smiled. "Let me load the gun for you and we can find out."

Roslyn blinked away tears and knew better than to say another word. Lyle left the kitchen through the backdoor and as soon as he stepped around the corner toward the garage, he spotted Joni sitting on an old tire with a cigarette in her mouth. Anger flashed through him as he closed the distance between them in four steps.

"Daddy, I didn't." She threw the cigarette in the grass with terror in her eyes. Lyle jerked her up, pulled her across his knee, and spanked her until she screamed. Spanked her until his hand hurt and she'd think twice before she took another of her mother's cigarettes to play with.

He yanked her inside the house. "What happened?" Roslyn said. Lyle took Joni to the basement door.

"No, Daddy, please." Tears fell from her face as he unlatched the lock. "I'm sorry," she said. "I'm sorry." Joni grabbed his shirt. He didn't feel sorry for her. She needed to be punished. She screamed as he left her on the top of the basement steps, the closed door between them. Not only was she afraid of the basement, she was afraid of the dark. This always served as her punishment. Last time he punished her, it was because he caught her snooping around his garage.

Lyle threw the lock in place, and she banged on the door. "You can stay in there all night as far as I'm concerned."

The banging stopped, but the crying didn't. He was doing her a favor. Teaching her a lesson, which was much better than what his mother gave him. "Daddy, I love you."

Roslyn said, "I can't listen to this, Lyle," and went for the lock.

"If you touch that door, you'll end up down there with her."

Roslyn shoved past him, and he grabbed her by the shirt and slapped her face. He had no idea why she was so shocked. He did warn her.

***

Two days later, the rain came down in sheets and spoiled Lyle's plans. "Play with me, Daddy." Joni sat on top of the coffee table with her legs underneath her. The storm was so bad it knocked out the electricity. For the most part, the house was dark except for all the candles Roslyn set out. Joni slapped her hands over her ears with each clap of thunder and it made Lyle smile.

"Come here." He pulled her into his lap. "Don't be a fraidy cat."

"I'm not." Her breath was warm on his neck. "Knock knock."

"Who's there?"

"Oink oink."

"Oink oink who?"

"Come on, are you a pig or an owl?"

Lyle laughed. "Knock knock."

"Who's there?"

"I am."

"I am who?"

"You mean you don't know who you are?"

Instant laughter. Then Joni said, "Daddy, that's lame."

"Sit here a second." He moved her off his lap, went into the kitchen. When he returned, he sat back down and pulled his daughter back onto his lap. As the candles flickered, she opened

11

the small brown sack and pulled out a necklace he'd bought at the gas station.

"It's so pretty," she said, and held up the necklace with tiny brown elephants. He helped her put it on. The elephants were the same shade of brown as Joni's eyes. Her blonde hair was a mess around her face, and Lyle smoothed it away.

A minute later, she looked at him, her eyes serious. "I don't like it when you lock me in the basement."

"That's why I do it."

Her body tensed and she looked away toward the window, and she sat there without saying a thing, which was something because Joni was always chatty.

He cupped his hands around her tender face and pressed his lips to her forehead. No matter how close they were, it was never enough. When he held his daughter on his lap, the monster was at bay and only at times like these, he wondered about himself. Could he be helped? Could he pour gasoline on himself and burn the monster out? Joni was okay, wasn't she? Roslyn screwed her up a lot and had her worrying about things she didn't need to worry about. Because of Roslyn, Joni had fear and Lyle wanted to teach her how to control her fear. There were so many things he wanted to teach her. Life was cruel and sometimes the people who hurt us most were family. That hurt was close, and he had his mother to blame for that, but it would be a bloody day before he ever let her hurt him again.

Lyle's life wasn't about her anymore. He did what he wanted, and if it wasn't raining right now, that's exactly what he'd be doing. The disappointment settled on Joni's face as he dropped her on the sofa and told her to tell her mother he'd be back later. Not bothering with an umbrella, he ran to the Cadillac and drove twenty minutes to a little sandwich place in Smyrna.

As soon as he walked in, the young woman behind the counter said, "Long time no see, stranger," and Lyle was happy she was working tonight. "You want the usual?"

"Actually, I was looking for coffee."

"Sorry." She wrinkled her nose with the words. Her name was Miranda and she must have been in her late twenties, possibly early thirties, but Lyle gave up on judging their ages long ago. "I could use a coffee myself, though. Apparently, no one likes sandwiches when it rains." Miranda sighed. "It's gonna be a long night."

"Okay," Lyle said, because he played right into his bright idea. "How do you like your coffee?"

"What?"

"I'm going to go get us coffee." At her protest about not being able to bring other food into the joint, he said, "Who's gonna know?" and swept his hands out to show how empty the place was.

"Fine." She pulled out some cash, but he insisted it was on him. Of course, it was. Why would he not buy her coffee? She told him what she wanted, and he was gone and back in fifteen minutes. The place was still empty, and they sat down at a table.

"You are soaked." Miranda dropped a handful of napkins on the table before she sat down. Lyle dried his face and took a closer look at her. An earring was pierced through her right eyebrow and he wondered if it hurt. Her blonde hair was tucked into a cap that had a sub sandwich on it, and the ponytail hung through the loop in the back.

"So how's your baby?" Miranda said.

"Just started walking. Looks like a drunk baby gorilla." Lyle held up his arms to demonstrate which made her laugh. He had no problem remembering the storyline he gave her months ago when he'd first started coming here. Told her about his little baby girl at home. How his wife died in a car accident right after she was born. Miranda felt real sorry for him. Got a free sandwich and a cookie out of it.

"Your boyfriend still missing you?" Her answer was an eye roll. "What's his name again?"

13

Miranda's jaw dropped. "John. The same as yours. How can you forget that?"

"I have a bad memory. But I remember you saying that you were trying out for a part in the Nutcracker for Christmas. How'd that go?"

Miranda frowned. "I didn't make it."

"That's too bad." He patted her hand. She'd told him one day how she and her boyfriend moved to Atlanta together, but then he ended up dumping her and she was not sure whether she wanted to move back to plain ol' Milledgeville or not, since she really liked the Atlanta area. And that's what attracted Lyle to her. No family around. No boyfriend. No one to miss her right away.

That's how easy it was.

For the next two weeks he continued to talk to Miranda, and because he was the logistics manager, he had potential meetings with sales reps, except he really wasn't going. He was stopping by the sandwich place during lunch.

On his way home after watching her one day, he stopped at the store and bought three gallons of bleach, then went to the hardware store for a roll of plastic wrap. Lyle backed the Cadillac into the garage, and sometimes he had to park in here even though he didn't like to, but it was the only way to make it look right. That way, when he really needed to park in his special garage, Roslyn didn't ask any questions.

When they'd first moved into the house twelve years ago, he'd built the detached garage to his liking. Inside, the place was mostly empty. The floor was concrete and a work table ran along the right wall with a deep sink at the far end. The walls were double insulated, and he added an air conditioner for the summer. He didn't mind the smell of sweat and blood, but he hated the smell of piss.

Lyle set the bleach under the worktable and looked around. Even though he visited the garage every few days, he hadn't used it in five months.

Five long months.

The garage sloped down; the back concrete wall was built against a small dirt incline outside. But on the inside, the dirt had been dug out and Lyle made a six-by-six-foot concrete hiding place that only came three feet high. From the inside, it looked like a normal garage with the slope barely noticeable. Lyle walked to the back and removed the false wall. It was like a small tomb in there.

Dark. Cold. Quiet.

Inside was a handmade table. The metal legs were bent underneath it and it was on wheels, and fit nicely into the hiding place. Lyle pulled the table from its hiding place, where it rolled to a stop, and he covered the table with plastic wrap. The anticipation rushed through his veins like a tidal wave.

Soon, he told himself. *Very soon.*

Chapter Three

Miranda lived in a nice apartment complex off of Windy Hill Road. From his car, he could see her front door, and he wondered for a moment what she'd do if he knocked. Would she let him in or freak out? Stick to the plan. The *plan*. The plan was perfect at this point, damn it, don't mess it up. Thirty minutes later, a pizza delivery guy showed up. As the minutes passed, no one else stopped by. She must have been eating alone. Lyle checked his watch again and cursed himself. Time flew when he was having fun. Too bad Roslyn didn't understand that.

The obsession with wanting to know where Miranda was at every second of the day was killing him. From work, he called the sandwich place three times, hoping Miranda would answer the phone. When she didn't, he'd hang up. On another day, she answered the phone, but he pretended to be a random guy with food allergies asking about how their whole wheat bread was made. His time at work was sporadic and when he was at home, his wife and daughter were getting in the way of being able to do what he wanted. When Lyle was in the zone, the only way he thought of his wife was a dumb bitch, and Joni was annoying. She came home from school wanting a dog since her cat died four years ago. Lyle's pets died too. He needed another.

On a Thursday, he called Roslyn at work. She was a secretary at a finance company in Marietta, and sometimes she worked late, so Lyle told her he'd pick up dinner if she was able to pick up Joni from after school care.

Just before five o'clock, Lyle parked his Cadillac next to Miranda's Civic at the back end of the parking lot, and he used a plastic wedge and coat hanger to break into her car. Once he was in, he pressed the hood release, then exited the vehicle. He yanked the spark plug wires loose and cut one of them in half.

He moved his car before he went to get his family dinner, but he didn't see Miranda. Where was she?

"What can I get for you?" a pimply kid behind the counter asked. While Lyle looked over the menu and ordered, he kept his baseball cap low on his head to cover his eyes. As he paid cash for the sandwiches, he spotted Miranda in the back, tossing her purse over her shoulder. Lyle left the sandwich place and heard, "Hey, John," and he turned to her. She looked at the bag in his hand and said, "You're hungry."

"My turn to bring my mother dinner." When the word mother came out of his mouth, his blood raged. Why hadn't he thought to say someone else?

On Thursdays, Miranda went into work at ten a.m. and left at five. "I hope you have a good night," he said, as they parted ways. She gave a quick wave and walked to her car and Lyle waited inside the Cadillac while she tried to start the car. None of this would have worked if he couldn't have broken into her car, but it worked last time, so he went with it. She looked under the hood as planned, but then he saw she had a black mobile phone pressed to her ear and he wondered if this was going to work.

"You okay?" Lyle slowed his car in front of her.

"My car won't start," she said, then spoke on the phone to someone about picking her up.

This work wasn't for nothing. "You want me to take a look?" He got out, nosed around under the hood and told her the spark plug wire was damaged, which she repeated into the phone.

Miranda listened, then turned off the phone. "My friend's in the middle of a class, but he'll be here in an hour."

"Do you want a ride home?"

"No." She waved him off, and Lyle shoved his hands in his pockets.

17

"It's not much to fix this. All you have to do is replace the wires. Shouldn't take more than five minutes."

"Really?"

"Yeah. There's an auto parts store down the road. I can see if they have them."

"Don't worry about it. Besides, you need to take your mother dinner."

Lyle smiled. "How about I go check the store and come back and let you know?"

Miranda chewed her bottom lip, then said, "Okay, fine. But I'm coming with you. You bought me coffee; I'm not owing you for spark plugs."

Lyle said, "You remind me of my sister," and they got into his car. He passed the auto parts store and pretended it was an accident and before he could act like he was going to turn around, he zapped her with a stun gun until her body fell against the door. Lyle set the device in the cup holder and drove about a hundred yards to a small wooded area with a narrow road. Once he was hidden from traffic, he moved quickly because she started to freak out.

Lyle opened her car door. "Get out."

"What are you doing?" Terror struck her, and he grabbed her by the hair.

"I said get out."

Three minutes was all it took. He had her feet bound, hands bound behind her back, tape on her mouth, then he used a cord to hogtie her, and attach it to an anchor screwed into the trunk of the car. With the pillowcase over her head, he closed the trunk and was gone before anyone could say, *hey, did you see that?*

Lyle backed the car into the garage and closed the door. Time was against him, but he kept calm. How many times had he done this? He got out and checked on Miranda. She was struggling against the ties, but she was still secure. She fought the whole time he tried to take her out of the trunk. He left the pillowcase on her head for now. If she'd calm down and stop fighting him, she could breathe better. He cut the cord that held her hogtied, and one limb at a time, he used zip ties to secure them to an eyebolt on the rolling table. Once she was secure, he rolled the table in the hole. When he took off the pillow case her eyes were wild with fear.

"Hi," he said. "Don't try to escape, there's no place to go." From a drawer, he pulled out his favorite knife, the one with the pearl handle, and then he ran it along the side of her arm, just barely pushing it into the skin. She said something against the tape and shook her head. "Shhh." He kept his voice soft and calm. "Don't waste your energy. You'll need it for tonight."

He set the false wall back into place and screwed it closed. The edges of the wall had gaps for air, but it was cool in the hole, she'd be fine for a while. But still, he didn't want her to die before he had time to get to know her.

***

Lyle put an extra sleeping pill in Roslyn's sweet tea, and by ten o'clock she was snoring like a freight truck. When he thought about Miranda alone and scared in the hidden place, he got an erection and let his mind wonder to that dark place as all the things he wanted to do to her began to play out.

Lyle installed different types of lights in the garage. Tonight, he flipped the switch for the red lights and the garage lit up with an eerie glow. He loved the term, *scared to death*, because when he went out to the garage and pulled the false wall away to expose Miranda, that's exactly how she looked. Can a person really be scared to death? So scared they die from their own fear? A person had to learn to control their fear so they didn't get scared to death.

"How are you?" He rolled the table out from the hole.

Her body was strapped down spread eagle to the heavy table, but he lifted the bottom end off the ground and pulled the

19

pins out to let the legs drop down, then did the same for the front. The legs folded inside themselves, so one leg at a time, he extended each one so that he had it about three feet high.

He took the pearl handled knife and cut her clothes off so he could see all that creamy skin she had hidden underneath, and loved how it glowed red under the lights. He knew his face was freaking her out. Every time he touched her, she screamed, the sound muffled against the tape. "I won't take this off until you can show me you'll stop screaming." Miranda nodded, and Lyle ripped the tape off her mouth.

Her breaths came in quick takes. "Please don't do this, John."

Lyle leaned in real close, watched the tears slide down her cheeks. "My name's not John." He swept his tongue across her lips. "Open your mouth and let me kiss you." Miranda shook her head and kept her lips tightly closed, so he squeezed her jaw tight in his hand until her lips parted and he flicked his tongue over her soft lips. "I bought you something." From a drawer, he pulled out the gift. It was a small snow globe with pink ballerina shoes inside. He put his face close to hers as he shook the little gift. "Isn't it pretty? I got this just for you."

The snow globe now sat on the shelf next to the other treasures. This one was number thirty-three. Thirty-three beautiful little gifts for his own pleasure.

"Please let me go," Miranda said, and she struggled against the ties.

"I will."

"I won't tell anyone."

"I know you won't tell." He ran his hand down her bare stomach. "You're a good girl, Miranda. A real good girl. Tell me you're a good girl."

"I'm a good girl."

Lyle smiled. She may want to play nice now because she was scared, and that was okay, but he knew she'd fight later.

"Let me kiss you," he said. "I want to feel my tongue in your mouth."

Miranda began to cry as he kissed her, sucked and pulled at her tongue and lips. Her mouth was beautiful, tasted delicious.

He went to the top of the table where her head was, and pulled her down so that her head hung off the edge. The skin covering her throat was soft and felt smooth like silk. He pressed the pearl handled knife to her, said, "Do you like being punished?"

For five hours he had his way with his little pet. For five hours he taught her what he liked and made her talk about what he did with her. For five hours he kept telling her he was going to let her go home, but she had to promise not to let anyone do these things to her. It was Lyle's special treatment for her.

He wiped the blood away from her nose and when he kissed her lips, he relished the fact that he could taste himself on her. After he slapped a piece of tape over her mouth, lowered the table and slid it back into the hidden place, he said, "I promise I'll be back."

***

Lyle couldn't focus on his work. Two shipments were late, and he had to adjust the cost for the client so that they'd continue to use their services. One of the bay doors wouldn't open and he had to call a repair guy to come out and fix it. An accident in Birmingham caused another truck to be late, which meant the hot freight wouldn't make it out on time. They lost thousands of dollars because of shit like this, but it was all out of his control.

His email was overflowing. Phone calls needed to be made. Diandra Norwood knocked on his door and wanted to know if he wanted to chip in for pizza. *No, I don't want any fucking pizza.*

"I have a phone conference at noon today. I'll grab something later."

"The door guy's here, said he should have it fixed in an hour." She turned to leave.

"Close the door, please?"

When everything was clear, he slipped out, but as he reached the side entrance, Roger Figgs held up some money, said, "We're ordering pizza."

"Yeah, I'll be there in a little bit. Hey," Lyle said. "After lunch, we need the back lot swept and scrubbed. You think you can manage that for me?"

"Sure thing, boss." Roger gave a salute. The man had to be nearing fifty and still worked like he was twenty. Lyle wasn't concerned about the concrete sweep, but he needed something to keep Roger busy so Lyle could cover his ass.

A padlock kept the garage sealed, and cool air hit him as he stepped inside. The place was quiet. Eerily quiet. And dark. No windows. Lyle unscrewed the false wall and Miranda appeared to be asleep, but as soon as he squatted down next to her, her eyes popped open.

"Missed me?" He rolled the table out and set up the legs. "You were late for work today," he said, and Miranda nodded. Surely by now someone realized she was missing, but Lyle was positive nothing could be traced back to him. Inside her purse, he looked through her wallet again. Found her license. Her name was Miranda McBean. Twenty-six. She liked watermelon bubblegum, had three packs of it. He'd turned off the mobile phone last night, but he wondered how many people tried to call her. How many people were worried about little Miranda?

While he watched her on the table, full of tears and terror, he stroked himself and made her watch. Two acres of land separated his garage from the nearest neighbor, and his wife and daughter weren't home. It was time to hear her scream.

***

At first, he wasn't trying to hurt her, he only wanted to let her know who was in control. He'd untied one of her hands so that she could fight him. She pulled his hair and his ear and scratched his neck. When he was done, he wiped his hand on the towel he put underneath her. They always ended up pissing on themselves.

Miranda had a beautiful body, and he closed his eyes so he'd never forget what it looked like. "How many days do you practice ballet?" She pulled her knees together, either from the pain or to hide herself. "You don't want to talk to me?"

She shook her head. Lyle squeezed her breast until she winced. He already knew the answer.

"Four days. Between work shifts."

These were the best hours to get her talking, as long as Lyle kept up the notion that he'd let her go. Within an hour he knew all about her family, where she took ballet lessons, that she was in beauty pageants when she was a teenager, that she missed John, was happy when her car wouldn't start, she thought it was time for a new one.

"Do you like sex, Miranda?" Tears fell from her closed eyes. "Come on. It's not that hard of a question. I like sex." Lyle slapped her face. "Look at me when I'm talking to you. I asked you a question. It's rude not to answer."

"I don't like this."

"Maybe I can change your mind." He took her free hand and made her touch him while he rubbed her smooth skin with the other.

"Please stop."

All the women were the same. First, they begged for him to stop and let them go, then they begged to just die. He was still being nice to Miranda, and she wasn't hurt enough to want to die. After securing her arm back to the anchor, he climbed on top of her and wished he had someone there to watch him.

Like he did with Mary.

23

Mary would watch him and drip with lust, and beg him to fuck her. To make her hurt. Mary and her begging eyes and soft lips. But then he let her go. He wondered if Mary ever took his advice and killed herself.

A noise came from beneath him and he realized Miranda was gasping for air. He released his grip from her throat and she coughed and coughed, and tightened her muscles around him until he released himself.

He climbed off of her and washed his hands in the sink. Turned when he heard her say, "I thought you were nice. You seemed so nice, and I fell right into your trap. I never thought you were a douche bag."

Her voice was raspy from screaming. Raspy from being choked. Lyle wiped away her tears. "Don't cry. You'll be able to go home soon."

She looked him in the eyes. "You're going to let me go?"

"As long as you play nice with me and don't tell anyone."

"I won't."

He gave her water. Changed out the towel beneath her. Slapped more tape on her mouth, and knew she didn't want to go back into the hidden place. The longer she stayed in there, the weaker her body became. That was the plan. Was he really going to let her go? Of course not. He wasn't crazy.

***

The knock came while they were in the middle of supper, and Joni jumped to answer it. "Daddy, it's the police."

Behind her, he said, "Go finish your supper," and remained calm.

One of the men flashed a badge. "Detective Trimclay with the Cobb County Sheriff's department. We've met before." Four years ago. Trimclay was as tall as Lyle, which put him around six foot two. "This is my partner, Detective Cyrus Kenner. We'd like to have a word with you, Mr. Chaskey."

24

"We'd like to come inside," Kenner said. His face was smoothly shaven and the dimple in his chin reminded Lyle of a baby's ass. He wondered if the baby detective was old enough to read his own badge.

"My family's having supper. We can talk out here." Lyle closed the door behind him. "What's going on?"

While Trimclay sized up Lyle, Kenner looked around at the property and stared right at the blue Cadillac. Lyle wiped his palms on his pants and said, "Is this going to take long? I got a little girl waiting for dessert." He almost let out a laugh at his own joke.

"I see you still own your Cadillac, Mr. Chaskey."

Which was the reason for his visit four years ago. "Yes, sir."

"Are you the only driver?"

"Yes." Trimclay asked a few questions about the minivan, but Lyle knew that wasn't his point of interest. *Come on*, Lyle thought. *Let's get this over with.*

"You still working at Staurolite Logistics?"

"Every day."

"Were you there yesterday afternoon around five?"

Lyle shrugged. "Left around that time."

"Then where'd you go?"

"Went to get my family supper. Why?"

The two men looked at each other. "Where'd you go get that supper?"

"A little sandwich place on South Cobb in Smyrna." Lyle let out a laugh. "What? Did I forget my change again?"

"Do you know Miranda McBean?"

Lyle made a production out of thinking about that and resisted the urge to look at the detached garage. "I don't believe I do, Detective."

The detectives didn't relax one bit. It was Kenner's turn to speak. "Miranda McBean works at Ike's. She was reported

25

missing this morning, and a kid we spoke with said he saw her getting into a blue Cadillac yesterday around five."

"Not in my car," Lyle said. "I went to get sandwiches, but I don't know anything about this."

"You didn't see anything?" Trimclay said.

"No."

Kenner stood stiff, like he was waiting for Lyle to give more details about something so he could ask questions because the detective obviously didn't know what he was doing. Trimclay, on the other hand, wanted to get to the bottom of this. "Someone broke into her car. Disabled it. I'm thinking so they could offer her a ride. You don't know anything about disabling cars, do you?"

"If you count putting sugar in my neighbor's gas tank when I was ten, sure." Lyle shrugged again.

A minute passed before Trimclay said, "This must all be a coincidence," and the baby next to him nodded.

Four years ago, Bonnie Hesledge went missing from Acworth, seen getting into a blue Cadillac. Lyle was questioned because someone got a partial on the license plate that matched his.

"And it was established that I wasn't even in Acworth at the time." Lyle pulled out his wallet, handed Trimclay his business card. "I was at work until almost five. You can call to verify that. I stopped at Ike's on my way home. I was home all night after that."

Staurolite was so disorganized yesterday with the late freight and broken door that no one would remember when they saw him. Last time Diandra saw him, he was about to have a conference call in his office. She'd be pretty sure he was there all afternoon. And Nelson Figgs would be sure Lyle blended in with the work crew of thirty-five warehouse employees while they all ate pizza, and Roger would be sure because then he went out to sweep the back parking lot while Lyle was in his office.

"I just find it funny, Mr. Chaskey, two girls have been reported missing within four years of each other and both seen getting into blue Cadillacs because their cars were tampered with."

"Well, I don't find it funny." Lyle looked Detective Trimclay in the eye. "Did you ever find out what happened to Bonnie Hesledge?" Always the polite citizen. He was nice like that.

"I think you know the answer to that," Trimclay said.

Lyle did. He made sure no one would ever find Bonnie. Lyle was going to have to stop taking women from Cobb County. "Well, I'm not the only one driving around with a late model blue Cadillac with the letters JKL. Tell me what I can do to help you out here, Detective, and I'll do it. Otherwise, I'd like to go finish supper with my family."

Chapter Four

Later that night, when Lyle had Miranda on the table, the thought about how close those two assholes had been to the garage turned him on. The red lights were on again, and he made her stroke him while he kissed her, and then he said, "I think your family is looking for you. You're not going to tell them about this, are you?"

Miranda shook her head.

"That's a good girl." He pulled off her restraints and made her lie on her stomach for a little while, which was a nice change for him as he let her legs dangle off the edge.

She seemed to like it when he spoke to her, told her how pretty she was and how good she made him feel. He wasn't gentle, but she wasn't screaming about it like before. "You're a woman who knows how to take it."

When she was on her back again, strapped down, she said, "You are the stupidest fucking asshole I ever met in my life." Lyle's silence made her struggle against the ties. "The only reason you can do this is because I'm tied down. You're a pathetic piece of shit." Miranda spit on him. "You have a small dick. My dog has a bigger dick than you."

"What's your dog's name?"

Miranda tried to muster up whatever spit she could, but nothing came out.

"Rex? Max?" Lyle hurt her until she cried, until she screamed the name was Rothbart.

As he washed the blood off his hand, she said, "I'm glad your wife died." Lyle smiled at her over his shoulder. A part of Roslyn was dead to him, and he no longer cared, but he wasn't going to

28

tell Miranda that his wife was in fact alive, and well, and asleep right next door. "I hope your baby dies."

The smile faded. "What did you say?"

"I hope she's dead right now."

Lyle punched her in the face. "Shut your whore mouth."

"I hope. I hope that someone takes your daughter and ties her up and rapes her until she dies." Miranda choked back tears and snot, and Lyle punched her again, this time busting her nose. "You rape her, don't you, you sick bastard."

"I got news for you. I don't have a daughter."

"Yeah, because no one wants to fuck you, that's why you have to rape people." Lyle pulled out his pearl handled knife. "What are you doing?"

While he leaned over her body, he shoved his forearm over her mouth, and shoved the tip of the knife into the fleshy part between her thumb and index finger. She bit down into him while he dug it in. He pushed his arm down to muffle the scream.

Lyle leaned in close to her, looked at those fluorescent teeth. "I think I was being real nice to you. Why'd you have to go and say something like that about my daughter? You don't want her to die, do you?"

She surprised him with a nod. He surprised her with another puncture wound.

Then he raped her again. Yanked out her eyebrow ring and watched blood drip into her eye. She said, "Untie me so I can do it better," and Lyle pulled himself off of her. He snipped off the leg restraints first, then the wrists. That's when she grabbed the pearl handled knife.

Miranda sat up and pointed it at him. He'd been in this position too many times to feel anything other than power. On her wobbly legs now, she walked backwards across the garage.

"Look," Lyle said. "I'm sorry. You can go, but I want my knife back. It's my favorite."

"Favorite for killing people with." Miranda was almost at the door.

"You can't go without clothes on. What are people going to think?"

As she turned for the door, Lyle closed the distance between them. He locked the door with a key for this very purpose. Couldn't be too safe. "I want out!"

Lyle was behind her, put his arm around her neck and took back his knife. She kicked against him, rubbing her bare ass against his open pants. Lyle threw her to the floor, where she tried to crawl away, but he kicked her in the ribs. He positioned himself between her legs and took her. He said, "I thought you were going to do better than before?"

Lyle wrapped his hands around Miranda's throat and squeezed until her eyes dripped with tears and looked like they were about to explode with blood. The best noises escaped from her mouth as all the life escaped from her body. This was the best part of it all. This is what he needed.

***

Lyle put Miranda's body in the sink. Filled it with water and a gallon of bleach and got to work scrubbing her body down. Washed her hair. Her mouth. Between her legs and toes. Her fingers were long and skinny, like a pianist, but she wasn't a pianist, she was a ballerina.

He was careful with her hand, the one with the small wounds.

He'd have the snow globe to remember her. As Lyle went to work with scrubbing her fingernails clean, he couldn't help but notice his own hands.

Big. Rough. Mean.

He dropped the brush in the sink and looked at the palms of his hands. All the hurt he caused with these hands. But not always hurt. He could be gentle. Gentle enough to hold a newborn baby. Gentle enough to pry open that tiny fist and examine her wrinkly fingers. Gentle enough to stroke the tiny hairs on her head.

Lyle pressed his hands to his mouth and choked back a sob. Why did he keep doing this? The pain hit him fast, and he slid down to the floor, curled into a ball and wept.

His sweet baby Joni. How did his sweet baby Joni end up with a monster like him as a father? He would protect her. Never hurt her. Life was so fragile. Control was the only way to stop bad things from happening. Nothing bad would ever happen to him again. Nothing bad would ever happen to Joni.

Fear swept over him. Could he protect her? Dads were supposed to protect their kids. Lyle didn't have a dad, never knew him. And his mother... that piece of shit he'd had of a mother denied him. Denied him what he needed most.

Lyle rocked and rocked and rocked. Everything was quiet and time slipped away. He closed his eyes while he cried about how horrible his life was. His breathing slowed down and minutes later, his body jerked awake. The floor was cold. A hand hung down from the sink and in that short time Lyle had forgotten what he was doing. The clock on the wall showed nearly two hours had passed since he'd put Miranda in the sink. He'd thought it was only minutes.

But hours had passed.

He needed to get moving. Lyle picked himself up from the floor and went to work. He finished cleaning Miranda's body, drained the sink, dried her off. Spent another hour cleaning the garage, washing everything down with bleach. He put the blood and pee-soaked towel into a five-gallon bucket. Balled up the plastic sheeting and put that in the bucket too. As soon as possible, he'd burn what he could. Her wallet and everything inside, work clothes and cap, purse. He removed all the keys from the key chain and pocketed them, then put the little ballerina key chain into the bucket. Every personal item had to

31

be disposed. He'd toss the keys out the car window a few at a time over several miles. Throw out the eyebrow ring. He bleached down the phone and would dispose of that too. Nothing to trace back to him.

***

Lyle drove back to Fayette County. That day Joni had fallen in the water at Starr's Mill he'd driven around the back roads until she dried off. Tonight, he went as far as Coweta County until he found a little road off of Highway 16. Last time, he didn't see any houses out here, so he figured it to be the perfect dumping place.

Lyle went as far as he could, hit a few potholes in the road, then stopped when the path was too narrow. He thought about dumping the body into the creek at Starr's Mill, but knew that wasn't a good idea. That's how the first ones were found, because he hadn't done a good job of hiding the bodies. And now Lyle realized it was stupid to shove cotton down their throats to quiet them, because all seven of the bodies they'd found over the past ten years had cotton fibers in their throats. But he'd done a good job of eliminating evidence and nothing had been traced back to him.

Lyle adjusted the headlamp on his forehead, then took the body out of the car, and walked about a hundred feet into the woods, her dead weight heavy in his arms. He cleared away some leaves and pine needles. That way, if he left the body out, it would decompose faster. This was all about taking chances, figuring out the best way to do things. This worked.

He left nothing on her body, and if she was ever found, hopefully nothing would trace back to him.

They called him *The Cotton Mouth Killer* after they'd found naked, decaying bodies in various places throughout Georgia with white fibers in their mouths. But it wasn't cotton, it was pillow stuffing, you idiots. To be quite honest, he liked the name.

Except he wanted nothing to do with it. This had nothing to do with vanity, so he stopped putting the pillow stuffing in their throats to quiet them while he watched them choke.

He'd found better dumping sites, and since no more bodies were showing up, the police believed the *Cotton Mouth Killer* either stopped killing, was dead himself, or was some other criminal they'd picked up.

They were wrong.

Lyle adapted. Isn't that how it worked? Follow the media to find out what he'd been doing wrong? He thought he was going to have a heart attack ten years ago when the first body turned up. But boy, oh boy, didn't he get away with murder?

Lyle was dripping with sweat from the night's heat. When he was satisfied with his work of dumping the body out of the trash bag and covering it with leaves, he thought this would be a nice place for Miranda McBean to rest. He placed both her hands on her belly and walked away.

***

By the time Lyle got home, it was six o'clock in the morning and he still had a few things to do. The outside of the car was clean because he'd taken it through a car wash in Riverdale. He needed to do something with his clothes and shoes.

"Where the hell have you been?" Her voice didn't even startle him. She was leaning against the front porch with a cigarette hanging out of her mouth. He pushed past her and she said, "Jesus, you stink like death rolled over."

"Baby," he said, trying to be the good husband. "I don't feel too good. I think I have a fever. Do I have a fever?" He lowered his head so she'd get the clue to check.

"No."

"I have the shakes and the sweats. Do you think I'm getting the flu?"

33

Now she was concerned. "Lyle, it's April. How can you have the flu? You can't be around Joni with the flu. Hell, what happened to your arm?"

Lyle looked at the circle of teeth marks on his arm. "I think I bit myself. I'm serious Roslyn, I think I have the flu."

She looked at him for a long minute, stubbed out the cigarette, then said, "Come on, I'll run you a bath."

***

For the next few months, things seemed to go back to normal. The anxiety slowed down. The itch went away. He hadn't been with a prostitute since what's her name—Mimi? Lyle could go back to being himself and playing with Joni and going on their Sunday trips. It was hard to let things in life roll off his shoulders, and sometimes at night he'd crawl into the hidden place in the garage and masturbate and then cry. He didn't know why he felt so sad and unwanted.

Staurolite Logistics was having their annual picnic at Stone Mountain Park. A volley ball net was set up in a grassy area and some kids used the ball for soccer instead. Joni was best friends with Amanda Flockhart. Amanda's dad, Wayne, owned the logistics company. Every time Lyle saw Joni with her friend, he wondered what it would be like for Joni to have a little brother or sister. He'd wanted a son, but then Roslyn had a girl, and he fell in love with her the moment he saw her. Her little body fit in the crook of his arm and her head fit perfectly in his hands. But a son would be nice too.

"What's going on, boss man?"

Diandra Norwood stood behind him. She was a tall woman with a million braids in her hair, and she was the complete opposite of her short, bald husband. Lyle shook the man's hand. "Hadn't seen you in a while," Gilly said.

Diandra introduced him to their son, Gilly Jr. The kid must have been about twelve, looked just like his dad. Stood like him, too, with his hands tucked underneath his armpits.

"Your girl's getting big," Diandra said, and they all turned to Joni and Amanda, tossing acorns into the woods.

Lyle chatted with them for a little while, bullshitting about work. Roslyn surprised him when she came over and put her arm around him. Most of the people who worked at the logistics warehouse knew each other. They'd all been together for years.

The piercing scream startled them, nearly breaking sound waves, and they turned their attention to the edge of the woods. Lyle didn't notice the dog right away. What he saw was Amanda Flockhart flinging side to side like a rag doll. Without a second thought, he took off to them and grabbed a big stick, hit the dog, but it didn't faze the animal. With no time to think, his brain shut off, and he only reacted. He tried to knock the dog's feet out from under him, but he was fast and jumped back. The dog was brindle and stocky, must have weighed eighty pounds. Amanda screamed and blood oozed from her shoulder, neck, and arms as it continued to attack her. Her little face was a bloody mess, too.

At least it wasn't Joni.

He was thankful it wasn't his own daughter.

Adults were screaming from behind. He grabbed the dog by the mouth, and when he did, the dog let go of Amanda and in a split-second chomped down on Lyle's hand, let go long enough to take a better bite out of his elbow, and went into attack mode. Lyle didn't feel any pain. He shoved his elbow down into the dog's jowls, used his leg to make the dog fall and when the dog was on the ground, Lyle went with him because the dog wouldn't let go.

Lyle fell on top and put all of his two-hundred twenty pounds of weight on the animal as the dog kicked and bucked underneath. With his arm shoved deep in the dog's mouth, he still tried to bite, but it prevented him from moving. With his

35

right hand, he moved it to the dog's throat and squeezed around the thick muscles until he got a good grip. Not giving up, the dog fought beneath him, legs kicking, nails digging into Lyle's stomach and chest, but Lyle didn't give up either.

He had no hard feelings about squeezing the life out of this beast. In fact, Lyle's brain didn't register much of anything except killing it. Minutes passed and slowly the dog went limp underneath him, and he didn't move for a long time.

Then he heard all the commotion behind him. Blood was everywhere. Amanda was on the ground, her small body shaking from blood loss while her mother cried. Lyle's heart raced in his chest and he felt like he was going to throw up.

"Daddy?" Joni stood next to him, shaking with her own fear, but she wasn't looking at him. She was looking back and forth between the dead dog and his arm. That's when the pain came.

"Oh God, Lyle." Roslyn was next to him now. "An ambulance is on the way."

"I'm okay."

Okay until he noticed his arm. Looked like shredded beef dipped in spaghetti sauce. He moved away from the dog and its dead eyes, and sat back as the dizziness set in. Blood seeped through his t-shirt from lacerations from the dog's nails. His hand and arm throbbed in pain. He wondered for a moment if he was going to lose his arm.

Chapter Five

The newspaper headline read:

HERO SAVES GIRL IN VICIOUS DOG ATTACK

It had been a month, and that day would remain fresh in Lyle's mind forever. His arm was intact, but he'd undergone two surgeries to repair the damage done to his elbow. Skin was stitched back in place. Muscle tissue saved. His arm looked like Frankenstein's monster's face. For now, he had limited movement in his left arm, but the doctors said only time would tell whether there would be any permanent damage.

And that was nothing compared to what little Amanda was going through. They thought she was going to lose an eye, but now she was doing better and can see out of it. She had over a hundred stitches on her head alone. Shoulder, arm, neck, chest; none of it untouched by the bites. She'd only gotten out of the hospital a few days ago, but would undergo more reconstructive surgery on her face soon.

Lyle was getting nothing but pats on the back about the entire ordeal, but he didn't like the attention.

"Daddy?" Joni stood next to him at the kitchen table with a pen in one hand and the newspaper article in the other. "Can I have your autograph?"

"Why?"

"Because you'll be famous one day." Joni was like that. Thinking the best of people. She kissed him on the cheek.

"One thing can change your whole life, baby. One thing."

***

Within the next two years, Lyle had only killed one other woman. He thought after the dog attack the itch would go away, considering the fear he endured for those minutes, which felt like hours, but it didn't. In fact, the woman he took ended up being hurt a lot worse than the others. Instead of going forward, Lyle went backwards because that's what he used to do. Hurt them really bad, but he'd stopped and now he was doing it again.

He thought about Mary Rancotti, the only woman he ever let go. She was before Roslyn and Joni. Before, the killing was perfect. Mary was the only one he'd kept for three months. She was his first, and he didn't know what to do with her. So he kept her locked in a basement.

Joni was twelve now and started middle school, and kept sneaking off down the street to talk to a boy named Brian who was in eighth grade. Lyle didn't like this one bit. He'd warned her once to stay away from him. He was too old to be her friend, and what was an eighth-grade boy doing with a twelve-year-old girl, anyway?

When he saw her sitting at the street corner next to him, sharing an ice cream cone, Lyle lost it. Her skinny bare legs stretched out of her pink shorts, and she wasn't even wearing any shoes. *No goddamn shoes.* He marched up to her. "What did I tell you?"

"Daddy, I didn't do anything," she said, and dropped the ice cream cone between her knees where it landed with a plop.

Lyle jerked her up, said to Brian, "If I ever see you around my daughter again, I will beat the shit out of you. Do you hear me?" The kid nodded. Good. He was scared. There was no telling what that kid had on his mind. "Did he touch you?"

"What?"

Lyle still had her by the arm as he walked her back to the house. When they got inside, he brought her to the bathroom and closed the door. He turned on the hot water.

"Daddy," she said softly, her voice already trembling.

Lyle found bleach under the sink and poured some in while the tub filled. "Take off your clothes."

A cry escaped her lips. "I'm sorry."

Lyle yanked her shirt off. "You will learn that when I tell you to stay away from boys, I mean it. They are bad." He pulled her shorts and underwear down and she stepped out of them. Next came her little bra, and she stood there trying to cover herself and cried. "You have to wash yourself."

"Daddy, I'm sorry."

He grabbed her arm and shoved her into the tub with a splash, then forced her to sit in the hot water. "One day you will understand."

"He's my friend."

"No!" Lyle grabbed a washrag and soap. "No, he's not your friend. He only wants to pretend to be your friend so he can do horrible things to you." With the rag soaped up, Lyle yanked away Joni's arm and began to clean her, to wash every part of her body the boy looked at.

"It's hot."

Her skin was red and slippery from the bleach, and he ignored her complaints as he scrubbed her clean. Joni had her knees pulled to her chest, and Lyle yanked the ponytail from her hair, shoved her back so he could wash her hair.

When she came up, she coughed out the water and said, "I'm sorry, Daddy. I'm sorry."

***

The police had no further leads about Miranda McBean's disappearance. They found nothing on Gina Loyer either. She worked at a grocery store in College Park. He'd taken her a year ago, had his fun, hurt her real bad, then dumped her in McDonough. Lyle sold the Cadillac around that time, too. Now he drove a '95 Buick Skylark sedan.

The trunk wasn't as big, but it was a nice family car.

***

Lyle was in a motel on Six Flags Drive with another prostitute. He didn't mean to kill her. Honestly, it just happened. He'd put his hands around her throat and it felt too good to let go. Now he had a problem. The chances of him walking out unnoticed with a body wrapped in the bedding were slim, so he drove to the store and bought bleach and rubber gloves. While he was out, he went to a nearby laundry mat on Austell Parkway to wash all the bedding and hoped her pimp wouldn't find her before he returned.

The motel was one of the scuzziest he'd ever been to. The body would be found eventually, and about a thousand hits of DNA would be all over the place. Lyle only wanted to get rid of his own. While the woman soaked in the tub, he got to work scrubbing the place down, paying special attention to everything he touched. When he was done, he washed her down as well, cleaned her fingernails and between her legs, then dried her and put her clothes back on. Once he had her on the freshly made bed, he took a good look around. He'd been raping women for twenty years, and he'd even gotten away with what happened to Mary, so he would not get caught about this.

When he checked into these motels, he never gave his real name and as long as he paid cash up front, the clerk didn't care to know who he was. How many men checked into this hotel with hookers? Lyle was no different from any of the other men, so he tried to act like everything was normal, slid the clerk the key under the plexiglass window and told her to have a good night.

Two days later, he didn't show his surprise when Detectives Trimclay and Kenner came knocking on his door. They were having supper, and Lyle heard Joni say, "He was home all day," and slam the door shut.

This time, they didn't want to talk to him in the front yard. They'd brought him down to the station and put him in a hot room for hours before they decided to question him. This time Trimclay didn't ask him where he was two nights ago, or if he knew a woman named Pamela Davant, a.k.a. "Cherry" the prostitute who was known for her rides near Six Flags.

"We have you on video at the laundry mat washing a hotel comforter."

Surprised, Lyle said, "The laundry mat can afford video cameras?" That was something.

"And when we brought a photo of you around to the nearby grocery stores, a kid said you bought bleach, yellow gloves, and a candy bar. Now tell me, Mr. Chaskey, what were you doing at the motel?"

"How'd you get a photo of me?"

"We can do this all night, asshole." It was Kenner that spoke. *The baby.*

For a second, Lyle looked at him. Then he said, "You sure it's not past your bedtime?" and waited for the detective to hit him, but it never came.

Instead, Kenner said, "I don't think he's ready to talk."

"You're right." Trimclay stood. "We can talk about Cherry's syphilis over pizza and beer."

Lyle didn't bite, and ignored the men as they walked out. They were able to hold him, and Lyle found himself in a smelly jail cell, but he was sure that they didn't have enough evidence to convict him of anything. The video image of him washing the bedding was grainy. The kid that sold him the bleach was a cross-eyed teenager with broken glasses. He was not going to prison; they had no proof.

Even when they got a warrant to check his house, they found nothing. They got another warrant to check the garage and found his hidden place and an old bag of pillow stuffing in a bottom drawer of a tool bench, along with a handful of small knives and the stun gun. The garage was clean, though. They could put together whatever evidence they found and nothing could be connected to him. He wasn't stupid. He didn't keep pieces of the women in his freezer. Didn't keep jewelry. Didn't keep a logbook of his crimes. They were all upstairs in his head. They had nothing, and Lyle was confident.

But a week later he was still in the Cobb County jail.

Kenner brought him back into the interrogation room, and Lyle laughed when he accused him of the crimes of the person dubbed *The Cotton Mouth Killer*. The whole theory amused him. "You came to this conclusion because of a bag of pillow stuffing?" Lyle asked. Problem was, when they'd first found some of these women, the collection and recording of evidence wasn't that great. Or maybe it was, but they didn't know what they were supposed to be looking for. "You have nothing," Lyle said.

"You want to tell me about this?" Although he was the younger of the two detectives, he looked to be the meaner, like he had the potential of not putting up with any bullshit, but he didn't have the experience to control it. Lyle knew a thing or two about control. Maybe he could teach something to Detective Kenner.

Kenner set some photos of the hidden place and the table inside of it on the table. "Why would you need a table with anchor bolts screwed to the sides? This is the sickest shit I've ever seen."

As though Kenner were ignorant, Lyle said, "You haven't been a cop long enough to know what sick is. Trimclay still hold your hand while you take a piss, Mr. Detective?"

"What'd you use the table for?"

Lyle was going to need an attorney. He didn't say anything.

Kenner said, "Was it your family? Your little girl, Mr. Hero," and just like that, Lyle became uncaged.

Still in cuffs, he threw himself across the table at Kenner and punched him. The switch in his brain turned off and Lyle swung his cuffed fist at him and connected with his jaw. Then the door flew open and deputies pulled him off.

Kenner straightened his tie, said, "You're dead."

The lawyer's name was Sterling Dingler, and he was confident that this was all a mistake, but after his first court appearance in which the judge set no bail, Lyle was to be locked up until the preliminary hearing. Suddenly, Lyle realized Sterling Ding-dong didn't know what he was doing.

Two days later, Roslyn served him with divorce papers. What bothered him was that when he got out, she'd want the divorce and take Joni away from him. That wasn't going to happen. It wasn't fair to keep his daughter from him.

At their next meeting, Sterling Dingler asked Lyle again to be honest with him and tell him about the table. So far, that was all they had.

"And the cotton filler," Ding-dong reminded him.

But that's not what they were going after, so forget the garage. The district attorney wanted him on the dead prostitute, and Lyle wasn't confessing to a damn thing. They'd brought him into a lineup and the motel clerk picked him out and said he was the guy who rented the room where she was found. Once the state had their shit together, they had a court date set, but it would be another month before that happened. He was rotting away in that stupid jail cell while the lawyers sat around twiddling their thumbs to figure out how to stack their evidence against him. He was stuck there through October and November. Lyle didn't take the plea bargain, which was to plead guilty and end up in prison for twenty years with a chance of parole. The prostitute wasn't worth it. If they were going to lock him up, they better damn do it for something that was worth it.

He told them, "You're not listening to me. I didn't do it."

43

He'd take his chances with a jury. Let's see how well the detectives and lawyers did their jobs.

***

They pulled Lyle out of his cell one day and brought him into another interrogation room, this one bigger than all the others. Sterling Dingler was there. Detectives Kenner and Trimclay were there. Two uniformed officers. Lyle didn't know what the hell was going on, but assumed this was all part of the process. It's not like he'd been charged with murder before and knew what to expect.

"Mr. Chaskey," Kenner said, because it appeared he'd taken over the case. Lyle wondered how his partner felt about that. "We've brought you in here because we have something to tell you about your wife, Roslyn." He said it like Lyle didn't know who his wife was.

Lyle looked at each of the men. Trimclay stood taller than Kenner, but they both had that cocky attitude about them. I'm better than you. I'm smarter than you. Right. Sterling Dingler's hair was fuzzy and red, and his brown suit fit loose on his shoulders and looked like red cotton candy sticking out of a brown paper bag.

Lyle was looking across at Sterling's papers when Kenner said, "Mr. Chaskey, we're here to inform you that around two o'clock this morning your wife, Roslyn, committed suicide."

Hot fear spread through his veins. "Where's Joni?"

"She's with the Flockharts right now."

"Does she know?"

Kenner cleared his throat. "She's the one that called 911. She heard the gunshot and called 911."

Lyle put his face in his hands and took deep breaths. What has Roslyn done? If there was a slight chance that he didn't get out of here, at least Joni would have been safe with her mother.

But now? Now, who was going to take care of her? "What's going to happen to her?"

"If no one steps up to care for her, she becomes a ward of the state."

"You have to let me out of here. I have to take care of my daughter."

Kenner shook his head. "It doesn't work that way, Mr. Chaskey."

Lyle took a deep breath, felt a sob catch in his throat, but refused to let his emotions take over in front of these assholes. "I have a sister. Her name is Lacey. She lives in Peachtree City."

Trimclay took a seat across from Lyle. "We've contacted her. She said she wants nothing to do with this. Can you tell us why your sister would rather your daughter go to foster care than with her?"

Lyle didn't answer, just looked blankly ahead. His sister hated him; said all the things he'd accused their mother of doing were lies. He hadn't spoken a word to Lacey in nearly fifteen years.

"Your mother lives in Jefferson—"

"Oh, god, no. No. Please," Lyle begged. "Don't let my baby girl go with her. I'll do anything."

Kenner offered him a smile. "We can only help you if you give us the truth, Mr. Chaskey."

That's when Lyle broke.

***

He admitted to killing the prostitute in the motel, told them it was an accident because it really was. Things got out of control. He strangled her then cleaned the room. They kept poking and prodding, so to keep from getting the death penalty he told the district attorney that Kenner was right, he'd murdered the seven women found over the past ten years. He raped them and put the stuffing in their mouths. He offered whatever information they needed as long as Joni was safe and didn't live within fifty miles of his mother. If the DA wasn't willing to make a deal with that, then Lyle was willing to offer them more, but apparently that was enough to make the plea bargain. Lyle would spend the rest of his life in prison without parole.

"I want to see my daughter."

It took them days to get permission to allow his daughter to see him. As soon as Lyle saw her, he draped his cuffed hands over her head and pulled her close to him, felt her beating heart against his own.

"I'm so scared, Daddy," she sobbed, into his neck.

He didn't let her go. Had hurt the one person he loved the most. "Everything will be okay. You look so pretty." She had on a light blue Easter dress, but had worn her filthy pink high tops.

"Mom died. The blood was all over." Her hair smelled like fresh strawberries. "They're saying all this bad stuff about you."

"Don't listen to them, baby. No matter what they say, don't listen."

"I want to go with you, Daddy."

"You can't, baby."

When they ripped her away from him, she was still yelling the same thing. *I want to go with you, Daddy.* He'd never seen his daughter so mad. She kicked the officer in the shin, tried to shove him away from her. Snot hung from her nose from crying and screaming. Lyle was at the door now. "It'll be okay."

Her hair was wild, and she pulled off her shoes and threw them at Detective Kenner, then she kicked him in the balls. "I hate you," Joni said. Then she threw a chair at him.

"Get him out—" Kenner tried, but bent over from pain instead.

The last thing Lyle remembered seeing was his daughter looking less like her angelic self and more like a feral child.

Part Two

Chapter Six

Clemmie's Diner was an old restaurant in the heart of Fayette County that had been built in 1952 when mom and pop places were everywhere. Back then, the county was small and Clemmie's was an affordable place to get a cup of coffee and pancakes or steak and eggs over grits and gravy. The restaurant was a white wooden structure with a front porch and the inside was L-shaped with red booths along the windows, and sixteen stools along the front counter. The floor was drab beige linoleum, but red tile covered the walls to give the place some color.

Joni had been working here for twelve years, rarely saw a stranger. The grandmas and grandpas, better known as the coffee crowd, had been coming here since Clemmie opened the place, but the young ones, the newer generation of the coffee crowd, stopped by from seven p.m. until nine p.m. for coffee and fries. Some opted for ice cream and pie. Rarely did they ever eat a supper plate.

It was Friday night, and the rain was coming down like someone opened a fire hydrant on the place. Three teenage girls sat in a booth laughing about how they were going to get out without drowning, and Joni wondered the same thing about herself. Clemmie's wasn't far from her house, and she usually walked to work when she could. Today hadn't been any different, except she wasn't expecting the downpour. Rain pelted the tin roof, and the place smelled like summer heat mixed with fried onions.

Other than the teens, two regulars sat at another booth talking about their newborn grandson. Teddy Glencoe rang the kitchen bell and Joni went back behind the counter to grab the teens' food. They had thirty minutes until closing, but it wasn't like they'd kick anybody out.

"There's no Wi-Fi?" one of the girls asked and made a pouty lip.

"Sorry," Joni said. "Old place." Archie Glencoe wasn't about to re-wire the place so people could park their butts all day and surf the net.

The teens went back to chatting, and Joni could have sat down with them and fit right in. Long hair. Youthful look. Slender, toned body. Except Joni wasn't a teenager anymore. That part of her life was long gone.

"What's it look like out there?" Teddy nodded toward the dining room. She'd already brought him all the empty dishes that needed to be washed.

"I'll have it done by nine-thirty."

Since eight o'clock, Joni and Teddy were the only two employees in the restaurant. The dinner crowd was long gone because of the rain, and it wasn't like they'd get bombarded, so she sent Val home an hour early. Joni finished cleaning the rest of her tables while the teens shoved their hoodies over their heads and made a run for their car.

"Y'all be careful," she said.

When the last of the customers were gone, she locked the front door at nine-fifteen, then went to the kitchen to fill a bucket of mop water. Teddy's back was to her as he stood at the sink washing dishes, his muscles stretching his shirt tight across his back. Light brown curls touched the collar of his black Clemmie's t-shirt, and his jeans were worn through the rear.

Joni filled the yellow bucket with disinfectant and looked again at Teddy. They didn't talk much anymore, and Joni wondered if he'd ever forgive her.

He turned around and caught her eye, held it for a moment, then looked away. There was nothing to say, so she went out into the dining room and began her nightly closing chore of mopping as she listened to Patsy Cline on the music station. Joni didn't like Patsy Cline. She sang too much about love, and what was love anyway? Sacrifice the elements of love, and life becomes full of pain. Commit, and love becomes nothing more than a mask to cover up the ugly desires that are hidden underneath.

Joni felt a sense of ease as she shoved the handle down on the bucket to squeeze out the water from the mop and wondered if anyone ever knew what true love was. The diner was dim with only the lights on from behind the bar area, and she had to admit that this was one of her favorite times of the day. Being in Clemmie's alone with Teddy, the quiet taking over her thoughts. No customers yelling for more ketchup.

The wet mop slid across the linoleum that was well past its life expectancy in the 80s, but don't tell that to Archie Glencoe, he says the customers like the place the way it is. Clemmie's hadn't changed in sixty years except for the changes the health department made mandatory.

Joni was almost done mopping when she heard, "What's this?" and Teddy held up a skinny tea urn she'd forgotten to dump and take back to be washed. Apologizing was useless. Teddy would still roll his eyes. He did a double check behind the counter, then went to wash the urn. When they were both done, they brought dishes back to the front and set up for Saturday morning, which was always their busiest day of the week. But thankfully Joni wouldn't experience it. She had other plans for tomorrow.

Shortly after nine-thirty, Teddy locked all the doors, and they stood on the front porch for a brief second and watched the rain.

"See you Sunday." Joni stepped off the porch, warm rain hitting her as she took off down Grady Avenue, and a second later Teddy pulled up next to her in his old truck.

51

"Get in," he said, and she did. It was one thing for him to offer, and another for her to ask. Joni shook the rain out of her hair and held tight to the sopping wet bag of leftover food.

Fayette County was home to the oldest courthouse in the state of Georgia. Even though it wasn't used today, it still stood proudly in the center of the city. Joni's neighborhood was considered to be historical even though there was nothing special about it. The tiny houses were built back in the early 1900s, and each had undergone many renovations as new people moved in.

Joni's yellow house was in the back of the neighborhood. The window boxes where she planted geraniums and impatiens were new. A huge live oak with its arms stretched over the house provided enough shade to keep the air conditioner use at a minimum. That was something considering Georgia's heat.

As soon as Teddy pulled into the driveway, two furry heads shoved back the curtains to see who was visiting.

"Thanks, Teddy."

"Sure thing." His southern drawl had no emotion in it whatsoever, like he could have been dropping a 'coon off at the taxidermist.

Joni pressed her damp palm to the door handle. "You want to come in?"

The truck's green glow shone over his face as he shook his head. Joni got out and Teddy was gone in seconds, regret eating at her heart like tiny maggots digging their way inside.

Clyde and Bubba bombarded her as soon as she opened the door, and because she lived so close to Clemmie's, she usually checked on them during a break at work, but the rain stopped her today. "I'm sorry," she said to the two German shepherds as they smelled the brown sack in her hand. They had a doggy door, but she still walked the dogs every night after her shift. What the hell, she thought, she was already soaked.

Joni entered the kitchen and nearly tripped on the overturned garbage can. "Who did this?" Clyde hauled tail down the hall. The garbage can had been on top of the table, but Clyde pushed a chair back so he could dump the garbage can over. The dog knew he wasn't in trouble because five seconds later he ran back to see what she thought of his job of destroying last night's spaghetti.

The umbrella was nothing against the rain as she walked the dogs down Redwine Road. She must have looked stupid to the people driving past her, but the dogs loved it. They would roll around in mud puddles if she'd let them. Even with the rain, they wanted to smell everything and peed to cover it up.

The rain smelled like pine as it came down and by the time Joni got home, she was freezing, but she had to dry the dogs first or they'd roll all over the carpet and sofa. She kept old towels in the carport, but knew it was no use, the dogs smelled like they'd been left outside for days and their fur wasn't easy to dry.

Both of the dogs had identical markings, typical brown legs with black backs, but Clyde's muzzle was darker and covered some of his eyes and ears. As Joni rubbed the towel over his back, he barked once and went on alert.

They heard something.

Joni did too.

Before she could yank the dogs back inside, Bubba jerked forward and Joni grabbed him by the collar. There was movement on the other side of the wooden fence and when both dogs started barking, two deer took off down the street.

Joni pressed her face into Clyde's, and let out the breath she'd been holding. She wouldn't hesitate to let them go if she ever had to. That was the whole point of getting them six years ago. By the time Joni got inside, her nerves were still on edge. She'd been living here for eight years and never had a problem with anyone, but every so often she'd get some stupid letter or email telling her she needed to die because her blood was poisoned. Once, she ended up with a brick through her car window.

Nothing was wrong with her. She was just like everyone else. Okay, so she had a serial killer as a father but that didn't change who she was inside, and even though the families weren't happy because he was still alive and their daughters weren't, it didn't mean anyone needed to treat her badly.

Still soaking wet, Joni pulled out a bottle of bleach to scour her kitchen floor. The smell of bleach was something she welcomed. It reminded her of her father.

***

The rain had yet to let up at four a.m. Joni wasn't the only one up, just the only one dumb enough to take the dogs for a walk again in a downpour.

She dried off the dogs, and put fresh food and water for them, which they chowed down like they were starving. After her shower, she put on a pair of blue jeans, a bra with no under wire, sneakers, and a sensible gray blouse that wasn't revealing in any way.

"I won't be back for a long time," she said to the dogs. "Play nice. And Clyde, stay out of the trash." She gave them kisses and ended up with dog hair on her shirt.

Joni grabbed a breakfast bar and was on the highway by five. The drive to Reidsville in Tattnall County took three hours, and she liked to get there early because sign-in sometimes took forever. If she didn't arrive before they did the morning counts, she'd have to wait for afternoon visitation. The parking lot was practically empty but would fill up quickly throughout the day. Joni checked her pockets, grabbed her license, and left with only her keys in her hand and a small clear bag full of quarters, and couldn't dodge the raindrops to save her life.

Georgia State Prison had three various check points for visitors before entering the general population visiting center.

The first was a metal detector with a hand wand—wouldn't want to provide a shank for the criminals, now would she? The second asked for her driver's license where her name and number were written into a log. They would return her license and keys upon check-out. The third was through another security area where she held her arms out and was given another hand wand job just in case they missed the shank or contraband the first time. At this point, her shoes were checked, and she had to lift her pants legs as far as they would go. This slow process took nearly an hour. The group of visitors was held in a small waiting area behind a gate. Joni had gotten familiar with some of these faces and found it comforting when she saw the same ones every other Saturday. She'd watched one little boy grow from a silly toddler to excited school kid who couldn't wait to see his dad.

Joni stood with her arms folded and waited for her name to be called.

"You bring all this rain with you?" Officer Simon was an older man with tiny curls all over his head. His green eyes sparkled, but the lighting in the prison didn't do them justice. This spot had been his home for all the years she'd been visiting. Considering what the officers had to put up with, they were mostly rude, but Simon was all right.

"I was hoping it would keep all the visitors away so I could have the room to myself."

GSP was a multi-security level prison, housing over fifteen hundred inmates that ranged from trusty to maximum. It used to be a death house, but now all the death row inmates lived in Jackson, but that didn't mean this prison was any safer. Joni never forgot how dangerous these men were. Her dad always told her never look any of them in the eye, which was a sign of weakness on her part, but looking a criminal in the eye was only a challenge to them.

Finally, her name was called and Joni sat at a metal table while her dad was walked in. He was considered an ideal inmate, no longer got into any fights since he'd maintained his status among the other inmates years ago. No one messed with him anymore.

She stood and hugged him tight, felt the roughness of his white jumper beneath her palms. Still a big man, her arms barely wrapped around his chest. They sat down across from each other and she noticed his hair was getting gray. He'd been incarcerated for fifteen years now and wasn't aging all that well. He was only fifty-six. Hooded brow bones gave his caramel eyes a guarded look. His cheeks were sunken in like little pools. He kept his hair short and his face shaved, his fingernails trimmed and clean. Every time Joni saw him, she wondered how he was making out without his bottles of bleach because he said that prison was a dirty place.

"We don't go out when it rains."

Joni ran her hand over her damp hair. "It's yucky outside."

"I'd rather sit in the rain than be stuck in concrete. Are you doing okay?"

Always worried about her. It was hard coming up with things to talk about sometimes because truthfully, nothing had changed in the last two weeks, but she was his only visitor. He received letters all the time from people obsessed with him, but Joni liked to think of herself as his only link to the outside world.

"I've been doing good," she said. "Are you still seeing the counselor?"

"I don't like to, but yes."

"What do you talk about?"

"You." Lyle touched her hand briefly, then let go when a corrections officer looked their way. More visitors and inmates were settling in and she would never get used to how loud the place was. Like voices buzzing from all directions in a school cafeteria. "My psychologist doesn't think I love you."

56

"Do you?" This was something he constantly confirmed for her. There was always a dialogue running through her mind about whether he truly loved her. "Or is it something that you tell yourself you're supposed to feel?"

His eyes met hers. "I love you, Joni. I wish I could prove that to you." A moment passed, and he said, "What about you?"

"I stopped going to the counselor because they think—"

"I meant; do you love me?"

"Of course, I do, Daddy." No matter what happened, she couldn't turn her back on him. He seemed pleased with her answer.

"So, no more counselor for you?"

"Not since Amanda."

"It's not every day your best friend screws you over."

"Yeah, well, maybe you shouldn't have saved her after all."

Her dad shook his head. "Don't talk like that."

Amanda Flockhart was nothing more than an opportunistic bitch who told nothing but lies for attention. Joni wasn't interested in talking to anyone about a damn thing. Not a doctor or even an old friend. Amanda wrote her lies anyway, based on police evidence. Isn't that how it always goes? Her dad still refused to talk about the specifics, never went into details about how he did things, and according to Joni, she felt like it was enough. She didn't want to know the details, and if it were up to her, she'd pull her dad out of prison and take him to a remote island to care for him. Prison was a sick place and he shouldn't be here.

"How's Aunt Lacey?"

Joni kept her answer short, and said, "She's fine," because talking about Aunt Lacey would lead to talking about Grandmother and her father didn't need to think about that woman ever again. Aunt Lacey was almost twelve years older than her dad and moved out of their house by the time he was six, so he didn't really know her all that well. Joni hadn't either

57

until she finally took her in. Living with Aunt Lacey was no skippity-do-da day, so she tried to keep her out of their conversations.

Her dad's left arm remained bent at a slight angle because he had two pins in the elbow and ugly scar tissue because of the dog attack. He had a habit of rubbing the scar and as Joni focused her eyes on his, she could see his fingers sliding over the indentions in his skin.

"Are you doing anything new?" she asked.

"They're still allowing me to help teach a business class. I enjoy it. Some men look to me for advice. I was on library duty last week and I hate it, but this week I'm back in the kitchen."

"Why do you like the kitchen? I don't remember you ever cooking, just mom."

She caught herself before she realized and looked down. The mom topic was never discussed, and Joni hated how her dad acted like Roslyn Chaskey never existed.

He ignored the comment and said with a smile, "Two new people wrote to me this month."

Two new people, plus the dozens of other crazies that sent him letters. "But you never write them back."

He shrugged.

Should she consider herself lucky to get several letters a week from her father? Of course, his letters consisted of everything he'd done that day, what he'd eaten, which inmates he'd spoken with. He never wrote men's names, just called them "this rat" and "this other rat." His headaches and stomachaches were a popular topic, and he swore the prison was trying to poison him.

Commotion from the right caught their attention. A woman slapped an inmate in the face and cursed at him. A moment later, the corrections officers were rushing to the table, and everything went dead quiet. More COs rushed the visiting center and told everyone to remain seated, and suddenly Joni was nervous and wondered what in the hell was going on. Both the inmate and the visitor were dragged out in different directions, but Joni couldn't help but notice the sick smile on the man's face.

She turned back to her father, and he was all relaxed like nothing happened. He was used to this. Before she could even inquire, Lyle said, his voice low, "Six years ago he killed his own son. Hacked him up and fed him to the family dog."

"What?"

"Shhh." Lyle shook his head, turned to check his back. That was all he was going to say about it.

The visiting center was a large room with vending machines but Lyle wasn't allowed to use them, had to remain seated at all times. "What would you like?" Joni grabbed the bag of quarters.

"Something sweet."

Joni returned with juice, donuts, two candy bars, a bag of chips, and some peanuts. They had to eat everything because he wasn't allowed to take it back with him. She wished she could bring him some home cooked food from Clemmie's, but that was never going to happen.

They talked about her dogs and their tricks. She'd sent Lyle a picture of them with a letter once, and he always asked about them. They talked about his routine and the time he spent outside, in his cell, with his counselor, with other inmates. Her dad talked a lot about himself, almost to the point that he rambled unconsciously. But Joni knew better. Her dad didn't say anything that he didn't want to, thought well before he spoke, even to his own daughter.

Joni spent the next few hours soaking up her dad's company in the cold, concrete room as other inmates' families came and went. This wasn't how their life was supposed to be, but she loved him all the same. When it was time for him to leave, she hugged him goodbye and hated this part all over again.

"I'm the only one you can trust," he said.

"I know, Daddy."

59

"Stay safe."

"You stay safe."

Arms spread wide, he said, "I'm in the safest place there is, baby."

***

The next day, Joni went through the swinging door to Clemmie's kitchen, where Archie and Teddy were working. "I got a meatloaf plate, gravy on the side. Broccoli instead of corn. Extra corn bread." Archie arched an eyebrow, repeated the order. "You got it," Joni said.

She grabbed two of her plates off the counter and set off to deliver them. It was one o'clock on Sunday and the church crowd was just cutting loose and the place was still busy with latecomers. Joni and Val worked the booths while Penny, Archie's wife, worked the counter and register.

"Miss?"

Joni turned. Mrs. Mason had a floral scarf wrapped around her head like it was freezing inside. "Yes, ma'am?"

"May I have more barbeque sauce?" she said. "And I'd like more tea, but just half and half this time."

The place was hustling, and as Joni filled the tea and grabbed barbeque sauce, she noticed two plates in the pass through.

"Your fried chicken is up," Teddy said.

She wanted to tell him she saw it, but kept her mouth shut. "Can you add another pickle to this one?"

"Why didn't you tell me before?"

"Because she forgot," Penny said, and stuck an order on the bar. "Get her a pickle spear and go." Teddy slapped a pickle spear on the plate and rolled his eyes. "I know," Penny said. "Must be a real stink havin' ya mama as a boss. I need a well-done burger." Penny flicked the order she put up.

"I can read," Teddy said, and Joni felt his eyes on the back of her head. She made her deliveries, then went back into the

60

kitchen, where she grabbed a handful of black olives and put them into a small bowl.

"Joni, what the hell are you doing?" Archie said, sweating at the grill.

"A kid asked for black olives."

Teddy threw two gloves at her chest. "I think that's grounds for termination."

"I forgot."

"You know," Teddy said to his dad. "It's only every other Sunday she's stupid."

"Fuck you, Teddy."

"Hey! We don't use that language 'round here," Archie said as she walked through the swinging door.

The Glencoes were good people. Pillars of the community. Went to church every weekend. Gave food to the needy. So good, in fact, that when Teddy ended his relationship with Joni, Archie didn't fire her for breaking his son's heart.

Five minutes later, when Joni tried to set down the meatloaf plate, she knew there would be a problem. First of all, the guy was a jerk for filling up a whole booth by himself when there were plenty of stools at the counter. But no, make a family wait so he could lounge in a booth and watch the cars go by. Second, he hadn't looked at her the whole time she'd asked him for his order, just chatted away on his cell phone.

He took the cell phone away from his face long enough to say, "That's not what I ordered." He had a newspaper spread out on the table, stopping her from setting the plate down. Joni repeated what he'd ordered, and he said, "Yes, but I also asked for a baked potato instead of mashed. That's why I didn't want gravy."

Joni didn't want to have to smack the shit out of this guy. The customer's right and all, but she was still going to get hell from Teddy. "I'm sorry. Everything else is correct except you'd like a baked potato?"

"You didn't write it down. I told you you'd mess it up."

But sometimes the customer was wrong. "Sir. You asked for gravy in an extra bowl because it was too runny. You even asked me if the mashed potatoes had garlic or cheese. Next time, I suggest you get off your cell phone when you order."

"Excuse me?"

"Would you like me to get you that baked potato?"

The guy looked down at the cell phone in his hand as someone on the other end was talking. "I'm here," he said into the phone as he scooted out of the booth. "You will not believe what just happened to me."

A second later Val said, "Good going," and took his newspaper.

As Joni watched the guy get into his car, another man caught her attention as he and his big dimpled chin walked in the front door. He looked at her directly, said, "Can we talk?"

Special Agent Cyrus Kenner was part of a team with the Georgia Bureau of Investigation that specialized in recovery and identification of human remains. He was also part of a response team for missing persons. The guy needed a psych eval because he was too obsessed with dead bodies and missing women, which was why he'd contacted Joni years ago because he had missing women files coming out the wazoo and was desperate to find out which ones were her father's.

Joni wished she would've locked the door before he had a chance to open it. Government officials were not her favorite people. Not after she'd seen firsthand the way they'd treated her mother like an accessory to what her father had done. The sound of the gunshot that night still rang true in Joni's ears.

"You see this name tag? It means I'm working."

"It's serious."

"I doubt that," she said. "I got a fresh meatloaf plate right here. No line. No waiting. It's all yours, then you can scoot a'loo on out of here."

She hadn't seen Cyrus Kenner in two years. He was nice to her, sure, but that was only because he wanted something. They had a love/hate relationship. Cyrus loved to get personal information about Lyle, and Joni just hated him. Today his face was serious, and he blinked once, then said. "We found a body."

"I bet that's just the icing on your birthday cake. Do you want this?" She held up the meatloaf plate.

Cyrus lowered his voice. "We need to talk outside."

Joni sighed, then asked Val, "Can you cover me for five minutes?"

Warm air hit her as they stepped outside on the porch where she folded her arms across her chest, and noticed now that he had a limp in his walk. Like maybe someone kicked him in the nuts. "Five minutes. Go."

"Last week, the remains of a woman were found in Tallulah Gorge State Park. She was between twenty and forty years old. Tiny white fibers were found in the throat. They matched the ones from the other bodies. We have him on this, but he's not giving us an identity."

"I haven't heard anything about this."

"It's been all over the news," he said as though she'd been under a rock. "I spoke with him two days ago, but he isn't saying a damn thing. Apparently, he still thinks I'm a two-year-old cop fresh from my beat."

Joni had seen her dad yesterday. Why didn't he tell her about this? "Cyrus, you're wrong about this. He said there were no more."

"And you believed him?"

"This isn't one of his, okay? He said there were no more."

Cyrus folded his arms. "Forensics don't lie. He's a serial killer—"

"Don't call him that."

"If it walks like a duck... Look, all I'm saying is that this woman's family deserves to know the truth." Cyrus stood still while Joni absorbed what he said. Why would her dad lie to her? If he said there were no more, then she believed him. Why couldn't they?

"Joni, her neck was broken. That wasn't his MO, so what happened? And this dump site was the farthest north from all the others. Can you at least talk to him?"

"You want me to do your job?"

"I just want her name. Something. I've racked my brains trying to match this woman to a file. Her dental records have given us no hope. For all I know, she could be another prostitute."

For the last fifteen years, Joni let none of this get to her. Her father was a serial rapist and only a murderer to cover it up. She never thought about the things he'd done, never asked questions, never talked about it with him. If she didn't talk about it, maybe it would all go away, vanish with the morning fog.

Her father ended up with four life sentences without parole. With his bargain, he'd escaped the death penalty. If they found another decomposed body with the same cotton fibers in the throat, then where did that leave him? And why did he lie? And why did it matter, he was already in prison.

"He said there were no more," Joni said, and felt her words catch in her throat.

"Come with me to GSP."

"By the time we get there, visiting hours will be over."

"I have my own special visiting hours."

Chapter Seven

Neither one of them spoke for a long time. Pine and Sweet gum trees passed in a flash along the highway as the sun played shadows along the dash. Today was Sunday, and the ride reminded her of all those Sunday drives she'd taken with her dad. Special Sundays. They never made it to Tallulah Gorge. Had he ever gone to the state park alone?

They passed Macon when Joni said, "Why are you walking funny these days?"

"Some bastard kicked out my knee a year ago. Busted my knee cap. I wasn't even working that day. I ended up with surgery. Not fun, I guarantee."

"You seem to have a problem with people kicking you where it hurts."

Cyrus's laugh echoed the SUV. "Yeah, Joni. I'm starting to reconsider my line of work."

"Can't be too bad. How long since you've been playing with the big boys?"

He gave her a hard look, like he was offended. "Long enough to know it's not the size of the foot that matters."

She wore her blue Easter dress the day they took him away. It was the same dress she wore at her mother's funeral that day. What kind of people made a little girl say goodbye to both parents on the same day? Someone had to pay, and Cyrus was a direct shot.

"Something clicked inside me that day. It was like I wasn't myself and I wanted to hurt everybody and I wanted everybody to hurt like me. Nobody understood what they were taking away from me and my mom had just shot herself in the mouth while I was in my bedroom asleep. Something just clicked inside me."

That click made her wonder about how her dad did the things he did. "Doesn't something click inside everybody sometimes?"

"Yeah, which is why we have prisons and psych wards. Do you feel clicky all the time?"

"Every time I see you, I feel a little clicky," she said, and Cyrus laughed. "I'm sure you're wrong about this."

Cyrus swallowed down the last of his to-go coffee he'd nabbed from Clemmie's before they left. "The fibers match."

"I don't think so."

"Are you really going to argue with me about this?"

Her mind settled down, and she realized Cyrus was right. Facts won't lie if the fibers match. Talking to her dad about it was going to be useless. Lyle said years ago he was doing the time for the crimes he'd committed. There was nothing left to say.

Now a body turned up and Cyrus wanted answers. "I tried to talk to him a few days ago."

"I saw him yesterday. He never mentioned anything."

"Why would he? He likes the way you have him up on a pedestal. We have the evidence, but he's not interested in giving the info."

"Maybe it's a copycat."

"The remains have been there for over twenty years. That's when your father was active. You're still in denial about this, Joni. Let me tell you about Miranda Nicole McBean. Her family said she had a gentle smile and trusting heart. She moved to Atlanta with her boyfriend so she could practice ballet. She was reported missing on April 10, 1996. Her car had been tampered with and looked like foul play. For eighteen days, we searched for her. Interviewed 565 individuals; family members, friends, ex-boyfriend, co-workers, neighbors. We checked phone records and bank records and dusted her car for fingerprints. We got nothing, Joni. And I know now, without a doubt, that the day I talked to your dad about her, she was in that garage or already dead."

"Cyrus, he said there were no more."

"I made a promise to the McBeans seventeen years ago, and I never found their little girl. This body is too old to be Miranda, but I want to know who she is." Cyrus breathed hard, and Joni wondered for a moment if he was trying to calm himself down or having a heart attack. "You need to understand what type of person your father was. He stalked women, held them captive, and tortured them, murdered them; all the while his wife and daughter were right next door in the house."

"Doesn't he need a lawyer to speak with you?"

When he didn't answer, she realized he was trying to get information before it came to that. Cyrus sighed. "I never believed for a second that there were no more. Too many women went missing without a trace, yet somehow Lyle Chaskey's name came into the picture. Tell me why?"

Joni didn't have an answer. "He's already in prison. What does it matter now?"

"Justice needs to be served. These families want closure. They deserve that."

***

Cyrus was right about his special visiting hours. They went through security checks, but this time they were led to a different room, down another hall, far on the left side of the prison. As they walked, one officer told them to stop and put their backs to the wall as a CO led a shackled inmate down the hall. Once the inmate was gone, they continued. Joni had the feeling she wasn't supposed to be there.

Her dad sat in a small room with a table and chairs, and Cyrus's plan was for Joni to go in and talk to him. He'd watch through the observation window. A minute later a blubbery man in a blue suit walked over.

"Warden," Cyrus said, and shook the man's hand. "This is Joni Chaskey, the inmate's daughter." She shook the man's hand.

"Lamar Parrino," the warden said. The man's face was round like a basketball. With his pasty skin and bow tie, he reminded Joni of Porky Pig. Strange how she'd been visiting here for twelve years and had yet to meet the man.

"Nice to meet you," Joni said.

"We will not upset my inmate today, Agent Kenner," Warden Parrino said, and looked between the both of them. Maybe the man wasn't so bad, Joni thought, and waited for him to stutter.

"I need answers."

"Maybe he doesn't have anything to give."

"His memory serves him perfectly."

Cyrus was right about that. Her dad could recall memories in ways that many people couldn't. The warden gave Cyrus a stern look, then he turned to Joni. "I know you are a frequent visitor. Please understand that these are special circumstances. We don't normally allow schedules to be interrupted with such short notice." Parrino looked again at Cyrus, then back to Joni. "I have to tell you that there is a camera on the wall and you'll be recorded. I'll give you thirty minutes."

"Yes, sir."

Cyrus sent her in there with some questions to ask, and it kind of felt nice to be important to his case even though she wanted it to be a different inmate.

Lyle sat at the table with handcuffs around his wrists, and an officer stood in the corner of the small room. "For her own protection," the warden had said, and she wanted to ask him if he was joking. Her dad sat facing the door and his eyes went huge when she walked in.

"What are you doing here?"

Joni sat across from him, the door to her back, the one-way window to her right, the black camera blinking in the corner. She offered a smile, but he didn't give one in return. "Daddy, I think you know why I'm here. Cyrus said you won't answer his questions—"

"Oh, *Cyrus,* sent you here. Well, *Cyrus* Kenner can kiss my ass. He had no right to bring you here."

Joni swallowed the lump in her throat as her dad's eyes went dark in a way she hadn't seen in a long time. She thought back to what the warden said about not upsetting his inmate, and now she realized what he meant. But she wasn't in any danger here, not with her own father. Inmate or not.

"Well, I'm here and I want to know if you murd—" Joni took a deep breath and suddenly her hands were sweating. "Did you dump a body in Tallulah Gorge?"

"No. I've never even been to Tallulah Gorge."

"Then how do you explain the cotton fibers?"

"You've been listening to too much of their bullshit."

Joni looked over at the window. Lyle said, "Is he watching?" and she nodded her head. "Kenner is nothing but a virgin detective looking to make himself look good at nailing every gone woman to the *Cotton Mouth Killer.* Well, I got news for him. He can keep trying." He looked down at his hands.

Joni's voice was barely a whisper. "Why are you so defensive if you didn't do it?"

Lyle met her eye. "They'd tac my dick to the board if they could."

"Why are you being like this?" Was he acting like this because the men were watching? Joni reached over to touch his bound hands, but the officer in the corner stopped her. "Did you do it?"

"Do what?"

"It doesn't matter now. They have their evidence and it points to you, and they want to know the woman's name so they can notify her family. Wouldn't you want to know if it were me?"

"You're smarter than they are, Joni, and you have to stay smart, so nothing like that happens to you. She wasn't mine. I don't know who that whore was."

"I don't believe you."

"What?" The coldness was back in his eyes.

"Why are you lying to me? I've never asked you about anything that happened. I've never blamed you, and I've always stuck by your side. But I want to know the truth about this woman. The least you can do is not lie to me. I deserve that."

"You deserve that?"

"A lot of bad things happened because of you and I've never blamed you directly—"

"I'm not to blame," Lyle said with a growl in his voice, and suddenly she understood the need for the officer in the corner.

"Daddy, you need to calm down."

"Have you forgotten who you're speaking to?"

Joni shook her head, but the respectful child he knew years ago died inside her a long time ago. "I won't come visit you."

That hardened criminal seemed to melt away as he put his head in his hands. "Please don't say that. I'll do anything. You're the only one I have."

A moment went by while Joni gathered her thoughts. If she thought he was guilty of the Tallulah Gorge victim, then she was asking him the wrong questions. After the first time Cyrus contacted her years ago, he'd told her all the gory details about the victims her father admitted to, even though Lyle was vague in his statements because he knew he was going to prison. But of what she did know, she used to her advantage.

"None of the other girls had broken necks. She tried to get away, didn't she?"

He lifted his head and rubbed his mouth with his hands for a brief moment then looked to be in a daze. A long minute passed before he said, "I jerked her head back too hard. That's not what killed her, though."

Goose bumps spread over the back of her neck. He lied to her. Flat out fucking lied. All the times when she was little, and he told her over and over never to lie. He lied to her, and that hurt more than anything. Joni swallowed down her emotions because now she wanted the truth, no matter how much it hurt.

"When was this?" Joni said.

He continued in his daze while he answered. "1984. I met her at a bar in Atlanta. We had drinks a few times. She had the silkiest brown hair I'd ever felt. One night, I asked her if she wanted to go back to my place. This is when I lived in Decatur. My house wasn't set up right, but I had to make do."

Joni nearly bit a hole in her cheek while she sat there listening to him. Listened to him talk in a way she'd never heard. Talked about this woman he murdered was nothing but a toy for his disposal.

"How'd she get to the state park?"

He shrugged. "Late at night. I parked down the road, and walked through the woods, kinda buried her there under the leaves and pine needles. She had a vine of roses tattoo on the back of her calf that went all the way to her ass. It was pretty."

As she fought against the tears, she said, "What was her name?"

"Melanie," he said, a smile on his face. "Melanie Pavroy."

"How many more?"

He looked up. "There are no more."

Oddly, she no longer believed him. When she exited the room, she asked for a bathroom where she threw up in the toilet and unleashed everything she was holding inside. She cried for all those women who never got a chance. She cried for her mother, who checked out because she couldn't handle the stress, and she cried because her mother hadn't shot her first.

Why did this hurt so badly?

When she went back down the hall, Cyrus was in the interview room with her dad because he had to get a statement.

The warden wouldn't let her in the tiny room with the one-way window, and that was okay. She had no desire to hear another word about Melanie Pavroy.

When they got back inside the SUV, Cyrus didn't start the engine right away. He was silent for a moment, and Joni wondered what the hell her father had said to him. "Thank you. I didn't think he'd tell you anything, but it worked."

"He lied to me."

"He's still lying to you. I'm going to find them if I have to spend the rest of my life doing it."

***

By the time Joni got home, it was dark, and she was a little pissed off and running with the dogs for five miles down Redwine Road didn't even put a dent in it. Back at home, she grabbed yesterday's mail out of the box and thumbed through the envelopes as she brought the dogs inside, where they gulped down a whole bowl of water.

Both the dogs ran outside, but when Bubba came back, he had a mouthful of figs that had fallen from the tree. "You're going to get diarrhea," she said, and took his figs away. She felt sorry for him as he pouted, so she offered him a bone.

In the pile of envelopes was a letter with no return address, but Joni recognized Mary Rancotti's loopy handwriting right away. The strangest part of Joni's life was Mary. Eight years ago, she received a letter from Mary telling her in gory details about who she was. A victim that had gotten away. Mary found out her captor's identity when he was on the five o'clock news, being arrested for the murder of a prostitute in the Atlanta area. Although Mary went to the police after her escape, she was so unstable that she couldn't even remember where she was held or specific details about the man. For a while, the police didn't even believe her. Mary Rancotti had been a mentally unstable woman and Lyle Chaskey didn't know that when he abducted her.

And now, she was worse off than a bear with its foot in a trap, her mental condition now holding her captive. Over the years, she had been in and out of the psychiatric hospital, and against her sister's wishes, she still continued to contact Joni.

In Mary Rancotti's own simpleness, her letter was not elaborate, consisted of only one paragraph asking Joni to visit. Placing the letter back in the envelope, Joni set it in a basket with all the others. When Joni told her father about that first letter, he'd gone rigid, but she also told him that no one fully believed what happened to her. All Lyle said was, "Stay away from that woman. She's crazy."

Which was proof he knew something. Had done something to her to screw her up even more. Half the time Joni was so confused with emotions that she shoved them out of the way and ignored them. What good would it do to try and figure stuff out?

Joni took a shower and put on a short denim skirt, a tight tank top, and some strappy sandals, then set out to find someone to play with.

***

The Fantasy Club was a strip club in Atlanta known for its fully nude dancers and high amount of alcohol. Even for a Sunday night, the place was loud and busy. It had two stages. The main stage was in the center, and a smaller one off to the left was for the preview. Joni sat in a red leather armchair against the back wall and watched two strippers take their turns on the pole as men tossed money on the stage and gave out cat calls.

Joni wasn't there to watch the women. It was just part of the setup. She'd given the bartender twenty bucks to keep refilling her water, and as she watched Coco and Bunny, she noticed a group of obnoxious twenty-somethings at a nearby table.

One guy was really cute, had brown hair that feathered across his forehead, and a killer smile. His jeans were tight, and he wore a bright blue Polo. When he turned his head, Joni caught his eye, gave him a wink, then stretched out her bare legs in front of her. A second later, she sashayed to the bar for a refill.

Joni's blonde hair was down and went to the middle of her back, and she ran her fingers through the strands as she watched the two girls on stage as Pretty Boy watched her return to her seat. When she caught his eye again, she put the tip of her finger in her mouth. Typical horny male, it didn't take him long before he walked over.

He sat down in the red chair next to her, said, "I couldn't help but notice you staring at me."

Joni offered him a seductive smile. "I wouldn't call it staring."

"Can I buy you a drink?"

"Before you even know my name. You have no class." The women on stage were bouncing their asses in different directions as the loud music played.

"I'm sorry," he said. "My name's Ben. What's yours?"

"Marie," Joni said. "And yes, you can buy me a drink."

They made their way to the bar. He ordered himself a beer, and Joni a vodka and cranberry. "You're here alone?" Ben said.

Joni made sure the bartender was out of earshot before she said, "I'm waiting for a couple of my friends to get off," and nodded toward the stage.

"Nice." And because he was a typical horny guy, he added, "You and your friends hook up?"

Joni shrugged. Let his imagination play its own games. "You live around here?"

"No, but I'm about to finish up my last semester at Tech. Thank God, I'm so ready to be done. Do you live in Atlanta?" Joni let him rub her leg.

"No, but I feel like I do."

This was moving on quite nicely, Joni thought, and thirty minutes later when his friends were leaving, Ben stayed longer and said he'd catch the MARTA transit home. She let him buy her more drinks, and didn't stop him when he kissed her neck.

"You smell so good," he said. "Like a fresh strawberry I could just eat."

How convenient a cheap motel was across the street. She pretended like she'd never even noticed it was there.

Joni didn't let Ben kiss her on the mouth, but they'd taken off each other's clothes in minutes and he was so adorably cute that she even wondered if he had a girlfriend. She straddled him on the bed, and kissed his neck, and bit at the soft, tender skin on his sides. Wasn't it every guy's dream to go to a strip joint and be picked up by a woman? Joni rocked Ben's world.

He flipped her over and when he tried to kiss her, she turned her head to the dingy curtain over the window above the rattling air conditioner. "You are so hot." He slid his fingers between her legs.

It was now or never, Joni thought, and slapped Ben across the face. "I can't do this," she said, and looked into his startled eyes. "Did you hear me?" She went to slap him again. "Get off of me."

He had her wrist in his hand and squeezed. "What the fuck is your problem?" She bucked her hips, but he remained there like he was trying to figure out what to do.

Come on, Joni thought. Let's see how well you play.

With her other hand free, she used it to shove her palm underneath his jaw and pushed his head back, then when he let go of her wrist, she punched him in the chest. Ben pulled his knees up to sit on top of her and held both her wrists above her head as his eyes darted all over her face.

Joni smiled. "Don't think I'm going to suck you off now." Was that enough for him to make her do it? She bucked her hips again, but he barely moved. "I bet you're not even that good." Joni pulled her wrist free and punched him in the chest again.

"You fucking whore."

Joni lifted her upper body off the bed and bit him on the chest. Ben threw his leg off of her, but she still had his flesh in her mouth, and he punched her in the face to make her let go. The blow hit her under her right eye and sent a sharp pain through her face like she'd been hit with a brick.

Ben pulled his pants on and Joni said, "Come on. I'm just playing."

"Playing? Look what you did to my chest." She didn't know what he was complaining about. The skin wasn't even broken. Ben grabbed his shirt off the floor, didn't even bother putting his shoes back on.

"Ben, you're no fun."

He was confused and didn't know what to say, just held his shoes in his hands and walked out of the motel room. Joni fell back on the bed, rubbed her cheek to ease the pain. He really knew where to punch. Ben was no fun. Didn't even put up a good fight.

Then Joni came down off the high, and she was really pissed at herself. Why did she do this to herself? She pushed them and pushed them, and what was she hoping to accomplish? One of these days, she was going to push it too far. Then what would happen? Well, screw them. She was going to be able to protect herself, unlike those stupid whores who couldn't get away from her father. It was their own stupid faults they were raped.

***

When Joni got home, she thought about burning her clothes but this was her best skirt, so she threw everything in the washer instead. Clyde and Bubba were at her feet, smelling her like they knew what she'd done. *You're so dirty,* she could hear them say. In the bathroom, as she ran water and poured the bleach, she began to cry because no matter what, she was truly alone in this world. Aunt Lacey didn't love her. Teddy didn't love her.

Her mother didn't have any family and totally abandoned her in this hopeless world. There was her paternal grandmother who now lived with Aunt Lacey and Joni despised.

She lowered herself into the tub and scrubbed away at her skin, the smell of bleach taking over her mind, tugging at memories that would never go away. He tried to drown her when she was twelve. It wasn't the first time, but it was the scariest. Something came over him and there had been no reasoning out of the punishment.

Joni lay back in the water until her face was fully submerged, and she held her breath for as long as she could. She knew then that if she fought against her father, he'd only hold her down longer, so she'd taken a deep breath while he held her under. Joni never again shared ice cream with a boy in a Braves baseball cap.

She wondered what he'd do about her little escapades at the Fantasy Club.

When she came up, her lungs burned and Bubba and Clyde were both looking at her. By the time she was done in the tub, her skin was red and raw.

Her right cheek was swollen and the soft part under her eye was now purple, and she pulled her hair back in the mirror to look at herself. Now that she was older, she knew she looked more like her father, but when she was a little girl, she looked just like her mother. Maybe that was the automatic response when people saw little girls. "You look just like your mama."

But she had his caramel eyes with flecks of darker brown around the iris, and his prominent cheekbones, his blonde hair and pointy nose. Her lips were full like his, and she even had a dark mole on her jaw line except Lyle's was under his eye.

Joni went into her plain bedroom and pulled on a pair of pajama shorts and a tank top. Her house was a modest three bedroom, two bath home on a quiet street. She only had the necessities to survive. That way, she never had to feel like she had anything to lose.

Teddy always said she was crazy, but he was proof she wasn't. He'd loved her once, didn't he? Through her own fault, she lost him, never deserved him anyway. Teddy was too good of a person for her. He was honest and sincere and his family meant everything to him, and Joni took it all for granted because she didn't know how to have a family.

She climbed into her queen-sized bed, where Bubba and Clyde were already snuggled into their special spots. Bubba slept next to her on the pillow, but Clyde slept at the foot. He had issues with being trapped under covers.

Chapter Eight

Because of the bruise on her face, Joni called out sick the next day, something she rarely did. She took the dogs on a long walk, fed them breakfast, and kissed them goodbye. The drive to Macon would take an hour, so she stopped at the Race Trac for gas, and grabbed a coffee and doughnut while she was there.

Ever since she was a little girl, she loved the fast pace of the highway, and how everything zipped by. Good thing she enjoyed car rides because she'd put many miles on her Honda Pilot going back and forth between Fayetteville, Reidsville, and Macon. Plus, Bubba and Clyde liked to go for rides and she'd take them with her to run the roads when she was bored.

90s Alternative blared through the speakers as she cruised down Interstate 75, and by the time she got to Macon she was hungry.

Mary Rancotti lived in a cookie cutter community and all the houses looked like gingerbread houses. They were all one level homes with fancy front railings and lattice work. Joni made her way to the front door and knocked, and spotted the pot of dead flowers on the porch, the brown petals in a heap inside the pot. Mary had good days, and she had bad days, and sometimes she was just plain nuts. Like today, she opened the door in a black velvet dress and said she was going to a funeral.

Joni stepped into Mary's messy house, and the scent of body odor and kitty litter overwhelmed her. "Whose funeral are you going to?"

"I don't know. I'm waiting for my dad to come and get me."

Thirty years had passed since her ordeal, and it was amazing how three months could ruin a person. According to Mary, Lyle made her watch while he raped two other women, then he killed

79

them, but police hadn't believed her because there was no evidence, no dead bodies, and she couldn't even remember the location. But she knew things. Things that were too personal for her not to have experienced what she had.

Joni used the bathroom and was disgusted by the filth. Not only filthy, but Mary was a hoarder, and kept every scrap of trash she had. Hundreds of empty toilet paper rolls were in a laundry basket in the bathroom. Towels were piled up on the floor where the cat kept peeing on them. It smelled awful.

When she walked back into the living room, she asked, "Did you eat breakfast?"

"No." Mary brushed her hair with the cat brush. "I'm going to eat at the party."

"I thought you were going to a funeral."

"Same thing." Mary sat down on the sofa. She wasn't confined to her house, and she usually walked down the road to Wal-Mart. She lived off of the government and ate well, but her sister helped provide medical care for her. Joni had only spoken to her sister Nina twice, and the woman clearly hated her.

"You want to watch TV?" Mary put her feet up on the coffee table.

"I think I'm going to clean up for you." Is this what it would have been like to care for an elderly parent? A special needs sibling? The sense of responsibility for Mary was ridiculous.

A fat orange cat jumped in Mary's lap, and she brushed him, too. The house was filled with balled up newspapers and tissue tucked in all the corners of the living room and kitchen. She kept all her mail in different cubby holes throughout the house. Empty cans of green beans were lined up on the kitchen counter, with their lids sticking straight up.

"Mary, what are you doing with these?"

She looked at Joni, said, "I'm going to kill Lyle with them."

Death by green beans. Joni took a deep breath. "Is that whose funeral you're going to?"

"Maybe yours." Mary nuzzled the cat.

"Don't talk like that. I'm your friend, and I'm here to help you."

"Sheila and Rachel were my friends."

Joni walked over to Mary, sat down on the coffee table in front of her. Both of Mary's wrists were covered in jagged scars where she'd tried to kill herself, but all four attempts failed. She'd also tried cutting her own throat and overdosed twice on sleeping pills. The biggest thing about Mary was that she didn't understand why Lyle hadn't killed her, and now she kept trying to kill herself. She belonged in a psychiatric hospital, but all the times she ended up in there, she checked herself out, said she was perfectly fine.

"Do you want to talk about it?"

Mary pet the cat as she stared off into the distance. "Do you think he loved me? Is that why he let me go?"

"Mary, he didn't let you go. You escaped. You got the handcuff off your wrist, you pried the basement door open with a screwdriver, and ran away. That's what you told the police."

"He smashed Sheila's face with an oil lamp." Sometimes Mary was panicky when she spoke, or even explosive. Today she was calm, almost melancholy in her thoughts. Joni had heard about Sheila and Rachel, but this was the first she'd heard about the oil lamp and it made her heart ache.

"Is that how she died?"

Mary kept petting the cat gently while he purred. "Do you know what it sounds like to hear a woman hurt? Like an animal. I tried to protect them."

"I'm sorry, Mary. If I could take all your hurt, I would."

"You could kill him."

"He's in prison and he's never going to hurt you again."

Mary went back to brushing her hair with the cat brush. "I'm done," she said, meaning she was done talking.

Joni knew better than to touch her because she'd cower into the sofa and start rocking herself uncontrollably. Her body was thin and frail, and she went days without eating. "Do you want me to make you some lunch?"

"No. You can go home now."

"Why did you write and tell me to come visit if you don't want me here?"

"I didn't," she said. "Rachel wrote the letter and Sheila put it in the mailbox."

"Okay." Joni hopped up and set out to clean up Mary's mess. Which was really Lyle's mess, but Joni did what she had to do.

***

The evening was too nice to waste away when she got home, so Joni put on some shorts and a ratty old t-shirt, and went to the front yard where she pulled weeds out of the flowerbed while Clyde panted his hot breath in her face. Bubba was in the driveway chewing on a bone the size of his own leg. The sun was warm against her back, and every time Joni scooted over to move to the next spot, Clyde moved next to her. He turned his head, cocked his ears and went on alert as Teddy pulled his beat-up truck in the driveway. Bubba didn't bother to move out of the way, just went back to chewing his bone.

Joni's heart pounded in her chest. Teddy had a brown sack in his hand and stood next to her. He had on blue jeans and a Clemmie's t-shirt, and a pair of black non-slip restaurant shoes. He said, "What'd you have, one of those half-day viruses?"

Joni kept her head down. "I was sick, okay?"

"My dad told me to bring you some lunch, but you weren't here. Did you go to the doctor? Is that why you feel so much better, you're out here gardening?"

"I'm enjoying the last bit of sunshine."

That's when he caught sight of her face. He tilted her head back to get a better look. "Who did that to you?"

If the maggots were doing their work properly, her heart would be gone by now. She yanked off her gloves, whistled to the dogs, and went inside. Teddy followed her, pulled off his dirty shoes, then set the brown sack down on the table.

"I brought you some chicken noodle soup to help with your cold. I also brought you some hand cut potato fries because they're your comfort food, and with you being sick and all... I even made you one of my famous grilled cheese sandwiches because—"

"Jesus, Teddy, shut up."

"I know when you get sick, you won't get out of bed to feed yourself." Teddy tossed the wrapped grilled cheese on the table. "I hope you get to feeling better, Joni."

She shoved a can of Coke into his chest, then sat down at the table. "I'm fine."

"You're fucked up in the head. That's what you are."

The insult made her think about Mary.

Teddy went to the fridge and pulled out a bottle of ketchup and sat down. He unwrapped a juicy hamburger, squirted the ketchup on the wrapper for fries, and began to eat. "It's so quiet when you're not at Clemmie's."

Another insult, but that was probably the nicest thing he'd said to her in years. Joni grabbed a spoon and began eating the homemade chicken noodle soup.

"I saw the news this morning about that body they found last week." Teddy shook his head. "Is that why the GBI guy came to get you?"

"He wanted me to talk to my dad."

"He's no good for you, Joni."

"He's my father."

Teddy dipped a nearly black fry into the ketchup and silently ate the rest of his burger. He dropped some fries on the floor for the dogs, but Clyde wolfed them down before Bubba even smelled them, so he gave Bubba a tomato instead. "You two are good boys," he said, and patted them each on the head. A minute later, he said, "So what happened to your face?"

"Let it go."

They broke up because of this. Because she cheated on him one night and ended up with a busted lip. Teddy had no idea what he'd gotten himself into with her. She'd only cheated on him once and once was enough for him.

"You're going to end up dead."

"Who cares, Teddy?"

Joni threw the soup cup away, then began clearing away the other trash. She wanted him to say that he cared. That there was an ounce of feeling left for her, but he didn't. She'd hurt him and he'd never forgive her for it. How could he? The guy never knew if she could ever commit to a relationship or not.

"When you were sixteen years old, you showed up at my house to talk to my dad and he watched you cry your eyes out because you had a fight with your aunt."

"I know your dad cares about me."

"And later that night, I snuck you into my room and promised you I'd never let anyone hurt you, except I didn't know I needed to protect you from yourself."

"Well, I certainly didn't take my own virginity that night."

Teddy shook his head and pushed Bubba away. He opened his mouth to say something, then stopped. She wanted him to defend himself, but he didn't. He got up and grabbed his shoes.

"Where are you going?" she said, because he couldn't just come in here and pick a fight and leave before it even started. Teddy slammed the door. That was all she was going to get from him, because he was too fucking nice to hurt her feelings.

***

When the seven o'clock breakfast rush hit Clemmie's, so did a news crew. A woman wearing a black skirt and matching blazer stepped out of the van, along with a cameraman, and

Joni's gut clenched. Because Clemmie's was a little mom and pop place, the reporter broke the boundary and stepped inside because she had no morals.

In the last fifteen years since her father had been in prison, Joni had taken her fair share of hate mail and threats. Most of the people who knew her were pleasant, but a few made rude comments that she learned to ignore, and her life had only been threatened a handful of times. What people couldn't seem to get through their heads was that Joni didn't do this, and she was a victim too. She didn't choose to be born to Lyle Chaskey or choose for him to be the person he is. What Joni chose is to ignore all the bullshit surrounding the situation because she had no control over the matter.

"You need to leave," Joni said, and pointed at the front door. "You have no right to be in here."

The restaurant was silent. The only sound was the sizzling bacon in the kitchen. The woman didn't bother identifying herself, tucked a loose strand of strawberry blonde hair behind her ear, said, "Miss Chaskey, have you spoken to your father since the discovery of Melanie Pavroy's body?"

"I have no comment."

The reporter took in the fading bruise under Joni's eye. "Has your father assaulted you?"

"Are you kidding?" Joni set down the coffee carafe she was holding to keep from hitting the woman with it. "You don't have permission to be in here—"

"How do you feel about the murder charges brought against your father?" The woman shoved the microphone in Joni's face.

"What the hell is this?" Archie's loud voice boomed from behind the counter. "Get your asses out of here right now before I press charges against you." He barreled his way from behind the counter.

As the reporter backed out, she said, "How many more bodies are out there?"

85

"Get the hell out of here." Archie stood in front of the camera guy to keep him from recording Joni. "You're lucky I don't bust you up right here."

The reporter and camera guy stepped outside but kept the camera rolling. Archie picked up the phone, said, "Yeah, this is Archie down at Clemmie's. I need Sheriff VanBuckle to send a deputy over ASAP."

Joni said, "I'm sorry, Archie," as soon as he hung up.

He patted her on the back. "Pull the shades."

For as long as Joni could remember, the shades at Clemmie's had never been lowered. The restaurant faced north, and the sun never blinded the guests but let lots of sunlight inside. Joni and Val pulled the shades and went back to serving their guests.

"It'll pass," Mrs. Lemon said, and her husband offered Joni a pat on the arm. She did not know why people were patting her like she needed to be consoled, but she let the old man pat away because they were a nice couple who ate breakfast with them every morning, which meant that Joni knew almost everything about them.

Coffee carafe back in hand, she said, "I was on my way to refill your coffee, Mr. Lemon. Would you like more cream?"

He gave her a nod, said, "You sure are a pretty little thing."

Joni leaned close to the man. "I told you not to flirt with me when your wife was here."

They got a laugh out of that. Another reporter had shown up, and the sheriff's deputy told them they had to stay at least a hundred feet away from the building, and to make himself clear, two more deputies remained in the parking lot. Clemmie's had been serving the Sheriff's department and Fayetteville Police for over fifty years, offering them free coffee and discounted food every day. Keep them happy and they were at Archie's service in a heartbeat.

Val let the shades back up and by lunchtime, the place was packed as usual. Five minutes later, Joni slammed back the

86

swinging door to the kitchen. She didn't realize Val was behind it and Val ended up with two slices of pie on her chest. "Dude," Val said. "Look before you fucking push."

"Language," Archie yelled.

Val was right, and that's why there was a window in the door. "I'm sorry." Joni grabbed the two plates from Val.

"Now I have chocolate pie titties," Val said, and Joni could tell she wasn't mad. "Take my tables for a second while I change shirts."

Joni was filling drink orders and slicing more pie when Val returned. She said, "That hot secret agent guy is here to see you." Cyrus stood at the counter.

"Not a secret agent, and he's not that hot." Val mumbled something, and Joni motioned him to the kitchen.

As soon as Archie saw him, he said, "Joni, what are you doing?"

"We'll only be a second." She opened the door to Archie's office, and they stepped inside.

"Smells like onion rings and lemon."

Joni closed the door, and they both sat down. "And pickles. You better love the smell of pickles to work here."

He smiled. "Is that a question on the application?"

Joni laughed, but the tension didn't escape her. She nodded at the file in his hand. "Is this about the woman?"

Cyrus set the file on top of Archie's cluttered desk and said, "We confirmed her identity."

Obviously, Joni thought, since the reporter this morning mentioned her name. "Does he have to go to trial again?"

"No. The state is going to tack on another fifteen years to his sentence, but the question remains whether there will be a trial if the prosecutor pushes for a death sentence."

"Oh." Those words hit her hard. Years ago, the deal was that her father wouldn't get the death penalty if he admitted to the bodies, but now they know he lied and there were more, so who knew what would happen. "What if he tells us the rest?"

"According to your father, there are no more. He lied to us before. How do we know when he's honestly at the end of his list? I don't think we'll ever know how many women Lyle Chaskey murdered." Cyrus went back to the thin file and pulled out a picture of an attractive brunette. "Melanie Pavroy was thirty-two years old when she disappeared in 1984. She was single, worked in a bar in Atlanta. She came from a good family. A month before she was killed, she went to Ireland for a friend's wedding."

Joni continued to look at Melanie's photo as Cyrus went on. Her dark hair hung over her shoulder. Sunglasses sat on top of her head. She had on jean shorts and a white t-shirt and she was leaning against a wooden fence, with large mountains behind her.

Cyrus said, "There are no similarities in the women your father chose. Over the last twenty-five years, we've got nine women that are as much alike as Miss Piggy and Madonna. They're mostly brunettes and blondes, but they're short, tall, blue eyes, brown eyes, green eyes. We've got a banker. A real estate agent. A grocery store clerk. They lived all over the state of Georgia. My point is that, with all the women that have disappeared, how do we know which ones came into contact with Lyle Chaskey?"

The whole situation was depressing. Depressing enough that Joni wanted to drink an entire bottle of something strong and crawl under the covers until it all went away. By the time Cyrus left, Joni's brain couldn't stay focused. She kept asking herself what she was supposed to be doing. Back in the kitchen, when she had three plates in her arms, it all ended up on the floor with a loud crash.

"Joni, go home," Archie said.

Her jeans, along with the wall, were covered in gravy and salad. "It was an accident."

"You know the rules here. You start dropping plates, you're done for the day. Too much on your mind. Go home."

"This is the first time I've ever dropped food."

"And this is the first time I've ever had to send you home. Now go. Come back tomorrow when your head's on straight." Joni bent down to pick up the plate. Archie said, "Not only am I taking that food out of your paycheck, but if you don't leave now, I'll find someone else to cover your shifts for the rest of the week."

Joni reminded herself that this man could have been her father-in-law. She was one of Archie's best waitresses, but he must really be mad at her to send her home like this. As she pulled off her apron, he said, "Take it one day at a time, Joni, and it'll get better." He offered a smile to soften his harsh words, and he was immediately the good man again.

Outside, she used her apron to wipe away the food from her jeans. Teddy pulled up in his truck, and while he gathered his things for the day, Joni hopped in the passenger seat.

"What are you doing?"

"Will you take me home, please?" God, she hated to ask him for something.

"No," he said, and started to open his door. "Why are you leaving your shift?"

Joni grabbed his arm. "Please?"

He hesitated a moment, then started the truck. "Maybe you should stay home for a few days."

"No."

Teddy drove away and nodded at her pants. "Not having a good day?"

"First, I hit Val with the swinging door, then I dropped three plates."

"Is he making you pay for it?"

89

"Of course."

"I'll fix it," he said. "Don't worry about it."

"Thanks."

When he pulled into the driveway, he said, "You shouldn't walk anywhere right now."

"You were going to let me walk," she pointed out.

"Changed my mind, didn't I?"

Why was it he could be such a sweet guy to her, then sometimes treat her like dirt? "Fine, Teddy."

The dogs were at the picture window, barking at them. Or so Joni thought. Peering closer, she saw only Bubba. "Where's Clyde?" Usually, if one or both of the dogs were outside, they would come to the wooden fence. Joni got out of the truck and unlocked the front door. "Hey, baby." She bent down and snuggled Bubba, then called out for Clyde. "Where's your brother?"

Bubba barked at Teddy as he clomped his way over to him. "Everything okay?"

"I don't know. Clyde!"

Bubba ran to the back of the house and straight out of the large doggy door. Joni and Teddy followed him, and as soon as she opened the door, Joni's heart clenched. Clyde was on his side under the fig tree and when she ran to him, he wasn't moving. Did the figs finally do him in?

"Clyde?" Joni pressed her palm to his chest, where she felt his heart hammering away. "Something's wrong."

Teddy scooped up the ninety-pound dog and said, "Get in the truck."

Joni put Bubba inside, then closed off the doggy door to keep him from eating any figs, then followed Teddy to the truck. He lay Clyde between them, his body limp, and Joni began to worry. "Oh, God," she said, and ran her hand over his face. Please don't let him die. His heart was pounding, but he wasn't moving. Joni opened his eyes only to see they were rolled in the back of his head. His tongue was dry, his nose warm.

The veterinary clinic was down the road near the old courthouse. Teddy carried Clyde inside, and Joni said to the receptionist, "Something's wrong."

Within minutes, they had Clyde in a little room and Dr. Barnes had a stethoscope pressed to his chest. "Goodness," he said. He looked at his eyes and inside his mouth.

"I found him outside like this," Joni offered. "He likes to eat figs."

"Figs would only cause severe diarrhea. Not this."

Teddy looked at the bottom of his shoe, then back at them. "There were piles of vomit in the yard. I stepped in it. I'll be back."

After Teddy left, Dr. Barnes began asking a bunch of questions. He knew the shepherd was healthy because he was their regular vet, but he wanted to know if he had been eating and drinking like usual. Acting funny? Nothing was out of the ordinary.

Clyde began to cough, which was the first movement he'd made since Joni had seen him. He swung his head to the side like he was dizzy and tried to stand, but the doctor and his assistant held him back down. Then he vomited up a brown sticky mess.

With a gloved hand, the doctor ran his fingers through it. Tiny green granules were inside. He said to his assistant, "Let's get him to a room and set up an IV." Then to Joni, "We're going to pump his stomach. This looks like rat poison."

Before Joni could ask another question, Dr. Barnes was gone, and she was left there to look at Clyde's stomach contents. Grass blades were mixed in with what looked like peanuts and tiny green chunks of poison. How did Clyde get rat poison?

A few minutes later, Teddy returned with one of her kitchen bowls filled with more vomit. "There were six piles in the yard."

91

"The doctor thinks he ate rat poison. I never used rat poison. How did he get it?"

Teddy brought the bowl of puke to the assistant, then they were escorted to the waiting room, where people were waiting patiently to see the doctor that would now be awhile, because he was caring for her poisoned dog.

A man looked at Joni, then hollered out to the receptionist, "This gonna take long? Boy, I tell ya."

"The doctor will see you as soon as possible, Mr. Finch."

She went outside and sat on a bench and put her head between her legs. When Teddy sat down next to her, she said, "Was Bubba okay?" and he nodded, and all she wanted to do was bury her face into his neck and cry.

For the hour they sat outside, thoughts raced through her mind. She'd never been so worried in all her life.

For some strange reason, Joni thought back to the day at Stone Mountain when her dad killed that dog with his bare hands. Amanda's face was disfigured on the right side, and after the dog attack, no one except for Joni wanted to be her friend. She'd stood by her side and defended her. Of course, Amanda didn't return that favor as a best friend when Joni's father was arrested. Not only did Amanda stop being her friend and writing to her when she moved in with Aunt Lacey, she went and wrote that crap book about her life being the best friend of the daughter of Lyle Chaskey. All lies, Joni thought. She didn't care about Amanda Flockhart these days.

TOWN HERO SAVES GIRL'S LIFE to TOWN HERO ARRESTED FOR MURDER. And then even better: TOWN HERO CONVICTED OF BEING THE COTTON MOUTH SERIAL KILLER.

How was that for irony?

The vet assistant called Joni back inside and they were brought back to the same little room where the vomit had been cleaned up and the only thing left behind was the smell of orange cleaner.

Dr. Barnes came in and said, "He's going to be fine," and Joni let out a sigh of relief. "I pumped his stomach and we're trying to flush his system. Joni, have you set out any mouse or rat traps lately?"

"No."

"He had lots of peanut butter in his system and it was mixed with rat poison granules that had been crushed. I thought maybe you had crushed the rat poison, mixed it with peanut butter and Clyde ate it?"

"No," Joni said again.

"Then you may want to consider that someone tried to poison your dogs. Is Bubba sick?"

Teddy said, "He seemed fine."

"Keep a good eye on him."

The privacy fence around Joni's house was locked. No one could get inside unless they climbed over the fence, and that person would have to be really stupid to climb a fence with two German shepherds on the other side. Which meant—

"Someone put rat poison inside the peanut butter and threw it over the fence. Clyde always gets the food first, and Bubba backs off because Clyde is the dominant dog. Why would someone try to kill my dogs?"

Neither the doctor nor Teddy could answer that, even though Joni had a pretty good idea why. Dr. Barnes said, "I'm going to keep Clyde for at least forty-eight hours while he undergoes treatment. You can go back and see him, and come back as often as you like tomorrow."

Clyde was on a metal table in another room. His leg was wrapped in hot pink sticky gauze to secure an IV line. Seeing him like this broke her heart. Clyde was a big baby. The one that thought he was a lap dog and didn't weigh almost a hundred pounds. "I'm sorry, baby."

Clyde didn't move his head, but his tail thumped against the table. "You'll be okay. You have to spend the night here." The

93

dog's eyes were sad. "I'm sorry you're sick, but you'll be okay. They'll take care of you."

Joni hated to leave him, but Clyde was in good hands, and she had to get back to Bubba. Teddy parked in the driveway and said, "I don't think you're safe."

"Are you going to stay and protect me?"

Silence. Must not be in that much danger. She watched Bubba at the window again and said, "You want to know what a serial killer once told me? That if someone wants to hurt you bad enough, they'll find a way to do it. They get creative. Make up stories. Jump through hoops. Nothing will come between them and their victims. In fact, if something gets in their way, they only look at that as a friendly challenge."

Teddy kept his eyes forward with his arm resting on the steering wheel. He never liked to talk much about her dad, so when he said, "You think this has anything to do with that body they found?" it surprised her.

"Who knows? A lot of people want my dad dead, so throwing a brick through my window or trying to kill my dog is how they send their message. I wish people would understand that I have no control over any of this."

"You probably have more control than you think."

"How's that?"

"You're the only one who has contact with him. If he gave you enough information, he could hang himself and get the death penalty. That's the only way these families get closure."

Joni's blood went cold. "It may be that easy for you, Teddy, but he's still my father and I can't do that. What kind of person do you think I am?"

"You can't see—"

Joni got out and slammed the truck door shut. When she got inside, Bubba's nose smashed against her leg, trying to figure out what was going on. The sun bounced off Teddy's windshield as he backed out of the driveway, and he gave one last glance at the picture window before he drove off.

Joni collapsed on the sofa, put her head on Bubba's shoulder and cried.

Chapter Nine

Marie went to the Fantasy Club again. Said she was twenty-two and could tell right away this guy liked his girls young. His name was Matt. Looked older than thirty, but who was Joni to call him a liar? Matt's hair was a little gray at the temples, and he had tiny laugh lines around his eyes. And laugh he did. Matt thought everything Marie said was hilarious. She should have been a damn stand-up comedian.

As they sat shoulder to shoulder next to each other at the bar, Joni realized the guy wasn't much taller than she was. She'd come to expect guys like Matt, and the questions they asked, and Marie was prepared.

"So, what kind of fun do you like to have?"

"Anything as long as you can keep up," she said.

Another easy target, but he was surprised when Joni mentioned the motel across the street.

"Seriously?"

"Why not?"

Once she was on the bed, she took off her sandals. Matt tried to kiss her, but she turned her head and he put his lips on her neck. He smelled of cigarettes and whiskey, and as he kissed his way down her neck, she let her mind run free. Thoughts of Starr's Mill, and how her dad caught her when she fell into the water. On another Sunday, he'd taken her out to a field with rusty old cars that looked like toasted marshmallows. And another time they went to a field that had cotton as far as the eye could see.

Matt lifted her shirt and kissed down her belly, leaving a trail of warmth as his breath moved over her body. They'd sat at the bar too long and the alcohol had worked its way to her head and made her floaty and giddy, and she giggled as his tongue tickled the skin on her ribs. Too bad this wasn't going to last.

Joni pulled Matt down, rolled on top of him and straddled him. Judging his movements, she was figuring out how she was going to play this out. Every guy was different, and she really had no plans to actually have sex with him. This was all about seeing how far she could go. That's what turned her on. For ten minutes, her mouth toyed with him while she avoided his desire to kiss her. By the time Matt rolled on top of her again, she'd had enough.

Joni shoved him back and said, "Get off me."

"What?" Matt was sweaty and out of breath.

She shoved him harder this time. "I can't do this."

To her surprise and delight, he said, "Yes, you can. It's easy," and gripped her wrists above her head.

"I'm serious. Get the fuck off me." She used her hips to push him away, but he only smiled down at her. Jerking a hand free, she slapped his face. Matt didn't flinch.

"Is that how you like it? God, that's awesome."

Once he gripped her wrists tight again, he bit her shoulder and used his knee to push her legs apart. Fighting only encouraged him, but he never hit her back, even when she used the heel of her foot to pound into his legs, or jammed her knees into his ribs.

He held her down with his weight, and whispered in her ear, "I'm going to tell you something." Joni's heart pounded as she froze beneath him. He held her wrists tight and positioned himself on top of her. His mouth was to her ear still, and he said, "I didn't think you were serious about the hotel."

Through clenched teeth, she said, "I wasn't."

Matt used a free hand to slide it down between their bodies. For a second, Joni thought about opening her legs, but that wasn't what she was here for. Instead, she readied herself, took a deep breath, and pushed him off with all her strength. Matt went to the side, held onto her, and got back on top. This guy wasn't going to give up.

Joni used her forehead to head butt his face and hit him in the cheek. To keep her head down, he pressed his cheek into the side of her face and now he had her in a position where she could no longer move.

"Matt, I'm serious. Stop."

He laughed. "Okay," he said, but then without giving her any room to struggle, he worked her legs open and pushed himself inside. She had to admit that he felt good. So he was going to finish what she started. Joni bit his shoulder and Matt pulled her hair. When her hands were free and he was rocking into her, she reached for his throat. But she was no match for him. He closed his eyes and moaned with pleasure.

He kissed the inside of her wrist, said, "I could fuck like this all day." And he must have been serious because he went at her like that for fifteen minutes. Without giving her room to get away, he flipped her to her stomach. Joni elbowed him in the face but once he was on top of her again, she was done, and in no position to free herself. Pain wasn't a problem, as he took what he wanted. *Okay,* she thought. *I guess this is what it's like.* Except she knew it wasn't.

Matt moved her hair away from her sweaty neck and kissed her there. He held her arms down and moaned like an animal, and thoughts of Mary swirled into her head. When her father's words came to her, she buried her face in the bed to hide the tears.

You take the pain you cause for yourself.

Joni was angry at herself and letting men abuse her only validated the thoughts. When was it going to be enough? When was she ever going to stop allowing her pain to consume her?

A second later, Matt pulled himself out and straddled her back. Thankfully, the guy was smart enough to finish himself off and when he did, all the warmth spilled on Joni's back. Before he could collapse on the bed, Joni turned beneath him, lifted her leg and kicked him in the chest so hard, he flipped over and landed on the floor.

He rubbed the back of his head where he'd hit the wall. "Fucking bitch."

Joni wiped what she could off her back, then threw the tissue at his face. "You're an asshole." She put her clothes on and ignored him while he breathed hard from the kick. Too bad she didn't break a rib.

"Well, you're no peaches and cream."

Joni pulled his wallet out of his pants, but he didn't have any cash. "Hey," Matt said, and got to his feet.

"Take it easy." Joni tossed him his wallet and left the motel.

She had just passed the Peachtree Street exit on the interstate when a little car came rushing up behind her. The driver flashed the lights so Joni moved into the next lane to let them pass, but when she looked over; it was Matt flipping her off. That's rich, she thought. He pulled back behind her and rode her bumper, and she thought about slamming on the brakes and sending him through the windshield.

Damn seat belts.

Joni wasn't about to drive home with Matt following her. The stupid game she played had taken a turn for the worse. No one had ever followed her before, and she wasn't sure what she should do. Maybe this rape fantasy thing was going too far. She could handle that. Being chased down by an angry guy on the interstate was something else.

It was almost midnight, and Atlanta was still busy. Joni slowed down to about forty then pulled into the emergency lane where Matt pulled up behind her. She didn't wait, figured she'd gain the upper hand right now, and jumped out.

"Stop following me," she said, and walked up to him where he stood outside his open door. "Take it for what it is, and leave me alone, Matt."

"My name's Sam."

"Who cares? Go home."

Joni turned and cars zipped by. He said, "And I know you're Joni Chaskey," and she froze. *Get in the car*, she told herself. *Just get in the fucking car*. Her father's warnings hit her full force.

"When did you figure it out?"

The guy nodded to the exit. "There's a lounge not far from here. Let's talk."

"I don't think so."

"I followed you to the club. I'm Sam Doolan. You figure it out."

Joni's blood went cold. Their meeting wasn't an accident. "The lounge." Joni got back in her car and cursed herself until she parked again. By the time they sat in the booth, she was looking at him differently. "Why?" she said.

A waitress walked up to them and Sam ordered them each a round of shots. He pulled out a cigarette, lit it, then slowly sucked in the nicotine and blew out the smoke. "I guess I could ask you the same thing."

"I don't have answers for you."

"Lyle Chaskey does."

And there it was.

Joni pulled a cigarette from Sam's pack and as she flicked the lighter, she thought about her father jumping out from somewhere and smacking the shit out of her for smoking. They sat in silence for a long time while they smoked, and when the waitress set the shots on the table, Sam lifted the tiny glass and said, "To being able to fuck the daughter of my mother's killer."

***

Smoke filled the air in the lounge and somewhere in the back, billiard balls smacked against one another. Joni swallowed down her shot of whiskey and asked for another while Sam threw his back, then leaned against the seat. For a long time, they sat there, Joni not knowing what to say as her

100

embarrassment settled in, her thoughts of what happened in the motel still clear. No wonder he never gave up.

You don't forget a name like Darla Doolan. She was one of the original seven, found in a creek bed in Oconee County during a land excavation in 1992 after a landowner sold some property to a home builder. She'd been there for years, her body decomposed, and the only thing discovered was cotton fibers embedded deep in the throat that were slowly disappearing as the body rotted away.

"When did you recognize me?" Joni asked.

Sam put another cigarette in his mouth and flicked the lighter to it. "When you started flirting with me at the bar."

"I was not flirting with you."

Sam shrugged, looked around the lounge.

Joni said, "You said you followed me to the club. How long have you been following me?"

"I recognized you at McDonalds. Followed you to the gas station, was going to say hello while you pumped, but I lost my nerve. You really surprised me when you walked into the strip club, thought maybe you were going to work the pole, but then you threw yourself at me. What was I going to do, say no?"

This wasn't happening. "Why didn't you tell me before?"

"Before you bruised my lung with that donkey kick to my chest?" Sam rubbed his chest with his hand that held the cigarette. "What's your problem, anyway?"

Joni didn't answer. Sam's blue eyes dilated, and he gave her an intense look. He was a good-looking guy, clean enough that Joni thought to take him to the motel. His nails were clean, his face shaved. A chain smoker, if she'd ever seen one. Joni stubbed out the cigarette in her hand and figured just this once she'd kill her own lungs and pulled another from the pack.

"Couldn't you tell right away that I have issues?"

This made Sam laugh, something he hadn't done since they'd left The Fantasy Club. "I was too caught up in my hard on to think about it."

Joni sighed. "What do you want from me?"

"I want to know why?"

"Why what?"

"Why her?"

"I don't have that answer for you."

"He does. I was four years old the last time I saw my mother. Do you know how fucked up my life was after she was gone?" Did Sam want to compare notes here? "No one in my family wanted to talk about her because she'd been hooked on drugs since she was fifteen years old. She was trying to get clean. She had a job, she was taking care of me, she had a chance. Then that asshole had to go and fuck everything up. I ended up living with family who never wanted me."

"Sam, I don't know what to say." Joni knew enough about her father's victims, knew their names and had seen pictures of them and she thought about them all, every day. She thought about their families and their grief. How could she not? Some of those family members still sent her the most hateful messages about how her father ruined their lives, and they would not have peace until Lyle Chaskey was dead.

"I'm sorry."

"One thing." Sam held up his finger. "One thing can change a whole person's life and I'll never know who I was supposed to be and I'll never know who my mother was or how much she loved me. Your asshole father took that away from me. He's the only one that can give it back."

***

The bleach and hot water left her skin red and raw, and the steam swirled from her limbs like ghosts leaving a lifeless body.

She willed herself not to cry. *Don't be weak. The fear is only an illusion of what you can't control.*

Had she hit bottom like her mother, or was her whole life some sick joke that she'd never escape? Living in a vortex of a world with maggots crawling through her veins, chewing through every ounce of her, never ridding herself of the overbearing guilt.

Joni got out of the tub and dried off, threw on some sweatpants and a tank top. She said goodbye to Bubba and grabbed her keys.

Guilt came so easily to her.

Everything in Fayette County was named something McIntosh after a revolutionary war leader who was part Creek Indian. Joni would like to see Chaskey all over everything, but no matter what she did in life, she'd always be known for her father's crimes. She'd never get streets named after her with that hanging over her head.

West McIntosh was dark and creepy at night, but a person couldn't get lost in Brooks, Georgia. Teddy lived on property he'd inherited from his grandpa. She hadn't been to his trailer since the day he'd kicked her out. Teddy's trailer was nice, but nothing had changed much since he'd bought it new ten years ago and had it delivered to the property.

Teddy had been the one promising thing in her life. He broke up with her over a night like this. An empty night that meant nothing to her.

Considering it was two o'clock in the morning, it took him forever to answer the door, and when he did, he didn't seem all that surprised she was there. He stepped aside, and Joni walked in. The place was freezing.

"What do you want?"

"Nothing. I—"

"I'm tired. It's been a long day."

"I'm sorry about everything."

He waved her off because he wasn't interested and turned to go back to bed. This was how he acted. Had to light a dynamite up his ass to get a response. She was supposed to leave. Should leave. Except she couldn't. A minute later, she was next to his bed. So many things she wanted to tell him. "Teddy?"

He had his arm slung over his face, ignoring her because he wanted her to go. Joni pulled off her shoes and pants and crawled into bed next to him, his warm body a familiar comfort. She swallowed hard and traced her fingertips over his throat, felt his pulse surging through his veins. He smelled of soap, but it was only hiding the sour milk and fried food smell that came with working in a restaurant. She breathed him in deep as she pressed her head to his chest.

He turned her to her back, studying the face he no longer wanted to see. "I want you gone before I wake up," he said, his voice throaty and sexy as hell.

Joni nodded, and he kissed her, so soft it was like butterfly wings touching her lips.

***

By the next afternoon Clyde was doing better but he wouldn't drink any water and still had the IV in his arm, and when he heard Joni's voice as she squatted down next to the kennel, he lifted his head to say hello. Confused eyes stared at her, and Joni wanted to pull him into her lap and hold him. She wanted him to be okay. He was still trying to throw up clear fluid, and the doctor was concerned because blood was leaking out of his rectum. Clyde would have to stay there until his vitals were normal, and he was eating, drinking, and pooping with no blood in the stool. How long would that be?

Joni opened the cage and gave Clyde a kiss on his warm nose. "I love you, boy."

Bubba was broken up about Clyde too and hadn't touched his food since his brother had been carted off to the vet yesterday.

One thing was for sure. Someone tried to poison her dogs.

***

On Saturday, the first thing her dad said was, "I wasn't expecting to see you two weeks in a row."

With the unexpected visit, he didn't look as nice as he usually did. Perhaps he put more thoughts into combing his hair and shaving every other Saturday. Joni was about to get right in to it when Lyle said, "What happened to your eye?"

It had been a week since Ben punched her and the bruise was practically gone, and she even covered the last remains of it with makeup, but her dad was too meticulous to miss it. The first thing she did was smile to play it off, close her eyes and shook her head while she thought of an answer. What was she afraid of? There were no basements here. No bleach. No spankings for the visitors.

No, it wasn't that. It was the sheer disappointment he'd have in her. Joni said, "I think it was Sunday. I was walking the dogs, and I tripped over Bubba when he stopped short in front of me." A smile went to her face again. "I'm such a klutz."

"You would tell me if someone was hurting you, right?"

For a moment she was worried he wouldn't drop the subject, and he was looking at her, really looking at her like he knew the truth.

"Daddy, I'm fine," she said. "Aside from a few reporters and someone trying to kill my dogs, I'm fine."

"Why would someone want to kill your dogs?"

With a serious tone, she said, "Maybe you could answer that. And while you're at it, do you mind telling me if you hit Sheila in the face with an oil lamp?"

105

All the color drained from his face. Only one person could have given such a specific detail. "I told you to stay away from Mary." He lowered his voice. "She's crazy."

"I wonder why, Dad?"

He looked down at his folded hands. Rachel Ikenbor and Sheila Graninch had never been found, even though they had both been reported missing many years ago at different times during the months that he held Mary captive. Without their bodies, her dad wouldn't be responsible for what he'd done.

"You made her watch while you raped them, and you made her hold Rachel down while you murdered her. Crazy is an understatement when it comes to Mary. She thinks they're still alive. In fact, we all four have lunch sometimes and watch soap operas. They write me letters to tell me about their day."

Lyle snorted his amusement. Joni said, "Before you took her, she was bipolar—"

"Tell me about it."

"With symptoms of psychosis. Now she's schizophrenic with severe post-traumatic stress. She wants to know if you love her."

"Don't listen to what she says," Lyle said.

"Did you even know you were taking someone with mental issues?"

Her dad's past was something Joni avoided. He was in prison, why talk about it? But since the conversation with Sam Doolan four nights ago, she hadn't been able to stop thinking about all the horrible things he'd done.

"Tell me," Joni said.

"You don't want to hear it."

"Either you tell me what happened or I'll go on believing Mary's story."

Lyle became quiet and looked around the visiting area. He sat there for what seemed like five minutes, and when he said nothing, Joni got up and went to the only barred window in the room. She thought about all her motel escapades and how she'd feel if she ever had to give the details about all the stupid things she'd done, so part of her understood her dad's reluctance about talking to her about his past. But Joni was the one who had to live with his choices. She had a right to know.

When she sat back down, she said, "Are you going to take it all with you to your grave? There's this part of you I know, that I deep down know, and there's this part of you I've never even seen. Never even had a glimpse of."

"Do you remember how I used to be?"

"You were the best dad a girl could ask for. You used to hold me when I was scared and talk to me like I was a person, and I miss that. And no matter how the rest of my life goes, my best years were when I was with you."

When he looked at her, she swore he had tears in his eyes. He took a deep breath, said, "Mary was going to be the first kill. I lured her from a park in Atlanta and brought her to this abandoned house. At first she wasn't even scared." Lyle lowered his voice and leaned closer to Joni. "I don't know why I couldn't kill her, but I couldn't. I think it was because she was my first, so I found another woman. That was Rachel. I didn't have any feelings toward her, but I enjoyed getting to know her. I wanted Mary to see what I was doing. A month later, I took Sheila. They were both easy, but after Mary, I made sure to find out about who the women were before I took them. That was always the fun part. Finding out who they really were."

Joni listened.

He said, "Mary and Sheila were tied in the basement, and one day Sheila was able to get loose." Lyle shrugged. "So, yeah, I hit her in the face a few times with the oil lamp. I broke all her fingers, too."

"She died?"

"No," Lyle said, and sighed.

107

The thoughts about Sheila's last agonizing days were brutal, and the whole time she was tied in the basement, Mary was down there watching.

What changed things? How did he go from keeping a woman captive for months to deciding to hold them captive for only a day?

Joni said, "I met Sam Doolan."

"Sam who?"

"Think about it."

Lyle did. Then he shook his head and said, "Don't know."

"Darla Doolan's son."

"No," Lyle said. "Darla Doolan didn't have a son."

Chapter Ten

What struck Joni as strange was the way he talked about these women like he knew them. He'd spent months with Mary. A few weeks with Sheila and Rachel. And days with his other victims. Yet in that amount of time, he'd learned so much about them. What was even more strange was that her dad remembered so much like it was etched into his brain like a picture.

When his garage had been searched, they found no mementos from the women. Nothing personal to tie him to a single one of them, yet he remembered them in detail.

"Darla would have told me if she had a son, Joni. Are you sure his last name was Doolan?"

"Daddy, I met him." *I basically let him rape me.* When she had Sam's wallet in her hand, she didn't think to look at his license.

"Darla was a cokehead."

"Was she high when she was with you?"

"Said she'd blow me every day for powder." Lyle shook his head. "I didn't give her a choice."

Sam said his mother was trying to get clean when she was taken, but then again, he also said his family didn't mention her to him, so maybe getting clean was what he wanted to believe. "If she was high, then maybe that's why she didn't mention her son."

"She mentioned a poodle. Not a son, Joni. He said his name was Sam?" Why did he look so confused about this?

"Yes," she said.

Lyle took her hand. "I begged you once to stay away from Mary, and you didn't listen, but you have to listen to me about this. Whoever this Sam is. Stay away from him."

"He wants to know why, Dad. Why did you pick his mother? Why did you do it?"

"Darla wasn't anything special." He brushed his thumb across the palm of her hand. "I just liked it. Killing them made me feel good about so many things. Once I started, I couldn't stop."

***

Everything inside Mary Rancotti's house was red. Red on the walls. Red on the entertainment center. Red on the carpet. Mary had on coveralls and a white t-shirt, and she looked bloodied from throat to feet.

"What are you doing?" Joni said. Mary sat on the floor in front of her sofa and had an open paint can on the coffee table. She was painting her sofa red. "You can't paint your sofa."

"Yes, I can."

When Mary acted like this, Joni wondered if she had a split personality, but she couldn't have because she was always Mary. Throughout Mary's house were painted canvases of abstract images that were left to the imagination, but to Mary, they were of all the things that were bad in her life. She painted to ease her mind; it was something she'd told Joni she'd done since she was a little girl.

Her orange cat sat near the window with red paint stuck to his fur. Mary had ruined her entire living room. Joni leaned down to take a closer look at Mary and ended up putting her hand on the coffee table and touching paint. The kitchen was a mess again. Joni washed the paint off her hand and turned around only to run smack into Mary. She didn't even hear the woman sneak up on her.

"Has anyone come to visit you?" Joni opened the refrigerator but didn't find any food. Mary stood in the middle of the kitchen with a paintbrush in her hand, red paint dripping down her arm.

"You want to help me paint?"

"No, Mary, you can't paint your furniture."

Mary slapped the paintbrush to her palm, then put her palm flat on the white refrigerator. "It's blood."

Joni groaned. "Have you eaten today?" Mary pointed to an empty can of cat food. "Not the cat. Did you—" Joni picked up the can of cat food. "Did you eat cat food?" Mary nodded.

How often did Mary's sister check on her? Mary didn't even have a phone because years ago, she kept calling 911 in a panic to tell them she was being held captive in her own home. Last week, Joni cleaned Mary's house and bought her groceries. Now the house was a mess again, and the woman was out of food. Mail was piled up on the counter. Crud was caked up on the counter where more cans of vegetables sat. Dishes were stacked on the table and in their place inside the cabinets were piles of magazines and newspaper. The half-gallon of milk had been left out long enough to curdle.

"What do you want me to do?" Joni said, and tossed the milk in the trash. That's when she saw the newspaper. Joni pulled it from the trash and read the headline about Melanie Pavroy being found in Tallulah Gorge.

"Did you see this?"

"I didn't steal that newspaper. This is all my newspaper. I only threw it in the trash because I didn't want it anymore." A clenched fist held the paintbrush tight while her voice went up.

"You're okay."

"That's not Sheila."

"No, it's not."

Melanie's photo was beneath the headline, and below that was a handsome photo of Lyle from when he worked at Staurolite Logistics.

"Is he going to get out?" Mary touched the paintbrush to her palm again.

"No. You're safe." Joni said, "Are you afraid?"

"I was safe when I was with him."

"No, you weren't."

"I was safe. Sheila and Rachel were not safe. I think about him a lot."

She wasn't about to tell Mary that her father realized he'd made a mistake and didn't care a damn thing about her.

"He gave me gifts, but I wasn't able to take them with me."

Gifts? Joni thought. Had he been trying to apologize to Mary?

"I write to him," Mary said, "but he sends them back. Maybe Sheila should write it."

"Sheila died, Mary, you know that." Joni pulled out a kitchen chair for her. "I don't know where he put her after he killed her. Did he say anything?"

"She's with her mother."

"Where?"

"At her house. He gave her back."

Joni wished now she would have thought to ask her dad where he'd held Mary. That was the issue the police had. Mary kept claiming that a man held her captive while he raped and murdered two women, but she didn't remember where she'd escaped, but it had been far away from Macon. Considering her past mental issues, they had her evaluated instead, and committed to another hospital. "Would you feel better if Sheila and Rachel were found?"

Mary's face brightened. "Yes," she said. "I'd love to talk to them very much."

***

Clyde was home from the veterinary hospital. Not back to his usual self, but he was going to be fine. He hadn't knocked the trash can off the table this time and Joni told him, "So you've realized that eating the wrong stuff will mess you up," and he and Bubba followed behind her as she walked them out the door for a long walk.

The only thing on Joni's mind was Mary. If Joni could find out where her dad dumped Sheila and Rachel, then maybe Mary would be okay. Not completely okay, but better.

When Joni returned home, she called Archie to inform him she'd be back to work tomorrow. Then she pulled out a cardboard box of copied notes and photographs Cyrus Kenner had given her. It wasn't all of it, but it was small bits of information on her father and everything they'd gathered on the women that Joni was allowed to have. Cyrus had everything organized, with each woman having her own manila folder and another on Lyle. Other than the fact that Sheila and Rachel had both been reported missing by their families, there wasn't much else to go on, and their disappearances couldn't be connected to Lyle. He'd never admit to anything unless they found the bodies. As Joni thumbed through a file, she thought about how her simple plan really wasn't all that simple. Finding those two women's bodies was going to be damn near impossible without her father's help.

The telephone rang, and Joni answered when she recognized the number. Sam said, "Hi," and there was this awkward silence that fell over them. "Are you there?" he said.

"Sorry. Yes. I wasn't expecting your call."

"Were you busy? I didn't mean to bother you."

His voice sounded unsure and she could tell he felt bad. "No, I was playing with my dogs." She looked down at the files.

Sam let out a soft laugh. "Do you really have dogs, or is that code for something else?"

"Real dogs." As if they knew she was talking about them, they both picked up their heads and wagged their tails. "You should see them. They think they're human."

"I'd love to," Sam said, and Joni hadn't meant that as an invitation. "I was actually calling to see if you wanted to go have drinks at the lounge again."

"You mean real drinks or is 'drinks at the lounge' code for something else?"

Sam laughed, said, "You got me."

Heat flushed over the back of her neck. "To be honest with you, I didn't really like that lounge."

"Me neither." Oddly, comfort settled in over her when she heard his laugh, but then he said, "I was wondering if you got a chance to talk to your dad today."

Remembering her dad's words made her want to grind her teeth, couldn't bring herself to say her dad thought he didn't exist. Instead, she said, "I did, but he didn't say anything new. I'll keep asking about your mom, though." A huge part of her wanted to talk to Sam about her dad because he seemed so interested the other night, but then there was the part of her that still didn't trust him.

She said, "I'm in the middle of something right now, but if you're not busy tomorrow night, we can go to that Japanese place down the street from the lounge."

"Sounds great, as long as I don't end up with a donkey kick to the chest."

"I have nothing to apologize for."

"Nor do I." His words were slow and somewhat seductive. Thankfully, he wasn't there to see her blush.

"I'll meet you there tomorrow night at eight."

"At the motel?"

Ignoring that, she said, "Bye, Sam."

Joni was in the spare room with the computer desk and extra-large dresser. This was the room where she stored all of her old things. In one of the dresser drawers, she pulled out a stack of her old diaries and found the old map hidden inside. By happenstance, she'd ended up with the map from her dad's glove box when she needed to find the name of the town they'd visited. Later, the police searched their house and took what they wanted for evidence.

It was nice reminiscing with all these old diaries. She didn't go through this stuff often. The creases of the map were worn, so she taped them together, then taped the map to the wall. Using Cyrus's notes, she circled where these women lived, where they were abducted, and where they were dumped.

She started with Melanie Pavroy, who lived in Duluth, was taken in Atlanta, and dumped in Tallulah Gorge. Cyrus already had notes typed up about each woman except Melanie because she was the one just found. Joni grabbed a piece of paper and an empty folder to make a file for the woman. Making a profile, she wrote: Brown hair, went missing in 1984, vine of roses tattoo, worked at a bar. For now, that was all she could remember. Of course, all she had to do was pick up the newspaper to gather more info, but for now, this was a start.

She found the file on Darla Doolan, circled the map and wrote down that she lived in Athens, was abducted from Athens, then found in Bogart in Oconee County. She was twenty years old when she disappeared. Which meant—

"Shit."

According to her birth year, she was barely sixteen years old when she had Sam. No wonder he never had the chance to get to know her. None of the files had personal information on the women, so Joni moved on.

Next was Summer Buchner, then Diana Ossen, Paige Folly, Flana Farrell, Heather Chewter, and finally Colleen Garrish, the very first victim ever found.

She was in a wooded area around Villa Rica, and according to the coroner's report, she'd only been dead about six months. The crime scene photo in the file was a photocopy. Her body had been found near a tree with her hands placed carefully on her stomach. It was after the third victim was found with the same cotton fibers in her throat that the media named him the *Cotton Mouth Killer.*

These files gave Joni the chills. The fact was, her father was a rapist and murderer, but the whole idea seemed so abstract to her. She could not, for the life of her, actually visualize him doing these things.

Joni looked at the map and figured that most of the women had been taken within a hundred miles of the Atlanta area and dumped in various wooded areas. So far, her father had driven as far as two hundred miles south of Atlanta to dump a body in Blakely.

Looking at all the places these women lived, and were abducted, and found; there were no similarities in anything. Cyrus Kenner really had his work cut out for him. Joni didn't have any information on Sheila Graninch or Rachel Ikenbor because as of date they were still just missing persons.

With another victim just now being found, Joni really wondered how many others were out there. Her head began to hurt, so she gathered up all the files spread from the floor and stacked everything back in the box. Then she thumbed through a couple of the diaries again and wanted to cry because of all the mean things she'd written about her mother. Had she really felt this way? Deciding to read them another time, she set them on a small bookshelf in the spare room, and when the spine of a particular book caught her eye, her blood went cold.

The blue paperback titled *Saved by a Serial Killer* stared back at her and Joni wondered how in the hell Amanda Flockhart's book ended up on her shelf. She grabbed the book, and a picture of her father was on the back. Underneath that was: *My Life and Friendship with the Cotton Mouth Killer's Daughter.*

Joni did not buy this book, and worse than having it on her shelf was seeing that the book was an autographed copy. Inside it read: *You can never be too careful*, with Amanda's name next to a heart. Amanda Flockhart's picture was not on the cover. *If I was that ugly, I wouldn't want the world seeing my picture either.* There was only one person who could have put that book here.

***

The night Teddy broke up with her, she was mad at herself, not him. The whole time they were dating, she wasn't stupid, but she went to a strip club one night, had some drinks, and met a guy. When she came home that night, Teddy was parked in her driveway.

He'd said, "Where have you been?"

"I had some drinks," she said, and he followed her inside her house. Then he noticed the small cut on her lip.

"Are you drunk?"

"No, Teddy, I'm not drunk."

"I've been calling you for four hours."

"Sorry."

"Sorry? Where'd you go?"

"Atlanta."

"Why Atlanta?" Like he didn't believe her.

"Teddy, I went to a bar to have some drinks. That's all."

Now he was looking her up and down. She had on a short skirt and a flimsy blouse. He said, "Doesn't look like that was all."

"It's no big deal."

"You know what, Joni? Fuck this."

Teddy left, and for a long while, Joni didn't know what to do. Except she did know what to do. It just wasn't what she wanted to do. She screwed up and had to fix it. So that night when she got to Teddy's, he was inside with the lights off except for the one above the stove, and he was folding laundry at the kitchen table.

"I was going to do those," she said, and knew he was pissed. They didn't fight much. A kiss usually fixed everything. But this wasn't one of those kinds of nights.

He said, "You've been acting strange for over two weeks. Are you seeing someone?"

"It's not like that."

117

"Yeah? Then what's it like?" He looked her in the eye when he said this, and it was like he just knew she'd done something stupid. Did he know her that well?

Joni said, "I either tell the truth and hurt myself or lie and hurt you."

"You don't think the truth would hurt me?"

She thought he would forgive her. Until then, she didn't realize how badly she could hurt him. Not until she saw the dead look in his eyes after she told him about the strip club and a guy that meant nothing to her.

"*I* mean nothing to you."

"Teddy, that's not true."

"Get out," he said, and before she could say another word, he yelled, "Get the fuck out!"

She thought he only needed to cool off, that he'd talk to her about it the next day, but when she came home from a grocery trip, she found all of her stuff from his trailer dumped in her driveway. Not in bags or boxes. It was as though he tossed everything in the back of his truck and dumped it in her driveway.

Clothes, shoes, DVDs, dishes, a blanket, extra dog food, a Clemmie's t-shirt, some jewelry. All dumped in a pile like it meant nothing. And she deserved it.

Who she didn't deserve was Teddy.

But tonight, she was really upset with him. Joni banged on his door, and he answered with a rough, "What?"

"Can I come in?"

"No."

She stepped inside anyway. The trailer was dark, the only light coming from the TV, the tail end of a Braves game on. Joni held up the book. "I wanted to return this," she said. "Did you enjoy it?"

"Yeah. Actually, I did."

118

She threw the book at his chest. Teddy didn't flinch, and the book dropped to the floor. "You want a beer?" he said and turned.

"No, I don't want a goddamn beer. You know how much I hate that book. She wrote nothing but lies about me, and she was supposed to be my best friend."

"People let you down," he said, his voice all casual. He had on green pajama bottoms and she tried to ignore the fact that he was shirtless, as he handed her a beer. A day's worth of stubble covered his face. She took a drink of the strong beer and stood there for a moment as the window unit AC pushed cold air into her back.

Teddy's eyes were tired, and he walked past her, kicked the book out of his way and sat on the sofa where he finished watching his game. Joni sat at the other end and was reminded of how many times they'd cuddled together on this very sofa.

"So what'd you do?" she said, not giving him a break. "Find her on the internet and ask for a copy?" He looked over at her and sipped his beer, went back to the game. "Or was she desperate enough to just start handing out copies? I hope that's the case, and you didn't pay for the book."

"Joni, shut up."

"You have to understand where I'm coming from, *Theodore*. If it were your father, you wouldn't want me reading a bunch of lies about him."

"My father is nothing like yours. People like your dad are all the same and they all deserve to be ass-raped in prison all day, every day. Just keep passing them down the line."

Joni wanted to hit him over the head with the beer bottle. "Why would you even read that book knowing you were dating the person the lies were about?"

"Have you read the book?"

"No."

"Then how do you know?"

119

"Because she contacted me before she wrote the book, asking about the times my father molested me. He never did, Teddy. Never. I have no idea where she got that information, but it's lies. No wonder you hate my father. You don't even know him."

"He's a murderer. Stop defending him."

"You know how upset I was when that book came out. I didn't come here to fight with you."

"I'm pretty sure you did, considering you threw a book at me."

They sat there drinking their beer, and Joni wondered why she came here in the first place. She could have thrown that book at him at work. "I'm not the person people make me out to be just because I'm his daughter."

"I know that. I just wish you'd see that being a part of his life is not good for you. That the longer you communicate with him, the harder it is to see what he's done."

"I know what he's done. I'm not living in a false reality, Teddy. I just wish things were different."

"Me too. And by the way, I've never seen that book before in my life," he said, and Joni groaned because he was only trying to make her crazier.

Chapter Eleven

The next evening, Joni got a visit from Aunt Lacey. She didn't like Joni's dogs, so Bubba and Clyde were locked outside in the backyard. Making her way back into the living room, she noticed Aunt Lacey looking around the house with a disapproving smile. At sixty-seven, the woman didn't look a day older than fifty. She was well dressed in gray slacks and a coral blouse with a teal necklace down to her belt. Her hair was dyed to its natural blonde, which she kept in a sensible shoulder length cut. The coral nail polish and lipstick matched her shirt, and her black pumps were shiny.

Joni did not know where she was going, and it didn't matter. Aunt Lacey would dress to the nines if she were going grocery shopping. The first time Joni had met her aunt was after her mother's suicide. Even then, the woman was bitter to her.

"You look nice," Joni said.

"Mother has a cough and needs some syrup. I was out and thought I'd stop by. You haven't been to see her in a long time." Years, in fact, Joni thought. "She hasn't slept well in weeks and has been asking about you."

"I've been busy."

Joni was twelve years old the first time she'd met her grandmother, and her father was furious. The woman was frail and harmless, but she avoided seeing her grandmother because she knew her father disapproved. Of course, when she lived with Aunt Lacey and they took drives to the nursing home where she lived then, Joni had no choice in the matter. When Joni was seventeen, Aunt Lacey moved the old bitty into her home, and a year later, Joni moved out and avoided any interaction with the woman.

With Joni's hesitation, Aunt Lacey said, "You're going to Reidsville this weekend, I suppose?"

Joni nodded. "That was the plan."

"I wish you'd stop visiting him."

What was with all the people in her life telling her this? "I'm all he's got."

"Through his own fault." Aunt Lacey kept her hands folded across her chest. "I haven't heard from you in months." Was it only Joni's responsibility to keep their relationship going?

"No news is good news."

"Except I have to find out how you're doing through reporters. I thought surely you'd have called me when they found this new body." Aunt Lacey looked at her pointedly. "Unless you believe that to be good news?"

Joni sighed and moved to the built-in bookcase to rearrange her elephant keepsakes. "Aunt Lacey, I hate arguing with you, but it's hard for me to talk to you when the only thing you have to say is something negative."

"I tried my best with you, but unfortunately I disapprove of the way you live." In the six years Joni lived with her, the woman tried so hard to change her into who she thought she was supposed to be. Aunt Lacey lived in an expensive house in Peachtree City, a house big enough for three families. The schools were supposed to be the best. The city was one of the safest in Georgia. But no matter any of that, Aunt Lacey only took her in because of obligation. Nothing more. With no husband or children of her own, the woman could focus entirely on herself and for some strange reason, instead of spoiling Joni rotten and turning her into the daughter she never had, Joni seemed to be nothing more than an inconvenience in her aunt's life. Joni had to remind herself that she wouldn't have the things she did without Aunt Lacey's generosity. Especially this house.

"Are all of those from your father?"

Six shelves were filled with elephants of all shapes and sizes. "He took me to the circus when I was six. Bought me elephants ever since." His gifts were to remind her of how strong the elephants were.

"Elephants are smart. And hard workers."

"Trunks up means good luck. This one's my favorite." She pointed to a large white elephant with amethyst stones on its forehead. Probably the most expensive thing she owned. Her mother wasn't happy when Joni opened this gift. Was never happy when her dad gave her any gift.

"I'm speaking with Amanda Flockhart on Wednesday. I'd like for you to be there."

Facing Aunt Lacey, Joni said, "What on earth are you thinking? She painted a horrible picture of us. Why let her do it again?"

"Apparently she's working with another publisher who's offering her a large sum of money, which, in return, I'm being offered a percentage which I'll donate to the children's home."

Joni had her fair share of offers in the past as well. She was just never interested. "You've never wanted your name associated with my father. Why are you doing this?"

"I've decided it's in my best interest. And Amanda Flockhart is such a sweet girl. It really is a shame what happened to her."

"If you do this interview, the rest of the media will be on us like flies. Why would you do that to yourself? To me?"

"They want to know about my brother. People have a right to know about the monster that their tax dollars are keeping alive in prison."

**

Joni was late when she met Sam in front of the Japanese restaurant in Atlanta, but he wasn't put out by it and smiled when she greeted him, and she tried to ignore how distracted she was with Aunt Lacey. The tiny waitress asked if they wanted the hibachi or sushi side.

Sam said, "Hibachi," and Joni said, "Sushi," and they looked at each other and laughed, and suddenly Joni's mood improved.

"I've never had sushi," Sam said.

"Then you are in for a treat." She pulled him along to the left side of the restaurant.

Sam looked over the glass counter where a chef was preparing fresh sushi rolls for someone and Sam turned his nose up. "It's really raw fish?"

"Not all of it. We can get a sampler and you can try a lot of different things."

By now he was looking at the menu and gagged and said something about eel and squid, and Joni laughed. "Why'd you agree to meet here if you don't like sushi?"

"I guess I'd go anywhere for a date?" Sam tilted his head sideways as he questioned this and looked much like Bubba and Clyde.

"This isn't a date."

"Not yet." He patted her leg.

By the time their sushi rolls arrived, she was laughing at Sam again. He was funny even when he wasn't trying to be. Joni dipped a roll in the wasabi and soy sauce mixture to try it and said it was delicious. Then she explained all the different things that were inside the rolls. The cucumber, avocado, carrots, salmon.

"And you eat this green stuff?"

"Yes." She dipped a piece of sushi for him with the chopsticks and set it on his tiny plate. "You have to put the whole thing in your mouth."

And he did, and he chewed, and he gagged, and he couldn't swallow it.

Joni hid her laugh behind her hand. He was making a production out of it and when the roll went down, he said, "It was chewy." Then he took his napkin and wiped his tongue. "I'm from the south. We eat steak down here."

"I'm from the south too, and I like a variety."

"Next time we eat steak."

Joni smiled. "Fine," she said. "But you have to taste these other rolls."

Their dinner went on like that for a while, and Sam kept unwrapping the rolls like he was unwrapping the world, taking each thing out and examining it, then tasting it for the first time. The more Sam made her laugh, the more Joni relaxed and looked at him as less of a stranger. She'd forgotten about their first night together until Sam said, "Where do you want to go after this?"

"It's getting late, and I don't think we have many options."

"It's Atlanta. We can go get a drink."

"Nah."

"Coffee?" Joni shook her head. "I know what you want to do. You want to go back to the Fantasy Club, don't you?"

She paused mid-bite. "No."

"Skip the club and go straight to the motel?"

"You think you're so funny? That's not going to happen again, for your information."

"Why?" He squeezed her leg again. When Joni thought about it, she realized that because of that first time together, Sam automatically thought they were at that stage, but Joni wasn't at anything with him except having good conversation.

She said, "Sam, this is fun and all, but anything other than this is awkward."

"It doesn't have to be."

"It will always be." Joni let out a sigh. "I'll do whatever you want me to and help you find answers, but that's all I can do." Then she lowered her voice. "You and I can be friends, but I think that deep down there will always be a part of you looking to blame someone, and I don't want to be that someone."

"I only blame who's responsible. I hate not having answers."

"And I don't know if I can get you answers, but I have a question for you. Your mom was sixteen when she had you?"

Sam choked on his Coke. He coughed until Joni pounded him on his back. Jeez, was he a newborn or something? "I'm okay," he said, through a cough. "I'm okay."

"Sorry. I didn't mean to catch you off guard."

"Went down wrong." Sam rubbed his throat for a minute. "She wasn't even sixteen. She was born in April 1969, and died June 15, 1988. I was born November 8, 1984."

His mind was a box full of dates. "How do you know the specific date she died?"

Sam took another sip of Coke. "He told me. Not me, the police. When he gave them all the specifics on the women. I need a cigarette. Do they have beer here?"

"Yeah," she said, and ordered them each a beer, which she regretted because it was served at room temperature. "So you're not thirty?"

Sam paused mid-sip and thought a second. "I think we both lied that night, don't you?" Joni nodded like an idiot until he said, "Tell me about your mother."

"Nothing to tell."

"We can both agree that we don't like talking about our mothers?"

"But I thought—"

Sam reached for her hand. "When they first found her body, I was angry, but I'm not anymore. I feel relief and a sense of connection to you, like you understand how I feel. All I ever wanted to know was why this happened to her. It's strange," Sam said, "and don't think I'm crazy, but when I'm with you, I feel like you are the last string that connects me to my mother."

Joni didn't know how to feel about that, but the feeling was probably the same for Mary when she thought Joni had access to Sheila and Rachel through Lyle. She surprised herself when she said, "Did you know that my father's first victim is still alive? Her name's Mary," and Sam choked on his beer.

***

A sense of relief washed over her with being able to talk about Mary and the other women with someone who was genuinely interested. Not interested because he wanted to write an article or gather evidence. His curiosity was sincere and as he asked questions about everything, he kept saying, "I never knew that," but in some odd way, Joni believed he did.

She told Sam most of what she knew about Mary's time with Lyle, but she spent a lot of time talking about the days she'd go to visit her. "Since I've known her, she's tried to commit suicide and went to the psychiatric hospital, and all she does is shut down."

"And she's like this because of what happened to her?"

"No." Joni shoved the empty plate to the side and took a sip of water. "Before this she was severely bipolar, but when she was on her medication, she was okay. Then, after everything she went through with my father, it sent her into a terrible state of post-traumatic stress, and now she's schizophrenic."

Sam was quiet for a moment, looked down at the Japanese writing on the counter. His voice was low when he said, "She told you this?"

The information Joni knew was supposed to be confidential, but she said, "After Mary went into the psychiatric hospital, she asked for me, so I went to visit her. I spoke to a nurse who told me a lot of things I'm not supposed to know because I'm not her primary care provider or whatever."

Sam took a drink of Coke and nodded as he listened, then he said, "Who takes care of her?"

"She has a sister."

"That's it?" Sam said, disappointed. "She doesn't mention anyone else?"

127

Not unless you counted the dead people she talks to. Joni shook her head.

"Why do you go see her? I mean, do you truly enjoy being around a woman like that?"

Joni didn't have to think too long. "I do care about her. I want to help her in any way I can. I guess it's the same reason why I'm here with you. I feel obligated—" Wrong word choice, she realized with the look on Sam's face. "I hate what's happened to everyone because of my dad, and I've spent a lot of time feeling like I want everyone to leave him alone. But when I met Mary, it really put things in perspective for me about what happened to her. It's horrible, and I want her to be okay. Nothing that I do will bring any of those women back, not your mother, not Melanie Pavroy. All the people in those families know that they just want justice. They want Lyle dead. But Mary, on the other hand, doesn't understand what's happened to her. She thinks those two women that were with her are still alive and I have to find them so she can get better."

Sam's eyes went wide. "You're going to find two more women that your dad murdered?"

"I'm going to sure as hell try. Mary needs that."

"I can help you."

"No," Joni said, and pulled out her debit card, but then Sam pulled out his wallet and handed the guy cash.

"I'm starving," he said. "I wonder where I can get a good steak around here."

***

Another week went by, and Joni had met with Sam a few times in Atlanta for dinner. He talked more about himself and being raised by his aunt. Joni could relate to all that.

By the time Saturday came, Joni had worked herself up to a point that she had so many questions for her father. She didn't want to waste the time she had at Georgia State Prison. Lyle looked like he knew she wasn't there for pleasantries and updates about her week at work or walk with the dogs.

"You still talking to that Sam kid?" Apparently, her father had questions of his own. She thought about lying, but couldn't, so she nodded instead. He said, "I remember she had a kid. Four years old. Used to get in her way all the time. You should be careful."

"Especially if he tries to share his ice cream."

"Joni," he said with a warning.

"Daddy, stop." That was such a stupid comment to make. Even from prison, he probably had ways to make people disappear. She changed the subject to something far worse. "I want to know where you dumped Sheila and Rachel. I made a promise to Mary and I need to find them." Lyle looked down at his hands, shook his head, a little surprised she'd asked. "Daddy, what you did is not a secret anymore."

"They are long gone. You won't find anything." Caramel eyes pierced into hers, and he gave her a sharp look.

"So what?"

"You won't find Rachel. She's in the Towaliga River in Jackson. I wrapped her in a tarp and tied her to a cinderblock, and dropped her off a bridge north of High Falls."

"Are you serious?" Joni stopped herself to keep her tone in check.

"Why would I lie?"

"Is that where you held Mary? In Jackson?"

"No." His tone was nonchalant, and she wondered if he spoke about his crimes to his prison mates. Like if they compared notes or something.

"What about Sheila? Did you drop her off a bridge, too?"

This time, when he looked at her, he waited a few minutes before he answered. "Why are you doing this? Can't you leave things alone? This isn't your business."

"I need to know."

"You're asking too many questions here lately."

"Are you ashamed of me learning the truth?"

"What do you want? Firsthand knowledge of how they felt when they died?"

Although she was sure she knew the answer to that as well, what she said was, "I want to know what you know. I feel like I'm stuck in this place in my life and I need to know about everything. I need to know what happened and why. It started with Mary—"

"*Mary,*" he said, nearly spitting out the name. "Mary told you all about Sheila, but did she tell you what *she* did to Sheila? I'll tell you what she did and how screwed up in the head she was. I went into that basement one day and there was blood everywhere. I'd never seen so much blood. Smelled like a damn slaughterhouse. Mary took the glass from the broken oil lamp and sliced her up. Used the blood to paint a fucking Picasso on the wall."

Her obsession with the red paint. "Mary killed her?"

"I had to put Sheila out of her misery."

"Oh."

"Tell me how she doesn't know. Joni, why do you do this to yourself? She means nothing to you."

"She thinks you love her." This brought a sick smile to her dad's face. The same one she'd only recently begun to see. "Is that what you told her?"

"I told her a lot of things, things I don't even remember."

Joni didn't want to get upset. She needed to keep her dad talking to get the information she needed. For a second, she believed him, but then again, her dad had a sharp memory and she realized he had to remember every little detail about his time with Mary. Why play like he didn't know?

"This is just between you and me," she said, and Lyle shook his head.

"It's not that simple."

Joni reached out to touch his hand. It was warm and rough, and she wondered how many times he'd wrapped those fingers around women's necks. The strange thought sent a chill down her spine, and she casually pulled her hands back. "Daddy, are you afraid to die?"

"A part of me is already dead."

"What do you mean?"

"You'd never understand."

"I'd like to. Aunt Lacey said your mother has been sick."

"I'm sure she'd tell you exactly what she wanted you to know."

"And what is that? You're so vague about her, and I can't figure out if you really don't want me to know about when you were a kid or if you think I can't handle it. What in the hell happened to you to turn you into what you've become?" Lyle looked past her as though he wasn't fully there. "You wish she'd die, don't you?"

"I tried to kill her once. I couldn't do it."

"Aunt Lacey doesn't believe those things you said about her."

"Maybe Lacey should have been the first on my list."

Aunt Lacey had a different father, and their age difference impacted the way they were raised. By the time the abuse began, Lacey was out of the house. That's what her father told her, and that's all she knew. When she mentioned this abuse once to Aunt Lacey, Aunt Lacey called her brother a hellacious liar who brought their mother nothing but grief.

For a while Joni let her mind wonder into that dark place as she thought about all the different things that possibly happened to her father as a boy. Abuse. Neglect. Fear. Control. Some people shouldn't be allowed to have children. They should have to undergo psych evaluations. She wouldn't be sitting here like this if her grandmother hadn't screwed up and ruined her own son's life. It was why Joni would never have kids. The disease was in her blood like a virus.

131

Joni said, "I'm sorry, Daddy, I wish you could have enjoyed your life better."

He surprised her when he said, "Don't think I didn't enjoy every bit of it. I had different aspects of my life. I could be whomever I wanted to be. I was the family man that you and your mother looked up to. I was the boss man that never let anyone down. I was a friend when I wanted to be. And I was also many other people. I enjoyed it while it lasted. And in here—" Lyle looked around. "People know who I am, just like I know who they are. But they don't really *know* me."

For that brief second, she felt sorry for him again, then it all changed. Proof that he killed women because he wanted to. He was compelled to do it to escape something else in his life. He had a choice.

Lyle Chaskey chose wrong.

"Daddy," Joni said. "Where did you dump Sheila Graninch?"

"Perhaps she's in a quiet place where her mother can still hear her sing," was all he said.

***

The drive back home would take three hours, and as soon as Joni got on the highway, she called Cyrus. "Rachel Ikenbor is in the Towaliga River, north of High Falls."

"None of the other bodies were found in water. That's not his method." This wasn't how she hoped he'd respond.

"Rachel was his first kill. Maybe the first ones were different. He said he wrapped her in a tarp and weighed her down with a cinderblock and dropped her off a bridge."

"Which bridge?"

"I haven't figured that out yet. I think my dad took me there. I remember going to High Falls, then later a bridge. I'm going to Jackson tomorrow."

Joni could have sworn she heard Cyrus banging his head. "You can't go to any dump sites."

"High Falls is a state park. I can go anywhere I want." She knew she sounded like a brat. "What I mean is that I want to go back there and see if I remember anything else."

"Then I'm coming with you. I'll meet you at your house at eight in the morning," he said, and hung up the phone without giving her a choice.

Chapter Twelve

"Does he have to breathe on me like that?" They were in Cyrus's SUV, and he hadn't stopped complaining about Bubba and Clyde since Joni let them jump inside to go for a ride. "This is a government issue vehicle. They better not pee on the seats." He had on cargo shorts, a plain t-shirt, and aviator style sunglasses. Joni had never seen him dressed down before.

"My dogs have better manners than most men, plus they keep my bed warm," Joni said. "That sounded a lot worse than I meant."

Cyrus pushed Bubba back and gestured to her diary. "What's that?"

Joni explained about her Sunday trips with her dad and how she used to write in her diaries about it. She had three, and this was the one about High Falls. "I was nine when we went. The waterfall was so loud and dropped with such force, I was scared to go near it."

"And the bridge?" Cyrus changed lanes and drove faster than he should have.

"That's the thing. After we left High Falls, he drove to this other place and made me look at this bridge. It was boring compared to the falls, but I don't know where it's at. I'll have to retrace my steps. Do you have to drive so fast?"

He slowed down a bit and said, "The faster we get there, the faster I can get him out of my ear."

Joni placed her palm to Bubba's nose and said, "Sit," in a firm voice. He whined, then obeyed. "He likes to see where he's going." Back to the diaries, she said, "I was reading my diary last night when something caught my attention. This one time we went to a covered bridge where the water was really rapid. It was in Blakely, Georgia."

"Early County," Cyrus nodded as he understood. "Coheelee Creek Covered Bridge."

In unison, they both said, "Paige Folly."

From his own memory, he said, "She was found west of the bridge in some woods. Paige was the fourth woman found naked with cotton fibers in her throat. She ended up being the farthest south of all the bodies."

"Kennesaw to Blakely is about three and a half hours. I know, I wrote about how it took us all day to get there. She was found in '92, and from the date in my diary, the body had just been found a few months before when my father decided to take the visit."

"Can I read your diaries? That would be a huge help."

"No. I can't have you reading about how I fantasized about the boy down the road."

"Do you think he was secretly taking you to visit the dump sites?"

"Or scoping out new ones." The whole thing made her sick. What kind of father did that?

"What did he act like when you went to Coheelee Creek?"

Joni closed her eyes a moment, let the memory come in. "I ran up and down that bridge for twenty minutes because I liked the way it echoed. The sound carried off as though it would travel to all eternity." Joni opened her eyes. "I was only six, but I drew a picture and spelled everything wrong. I had to go to the bathroom, so guess where he took me?"

"West of the bridge?" Cyrus worked his jaw.

"He seemed happy that day. Excited even. I guess by then he knew there was nothing to link him to Paige Folly, so he figured he'd gotten away with it. That's how I know Rachel is under the bridge."

135

"The possibility of finding anything after thirty years is slim. We're talking about a river. I checked records after you called yesterday. There haven't been any unidentified bodies or remains found in this area, either."

Did that mean all hope of finding Rachel was lost?

***

High Falls turned out to be even more beautiful than Joni remembered. The waterfall cascaded down large millstones and dropped over a hundred feet into the river. The trees were magnificent and reached to the clear blue sky. The only thing missing was a bald eagle flying overhead.

"I can't believe I've never been here," Cyrus said. "I should get out more often."

Wooden stairs brought them down to the waterfall level, where a barricade kept them on a path. The dogs followed as Joni and Cyrus continued walking along the path to the old grist mill and powerhouse. This town used to be a prosperous place until the railroad bypassed it. Strange how all the mill towns become nothing more than shadows when they're no longer used.

This is one of Georgia's hidden places. So perfect and pure it took Joni's breath away. The powerhouse walls were crumbling and covered with graffiti.

"Feels weird being here," Joni said. "Like I was supposed to do all these great things with him, but he's not here. My dad used to say that it wasn't where you were going, it's how you felt when you got there. Since Melanie Pavroy, all I feel is doubt about everything I've ever known. I have to find Sheila and Rachel."

Whether he meant to or not, Cyrus pet Bubba's head, and Joni noticed how the dog relaxed into him. "Your dad is a killer." He'd told her that before, but this time his voice was soft. "He

136

will make you feel however he needs you to feel to get what he wants. His emotions aren't real."

"My dad loves me."

"Because he says so? Look what he's done to you. Better yet, look at what he's taken away from you."

"Don't talk about my mother." Joni looked away.

"I'm talking about *you*. He took away a part of you. And why don't you want to talk about your mother, she was a victim in this as well."

"She bailed on me. Do you have any idea what that's been like?"

"You're blaming the wrong person."

So many things went through her mind. Years of emotions smothered her to the point that her very existence no longer mattered. Cyrus didn't understand any of this. "Can we get out of here? I'm feeling a little clicky."

***

They were back in the Expedition, and Joni said, "My father stopped at a gas station," and flipped open the diary. "No. It was a bait shop. Snapper's Bait Shop."

Cyrus used a mini-laptop to search for the location. "No Snapper's."

"Maybe the place is so old it's not registered."

"Or maybe this isn't the location, because your father is a liar." The smile he gave was fake.

"Or maybe your Scooby-sense doesn't work and you don't know how to detect. What's so special about you, anyway?"

He feigned offense and put his hand to his chest. "There are a lot of special things about me that have nothing to do with my job title."

"Name one."

"I've never gotten a speeding ticket."

137

"That doesn't count," Joni said, and moved on. "Snapper's had a purple worm on the sign, and a torn screen door. If we can find the bait shop, we can find the bridge. Go left and follow High Falls Road."

At the end of the road, Joni told Cyrus to stop at the gas station. After he put the SUV in park, he said, "What do you need?"

"Directions."

"I have GPS, you know?"

Inside, Joni grabbed two Cokes, two Snickers, and water for the dogs. The man behind the counter spit tobacco juice into a coffee mug filled with stained napkins. The mug read, *I Survived the Zombie Apocalypse.* He gave her a toothless grin and totaled the purchase.

Joni handed him ten dollars and said, "Do you know where I can find Snapper's Bait Shop?"

He coughed, said, "Snappy closed that place about ten, twelve years ago. I got worms if that's what you need." He turned to the window; his look suspicious of the black government ride in his parking lot.

"No, thanks." Joni grabbed the bag. "I haven't been there since I was a kid. Do you know what's there now?"

"Nothing. It's still there. Take a left on the highway and go down a ways. You'll see it." He spit more tobacco juice into the mug.

***

The bridge, Joni thought as Cyrus drove over it to get to Snapper's. He parked in the lot and left the engine running for the dogs while he and Joni got out. Relief washed over her as she stood there looking at what she knew to be the bridge her father tossed Rachel over. The river at this point was about a hundred feet wide, with a twenty-foot drop from the bridge.

"You sure this is it?" Cyrus said, and shoved his sunglasses to the top of his head.

"I was nine, and I stood right here when he said to me, 'The easiest ones were the ones who didn't know they needed controlling'."

"What's that mean?"

"That he thought Rachel was weak."

***

Under the bridge the next afternoon, what they found was a cinderblock and a broken piece of rope. Since the water level under the bridge was only fifteen feet, it was supposed to be a simple search, but the media got word and it turned into a shark frenzy.

Joni and Sam leaned against Cyrus's SUV behind the police barricade in Snapper's parking lot. It was impressive to see Cyrus in action, giving orders to his four-man team and thwart the media at the same time.

After they pulled up the cinderblock, two divers began searching for any remains nearby, but Cyrus didn't look hopeful.

"How can they see?" Sam said while smoking a cigarette. "It's like emphysema black down there."

Rachel Ikenbor was twenty years old when she disappeared. No one knew what happened to her and by the time Lyle was sent to prison, she'd been missing for sixteen years. There was absolutely no connection between them except for Mary saying a man held her captive and killed Sheila and Rachel. No one put the two Rachels together, and Mary never came forward again.

Reporters were trying to get Joni's attention. She'd been caught twice by someone asking her questions and twice she'd said she had no comment. The strawberry blonde that stepped into Clemmie's was also there. How the hell did people find out about this stuff so fast?

Cyrus walked up, and didn't look happy. "I don't know, Joni. My Scooby-sense is telling me not to trust the serial killer."

Sam said, "Don't you mean your spidey-sense?"

"Who are you?"

"This is Sam—"

Joni stopped when Sam squeezed her shoulder. He said, "I'm Sam. But I'm going to get out of your way."

When Sam walked away, one reporter yelled, "Is it true that you're looking for a victim of the *Cotton Mouth Killer*?"

Cyrus said, "At this time we have no comment."

"Then why is Lyle Chaskey's daughter here? Can you tell us what's going on, Miss Chaskey?"

Cyrus blocked Joni from the camera crew. "I asked you to stay out of the parking lot and not to film from the bridge." Then he opened the SUV door and shoved Joni inside. "Why are you here?"

"I found this place."

"Really? I thought maybe the Creek Indians did that."

"At least you have proof she was here."

He paused a moment too long, and bit his lip before he said, "Remains at this late stage are far and none. Decomposed and brittle bones. Flesh, muscle, tissue; all gone. Do you know how hard it is to find a sliver of a piece of evidence in water like this?" Joni shook her head, and Cyrus pointed over his shoulder to the team. "They think I'm crazy. Do you think I'm crazy for doing this?"

"It's what you wanted. You've been after these bodies for years."

"We'll test what we found, but whatever was tied with that rope is long gone. I'm sorry, but I don't think we'll find anything else. I'm pulling this at five o'clock."

Perfect, Joni thought. Just in time for the news to catch the live coverage.

***

The next day, Joni sat at the computer, searching for what she could find on Darla Doolan. For a drug addict, her parents had nothing but nice things to say about her. How sweet she was. How loving. How much she loved life.

What about her son? Was he being excluded to protect him? There was only one way to find out. Darla's mother died several years ago. One sister lived in Birmingham, the other in Athens, with no address to her name. The father still lived in Athens as well. Joni put the address on her phone's GPS. Back roads would get her there in less time.

The dogs began barking, and Joni went to check on them. A new mustang was parked on the street, and she was surprised at who dared show her face here. Out of spite, Joni swung the door wide open, but instead of going into protective mode, Bubba and Clyde wagged their tails.

Their hearts were too good to sense the lack of danger.

Amanda Flockhart handed over the mail. On top was a letter stamped with Georgia Department of Corrections.

"Would die to know what's in there."

"Keep dying." Joni locked the dogs in the house and stepped outside. "What do you want?"

"I just finished my interview with your aunt."

The right side of Amanda's face was whiter than the rest. Her eye drooped lower because the whole eye socket had been reconstructed where the dog bit into her face. Through surgery, the right ear, her nose, and part of her lip had been attempted to be put back to normal the best way possible. But in Joni's opinion, it looked as though Amanda had recently undergone more surgery to make herself look even better. She was dressed in nice jeans and a turquoise blouse. Even with her face messed up, to Joni, she would always be that popular school girl.

"I have nothing to say to you."

"Hear me out."

Joni walked down the steps toward the Honda Pilot, her old friend right on her heels. "Amanda, I have nothing to say to you, and if you don't leave right now, I'll call the police."

"Oh, get over yourself, Joni."

Joni turned to her. "Let me remind you of something. After you got out of the hospital and went back to school, you were no longer popular, Amanda Flockhart, and I was the only one who stuck by your side. I defended you, and I never looked at you any differently. But you? You're no friend. As soon as I moved away, you wanted nothing to do with me. And now this?"

"My dad wouldn't let me write to you anymore."

"He had no control over you once you were an adult. And he had no control over the lies you wrote about me."

"They weren't lies. I got that information from one of the detectives working the case."

"Who was only speculating," Joni pointed out, "because of what my father had done to these women."

"Well, yeah."

Joni threw her hands up. Amanda would write whatever she wanted, and she was going to do it again.

"I'm doing a lot more research and visiting all the places he dumped those women that were found. I've been travelling for months and interviewing a lot of people. I'm trying to get your side of the story," Amanda said, and handed Joni a plain white business card.

"You couldn't do it right the first time, so now you're trying again? Don't bother. Liars always lie."

"Harsh words from someone who's got it running in her blood."

For the first time in her life, Joni struggled against causing another person bodily harm. How good would it really feel to punch Amanda in the face? "You know," Joni said, and took a step forward. "That day in Stone Mountain? I never told a single person what you did."

Amanda's face went still. "I never did anything."

"You provoked that dog—"

"I did not." Amanda tried to walk away, but Joni grabbed her arm.

"You threw acorns at him and poked him with sticks."

"Now who's lying?"

"He was an innocent dog who had enough and only defended himself. Look what happened to him."

"No," Amanda said. "He attacked me for no reason, and your father choked him to death. I guess by then he'd had lots of practice."

"I'm warning you now not to write another thing about me or my father."

Because Amanda Flockhart was provoking another dog.

When Joni got into the car, she crumpled Amanda's business card and threw it on the backseat. Then she ripped open the letter from her father.

My Dearest Joni,

With every passing day, I miss you more and more as though you've never been here at all. I forgot to ask you to send another care package, if you will, please? Aspirin and more white socks will make my life so much easier in this hellhole. Also, I'm running low on soap and my favorite cinnamon mints.

Do you remember Marshmallow? How could you forget? You used to carry that cat in a basket as though it were a baby. You used to dress him in bibs and bonnets and wrap him in your old baby blankets. I thought you should know that when Marshmallow died; I buried him under your swing set. Right under the slide. That way, no matter what, he'd always be with you. At least now you know the truth. Knowing now is better than never

143

knowing at all. Sometimes the ones we love are right under our feet and we never even know it.

If you get a chance, can you throw in a chocolate bar of some sort? I'm having a craving.

Love,
Daddy

She cried for weeks after Marshmallow died and begged her parents for another pet for years. Of course, when she was only six, she hadn't noticed the patch of grass pulled up under the slide. She was too little to have paid attention to that.

Why did he lie about where he buried the cat? It was something so dumb.

And she realized he was being truthful about it because when the police searched their house, they also dug up the backyard and found a tiny set of bones. Animal bones. Joni never thought much about it. Why was he telling her this now?

***

The Clover Leaf town homes were outside of Athens, looked to be well established with a warm, cozy feel to it. From the look of things, it was more of a retirement community than anything. Two old ladies were in front of their homes watering plants and probably chatting about their grandkids. Another old lady sat on her swing while her husband washed the car.

Joni parked at the address and felt many eyeballs on her. Couldn't commit a crime here if she wanted to. On the porch, a UGA flag hung from a pole and looked like every other residence in the city. Home of the Bulldogs. Joni rang the bell twice before a little old man answered. Couldn't have been but five feet tall. Had she mistaken the house for the Keebler elves' tree? The old man was cute. She had to give him that.

"Are you Mr. Ira Doolan?"

"Yes, yes." He opened the door wide, said, "Come on in," and Joni was confused with his easiness to trust a stranger. Did his daughter have the same trait, and so easily trust Lyle? Joni hesitated a moment until she saw a little girl peek around the corner. "That's my great granddaughter. Emily, say hello."

"I'm four. You wanna play with me?"

The old man laughed, tickled by her antics in a way only a great grandfather could be. "She's just here to talk to Popsy, sugar." How'd he know? He leaned down to Emily. "You be a good girl and go work on your puzzle, and I'll be there in five minutes."

"Okay," Emily said, and ran into the other room.

Ira said, "You can come with me," and turned toward the kitchen. Totally confused, Joni followed him, was about to ask if he was expecting someone else when he said, "You didn't bring the cooler? The other nurses always bring a cooler. I put the container in a brown sack so Emily wouldn't see it." He dug into the fridge and came out with a brown paper bag, handed it to Joni. "That stool is about an hour old. I'm glad you could get out here so soon."

He was giving her a stool sample?

Joni set the bag on the table, disgusted. "Sir, I'm not a nurse." It was his turn to be confused. "I only stopped by to ask you a few questions about your family."

The man swallowed hard, his face suddenly going cold. "You're a reporter? I already told that little Flockhart girl I have nothing more to say."

"I'm not a reporter. My name's Joni Chaskey—"

Ira Doolan fell back, hitting the counter as his feet slid to steady himself. "You stay away from us." He continued to move away, faster this time, until he reached the doorway. "Emily!"

She was such a moron. "I'm not going to hurt you."

Right outside the kitchen was the living room, and Ira Doolan stood shaking with Emily wrapped around his leg, too weak in

145

his old age to even pick her up. She began to cry, and Joni knew that cry. Pure fear from being too young and not understanding why the adult who was supposed to care for you was upset.

"It's okay."

"You go away," he said, and grabbed the fireplace poker.

Joni held up her hands in surrender. "I only wanted to ask you about Darla and her son." He fell back onto the sofa, Emily holding on for dear life as she cried. "I'm—"

"You get out of my house, you bitch."

She was traumatizing both of them. For what? She should be interrogating Sam, not Ira Doolan. "I'm sorry," she said, and there was a knock on the door, probably a nosy neighbor who heard Emily screaming.

Joni had to get out of there. At the door, a woman in regular clothes and a nurse's badge clipped to her collar stood there with a smile, holding a zippered cooler. "Hi, I'm—"

"On the table," Joni said, and got the hell out.

***

The one-way streets in the middle of Atlanta weren't easy to navigate, but Joni knew her way around well enough to find Sam's rental with no problem. The small house was in Grant Park, and his rent had to be close to two grand a month, and she wanted to know what the guy did for a living to afford it. She parked in front of the single-car garage and made her way to the door, where two large clay flowerpots sat with gorgeous white hydrangeas. They were fake.

Sam had the door open before she knocked, and without hesitating, she went inside. "Are you baking," she said, at the scent of sugar cookies, and tried to pretend everything was okay.

"Hell, no," Sam said. He closed the door, then pointed to a nearby candle.

"Should have known."

146

Although the entire living room was jam-packed with antique furniture, it all seemed to have a place. The house was cozy and moderately decorated for a bachelor. Strange how this very house reminded Joni of her own. Three bedrooms, two baths, maybe fifteen-hundred square feet, yet Sam's house had to cost triple what Joni's did. All because of location.

"Your house is so cute," Joni said.

"That's exactly what I was hoping for. A cute house," he said, his voice full of sarcasm.

Joni eyed an antique pie safe and ran her hand down the front. "I always wanted one of these." Jokingly she said, "Can I have it?"

"That piece is over a hundred and fifty years old, and belonged to my great-grandmother. Her father gave it to her as a wedding present when she moved from Savannah—" Suddenly he stopped as though he was about to tell her something she wasn't supposed to know, blinked twice, then said, "Come on," and motioned her toward the kitchen. "I told you I'd drive to you."

"And I told you I had plans."

"Secret plans?" he said, and waggled his eyebrows. "You want to go to that Japanese place you love?"

"Sure."

"I was kidding. You'd have to drag my dead body in there."

"Oh." Joni smiled and took in the recently remodeled kitchen. The walls were painted a light shade of blue and trimmed in white. Stone tiles covered the floor and matched the backsplash, which looked great with the granite countertops and stainless-steel appliances.

"You want to order a pizza?"

"Sounds good to me." She set her purse down on a barstool while Sam picked up the phone. He was in a pair of jeans and a black t-shirt, and Joni realized that the gray at his temples was gone. Did he color his hair?

The pizza was from a hole in the wall place, but it was delicious, better than she'd ever had. The pepperoni was crispy, the mushrooms and onions sautéed. After they'd scarfed down half the pizza, Sam said, "You're distracted."

Because I think you're up to something, she wanted to say, but smiled and pointed to the pie safe. "So, how much do you think that's worth?"

"You're going to steal my pie safe, aren't you?" Sam lit up a cigarette and blew smoke away from her.

"You caught me," she said, and pulled out one of his cigarettes. "You mind?" He shook his head and used his own to light hers, the intimacy a bit too close. "How long you been smoking?"

"My grandpa gave me my first cigarette when I was fifteen." Sam laughed. "One day I went into his room to find more, but I found porn magazines instead. When he caught me, he was so surprised he fell right out of his fucking wheelchair."

After today, she could picture that reaction, but why was Ira Doolan in a wheelchair? "Was the wheelchair temporary?"

"Hell no. The bastard was in a car accident and ripped off both his legs. They don't grow back, ya know?"

***

The game was simple to play once the rules had been established. Question everything he said, and he'd ramble on in an unconscious stupor, talking himself into circles and corners. What he said was not what he meant, and when he became frustrated with his own lies, he said both his grandparents were dead. It was easier not to talk about them.

Although she hadn't learned anything new, except that Sam Doolan was a liar, she played along into his illusion because he'd tire of the lies before she tired of the game.

Her dad taught her well like that.

The last bit of daylight turned the sky soft pink and purple, and this was what little girls' dreams were made of. Life in the clouds where everything was safe. Joni drove home with a lot on her mind.

Everything in life was a puzzle, a piece of something greater than herself that she had to figure out or feel like a failure if she didn't. People's motives, for example, were the greatest puzzles of all. Joni didn't like this particular game, because just when she thought she had her father figured out, he sent her another piece.

That's when it hit her, those last few pieces snapping together almost perfectly. Her dad's letter made little sense, but put it together with Mary's words and it all fit.

Chapter Thirteen

Cyrus laughed at her before she even finished with her theory. "This is serious," she said, and shut the door of his small office. It was almost six p.m. She was surprised he was even here.

"And I could never get a warrant to dig up property based on the fact that your father buried your cat under your swing set. I appreciate your help, but that's insane."

"He wants me to figure this out without incriminating himself. Can't you at least look into it?"

"And say what to Sheila Graninch's mother? We have reason to believe your daughter is buried in your backyard?"

"Yeah," Joni said. Why was that so difficult for Cyrus to do?

"The bridge was a bust. I believe he's leading you on a wild goose chase. He's playing with you, Joni."

Her father wouldn't do that. Not to her. "Mary Rancotti thinks they're still alive." Cyrus grabbed a pen and put his serious face back on. "I said *thinks* they're alive. There is no chance in hell of that. He told me himself that he killed them. Crushed Sheila's face with a heavy oil lamp. I know they're dead. I just want Mary to know the same thing. And don't you think her parents should know after all these years? What if she's right there, Cyrus? Right there?"

"I want to find these women as much as you do, but at this time, since Melanie Pavroy's body turned up, I've got people all over the state of Georgia looking for more *Cotton Mouth Killer* bodies." He held up a stack of papers. "Today alone, we got seventy calls into the tip line from people who have all these ideas about where I should look for more bodies." Cyrus thumbed through the papers. "This one man called to tell us that his grandpa claims that back in 1994 he had a run in with a man who fits Chaskey's description, and Chaskey was in the middle of burying a body." He let the papers fall to his desk. "And because it's my job, I have to look into each one of these calls. They think they're helping, but they're not. Now you want me to dig up Sheila Graninch's mother's backyard? Don't kick me in the nuts over this, but I got work to do."

Joni felt bad, but this was the job Cyrus chose. He had to be used to it by now. "How hard can this one thing be?"

"This one thing? Part of me didn't have high hopes for under the bridge, but when all we found was a cinderblock and a broken rope, I have to say I was a little disappointed." He pressed his fingertips to his forehead. "The divers are still looking but I don't know for how long. This kind of stuff rattles people, okay?"

"Cyrus," she said, playing her last card. "What if it was Miranda?"

That's all she had to say. He leaned back in his chair and looked at a bunch of photos of missing women taped to the wall. "I'll see what I can do."

***

The morning sunlight poured through the shade and Joni opened her eyes to a wet nose against hers, and Bubba snoring like an old man. Sleep didn't come easily last night, and she kept wondering what Cyrus would do about Sheila. He'd been after her father's victims for years. Why not believe her? Maybe because all his faith drained out of him when he couldn't pull Rachel Ikenbor out of the river. What would it be like to have reported a daughter missing and never know what happened? Then years later the body is discovered, only to find out it was murder? Joni thought of Melanie Pavroy's family. They were on the news talking about being thankful that they could now have peace with knowing, but with that peace came rage. They wanted Lyle Chaskey to pay for what he'd done, and sleeping comfortably in a jail cell and eating hot meals wasn't enough. To

151

top things off, she couldn't get the look on Ira Doolan's face out of her mind.

The first thing that came to her mind was whether the Graninches still lived in the same house. She made coffee and let the dogs outside, then turned on her computer. The internet had information on Sheila's disappearance, but everything else was minimal. There was an article on an arrest. It was about Sheila's brother Henry, who'd gotten into a fight at a sports bar in LaGrange. The mother's name was Ellen, and a telephone number was listed in the online yellow pages. Just as Joni picked up the phone, the doorbell rang. It was Sheriff VanBuckle.

She locked up the dogs and answered the door. The first time she'd ever met him was at Clemmie's and she'd dropped a bowl of banana pudding on his shoes.

"A bit early for house calls, Sheriff."

"I don't usually make house calls, but I promised a friend I'd make this one personally." Joni nodded at his serious tone and started to wonder if something happened to her father. "Did you visit Ira Doolan yesterday?"

She breathed, then nodded.

"Don't do it again," he said, wagging his finger at her. "He has a lot of important friends in high places, if you know what I mean. He was this close," he said, and pinched his fingers together, "to getting a restraining order against you. I said I would take care of it. So I am. *This* is taking care of it. Is that understood?"

"I never meant any harm."

"Is it understood?"

"Yes, sir."

"Good." He turned away, and said, "I'm sure I'll see you when pie is served."

Joni closed the door, let out a nervous breath, and knew she had to do it again. She dialed the number, and a man answered. Joni said, "May I speak with Ellen, please?"

"She don't live here no more. Who's this?"

"Who's this?"

"Well, who did you call, dumbass?"

Joni hung up the phone and groaned. Not only did the family not live there, but another one did, and the guy didn't sound too friendly. She needed to know where Ellen Graninch lived, and who lived in her old house.

God, she felt like Amanda Flockhart looking for personal information on these poor victims. Well, Joni was trying to help them. If Sheila was buried in that yard, wouldn't they have peace as well? Wouldn't Mary? She had to; she told herself as she walked into the kitchen for more coffee.

***

Joni called the grumpy guy at the old Graninch place twice, but he didn't answer the phone. Probably at work, she thought as she took the forty-five-minute drive to Hogansville. The town was small and easy to navigate, and she found the neighborhood off of Hogansville Highway. Most of the houses sat on an acre. If her dad buried Sheila in the backyard, someone would have seen him, right? The house was a simple ranch style, except it looked like no one lived there. The grass was high, and the two shutters were hanging on their hinges. Joni knocked on the front door and waited and waited. All the other houses seemed to be in better condition.

Joni went around to the back, where there was no fence to keep anyone out. A green hammock hung from two trees. A small tin can was being used as an ashtray and a few empty beer cans littered the grass. An overgrown garden was stretched the length of the back of the house. Large flower pots sat beneath a wooden frame that was also being used to hang plants. A rusty motorcycle lay on its side, past the hammock. A garden hose was tangled. A broken dog house was off to the right with a huge roll of fencing supplies next to it. No swing. On the right side of the backyard was a cream-colored shed, and Joni froze when she saw a rusty green leg poking from behind. Her skin prickled, and she almost lost her breath. When she finally moved closer, she saw that behind the shed was an old child's A-frame swing set. Just like the one she had as a girl.

His voice startled her, and Joni turned around to see a heavyset man with a beard to his chest. Words slurred as he asked something again, and when he pointed his finger at her, his eyes weren't friendly. "I know you. You been on the news."

Great, the guy was drunk.

"Do you live here?"

"Who wants to know?"

Joni held her palms up. "Obviously me, if I'm the one asking. How long has that swing set—"

He slammed himself into her and Joni landed on the ground three feet from where she'd stood. Before she could get back up, he was on top of her, and Joni found her face smashed into the grass. Two-hundred fifty pounds easily held her down. She could barely breathe, and kept feeling his beard tickling her neck and arms. Cold fear rushed through her as he moved on top of her, then she heard him pressing buttons on a cell phone.

He said, "My e'mergincy is that I got that serral killer's daughter trying to steal my swing... I don't know." Then, to Joni, he said, "Why are you trying to steal my swing?" Joni couldn't breathe, much less talk. Then he said, "I'm fearful for my life... No, I don't see a weapon, but serral killers don't need weapons... I'm Henry Graninch, that's who I am. If she tries to kill me, I'ma kill her first... No ma'am, she ain't going nowhere. I got a hole a her like a snake."

When Mary told the police that a woman named Sheila had been taken and held with her, they had no information on Sheila except that a woman named Sheila Graninch had been reported missing. Mary confirmed it was the same woman through a photograph, but without a body or the identity of the man who'd done it, the police were unsure about her story. And with her mental state, well, the police didn't know what to believe.

Then years later when Mary said the man arrested for killing the prostitute was the same man that held her captive, the police looked into it again but still had nothing to go on except Mary's word. With all the talk, and putting some pieces together, the Graninches assumed that Lyle Chaskey had murdered their daughter. Joni remembered them from when she was younger, seeing them on the news and wanting to know what happened to their daughter.

Henry Graninch was still on the phone when the police arrived. "You're in trouble now," he said to Joni after he'd hung up. This wasn't going according to her plan.

Two police officers walked up slowly. One had his hand ready for his gun. "Sir, can you get off the young lady, please?"

"I want her arrested," Henry said.

"We'll sort this out, but for now, I need you to remove yourself from her."

Her bones nearly broke with the release of his weight. Finally, she could breathe.

"Do either of you have weapons?" the second officer asked, this one much shorter than the first.

"Define weapons," Joni said, and made a fist at Henry, who was on his knees next to her and swaying sideways.

"You know who she is?" Henry said.

Officer Shorty asked, "Ma'am, do you have an ID on you?"

"Yes, it's in my car."

"Don't let her go," Henry said. "She'll run."

While Officer Shorty stayed with Henry, the other one escorted Joni to her vehicle, where she retrieved her license and handed it to him. On his shirt was the name Colbert. "Are you Lyle Chaskey's daughter?" he said. Joni nodded. "And you were trying to steal a swing set?" he said, confused.

"That's ridiculous. I was looking at it when Attila the Hun dropped me."

With no patience, he said, "So, what's your business here?"

Joni thought about answering, then said, "I'm not saying anything else until you call Cyrus Kenner. He's with the GBI for the Atlanta region."

Instead, Colbert called his sergeant. Then he said, "Miss Chaskey, I'm going to ask you one more time what you were doing here?"

"I suggest you call Special Agent Kenner." She felt so stupid. How did she get herself into this mess and bring Cyrus's name into it as well? He was going to kill her.

Officer Shorty and Henry walked over—well, Henry shuffled—and Officer Colbert said, "Henry, you take the day off?"

Great, Joni thought. Nothing like being in good with the local cops. They were probably drinking buddies.

Henry said, "I called in late."

"Why's that?"

"I was out of milk and went to the store for breakfast. I can't work on an empty stomach."

"Which store?"

"Wal-Mart. Why are you axin' me questions? Shouldn't you be arrestin' her?"

Colbert moved out of earshot and spoke into his shoulder radio while Henry stared Joni down.

"Are you pressing charges, Henry?" Officer Shorty said.

"Hell, yes, I am."

Joni groaned. "Will you please call Agent Kenner? He can clear up this whole thing." If not, Joni was going to have to tell Henry why she was there, and honestly, he was in no condition for that.

The sergeant arrived shortly, and asked her the same questions, told her that Cyrus Kenner was on his way, and Joni felt like she could breathe again. The truth was that she didn't do anything wrong except go on someone else's property, and there was no private property sign posted. So really, what could Henry do about it? The problem was that they were only holding her here because of her name, which was a shitty reason. They could run her license and quickly find she hadn't so much as gotten a speeding ticket in her life.

Guess Cyrus was right. That was something special.

He showed up and seemed to be really pissed. He and the sergeant were arguing off to the side, away from everyone. If Cyrus would just tell him about the backyard, this would clear everything up.

What if her dad was lying?

But what were the chances of the Graninches having the same swing set?

Cyrus walked over, said, "I can't believe you came here," then he shoved a paper to Joni's nose. "This is a request I put in for a warrant to take soil samples. Couldn't you wait for me? I spoke with Sergeant Anderson, and right now, this does not look good for you. Get in your vehicle, and go home." She'd never seen him so mad before, but Joni had seen worse.

Henry called out from the yard, "Why y'all lettin' her go?"

"Henry," Sergeant Anderson said. "Don't waste my time. If I arrest her for being on your property, I'm arresting you for DUI."

"What?" Henry said.

"You have to tell him," Joni said. "You've done stuff like that more than me."

"Then why did you come here?" Cyrus said.

"I was going to tell him, but I didn't think he was so... angry."

"Tell me what?" Henry called.

"I have no facts that tell me to dig here," Cyrus said. "Now get in your vehicle and go home."

"Dig here why?" Henry walked over.

157

Cyrus turned and gave Sergeant Anderson a look, then turned back to her. "This family has been through enough."

"They should know. Tell him."

"No," Cyrus said, and got in Joni's face. "You tell him."

Joni felt too close to answers to go home. Turning to Henry, she said, "Where was that swing set in 1982? I believe your sister was buried under it."

"Hell, no, she ain't," Henry said.

By now, Sergeant Anderson had walked over. "How do you know this, Miss Chaskey?"

"My father told me."

"No, he didn't," Cyrus said, and gave her a look. Did Cyrus have kids of his own, because he did that look well.

"You're crazy," Henry said.

"They never found her," Joni said.

"I knew it." Henry spit on the ground at Joni's feet. "I knew he did it. Dig her up." He gestured to the police. "Dig her up."

"We can't," Anderson said. "We don't have any evidence to support that to get a warrant."

"I don't need no warrant," Henry said. He yanked his keys out of his pocket and stumbled to the shed. This was not how Joni imagined things would go. Henry pulled out several shovels from the shed and walked to the middle of the yard. He looked around for a second, moved closer to the house, and dug the shovel in while everyone watched. He said to Joni, "Don't just stand there. Start digging." She picked up a shovel.

"Put that down," Cyrus said.

"I can't."

They dug and dug until Joni's hands were red and blistering. She and Henry were sweating and filthy from red clay dirt. "I need to lose weight," Henry said, breathing hard.

"And stop drinking," Joni suggested.

"What do you know?" Then he added, "Little serial killer."

"You don't even know me."

158

"Don't need to."

They dug for thirty more minutes when Joni realized they couldn't dig like this all night. "Are we even digging in the right place, or are you too drunk to remember where your swing set was?"

"It was right here," Henry said, and flung a shovel full of dirt in Joni's face. She spit out what went in her mouth and tried to wipe the rest off her face. "My mom used to sit right over there and watch us play. I could touch the tree branches when I climbed on top of the monkey bars."

Joni looked over to where all the dead potted plants sat under the wooden frame. It looked as though it hadn't been used in years. She walked over there and moved the plants out of the way.

Her mother could hear her sing.

Henry walked over. "What are you thinking?"

"That we should dig here." They took down the hanging plants. "Was your sister a singer?"

For the first time, he smiled. "I hadn't heard her sing in a long, long time."

Cyrus said, "You going to dig up the whole backyard?"

Joni ignored him. To Henry, she said, "For what it's worth, I'm sorry."

"She disappeared. Was just gone. There aren't enough *sorrys* to make up for what this did to my parents. And if your old man had anything to do with her disappearing, I will personally hire another serial killer to kill him in his sleep. Yes, siree."

Joni didn't bother telling him it was a hitman he needed, not a serial killer. Instead, she dug.

Henry's beard was covered in dirt. The ground was nothing more than red clay stained with vengeance. "Mama thinks I should quit drinking."

"You should listen to her."

159

When the hole under the swing was four feet deep and four feet wide, Joni stumbled backwards with what she saw. All she remembered next was Henry screaming like a girl.

***

They'd brought out a crime scene unit and some forensic guys who were now finishing up with the dig and trying to keep the body intact. They were taking photographs, but there was nothing to bag near or in the site. They were taking samples of the dirt, hoping to find a trace of something. The entire area had been taped off with crime tape and, for the most part, the men were quiet while they worked, only making comments here and there about what needed to be done.

The Hogansville Chief of Police showed up and he and Cyrus were arguing off to the side. Henry sat in a moldy wicker chair near the back door of the house. He had his head in his hands and had been on the phone for the last hour making calls. He tearfully said, "No, I know it's her. It has to be her," and Joni felt sad that after all these years Sheila was right under their feet. Her heart ached for them and grew suddenly cold to her father.

She never even heard Cyrus walk up, just his voice behind her. "Are you enjoying the show?"

"Don't be like that." The *show* was a bit morbid, but Joni couldn't help the anticipation of them taking the remains from the ground. For the first time, she was experiencing this surreal situation first hand.

"There better be evidence in that grave because I have nothing to connect him to this except your word. You need to get me that letter. The one about your cat, Marcia."

"Marshmallow. And why are you mad at me?"

"I'm mad at you because you never should have come here. Henry could have been dangerous. You can't go around trying to find your dad's victims. It looks bad."

160

"I don't care what this looks like." Joni folded her arms across her chest. "I was only trying to help."

"We'll have to go through the same process we did with Melanie Pavroy," Cyrus said. "Thankfully, we know who this victim is, but we'll still need to confirm it."

"I'm sure," Joni said, "that if you go look at those bones right now, you'll find all her fingers broken, along with a crushed face."

"I want to talk to Lyle about this."

"Good luck with that."

Her dad was going to deny it all. He was going to pretend he did not know what they were talking about, and even though there was a body, the state was up against the wall with circumstantial evidence. Of course, there was always his history to back them up.

"We can get another statement from Mary Rancotti. Her testimony would be crucial to this case."

"Oh, now y'all want to believe her?"

Chapter Fourteen

The hardest thing Joni ever had to do was tell Mary. Her plan was to wait until the identity was confirmed, but she didn't want Mary finding out about any of this in the news. Mary didn't take the news too well, cried, then blamed Joni for everything. "I thought this is what you wanted," Joni said. "I thought this would help you get through what happened to you."

Mary's face was tense, her eyes dark, and something mean came over her. She said, "You only wanted to find her so you could kill her. You did this to Sheila, and now you want to kill Rachel."

Joni was tired of the niceties. "Why can't you get it through your head that they're dead? What do you need? To see their dead bodies again? Tell me, Mary. Did you cut Sheila with the broken glass?"

"She was hurting so bad." Her eyes shifted to the left and her body went tense again. She said, "I'm going to tell him everything you did to them. Everything." Then she looked out the window as she continued to brush her cat and didn't so much as give Joni another glance.

***

Two days later, Joni wanted to know the progress of the case. The Georgia Bureau of Investigation was in the heart of Atlanta on Forsyth Street. The building was one of the oldest in the city and looked like a Renaissance castle. She had to go through a security check at the front doors to get in, and then they called Cyrus to confirm her clearance.

Many government agencies were in the building, with the GBI on the third floor. Cyrus was waiting for her in his tiny office. "If you can believe it," he said, "this office is bigger than my last."

Joni smiled. Cyrus had a picture of himself and a man that must have been his dad framed on the wall. They were both in suits and looked nice together. Almost identical. It was strange how strands of DNA worked. How some kids looked just like their parents, some not so much. Some were spitting images of a grandpa, like Teddy and his Grandpa Theo. Joni looked like her dad, could see it in her cheekbones and eyes, and here Cyrus was, an identical younger version of his father.

"He's a good man," Cyrus told her and nodded at the picture she was looking at. Joni handed him the letter her dad sent, and he said, "Thank you."

"Cyrus," Joni said, and found herself ashamed. "I'm sorry about everything. I hope I didn't get you into any trouble."

Cyrus shrugged. "They're rushing evidence, but it's still slow. I have other cases I'm working on, so until then I can only sit and wait."

Joni told him about her conversation with Mary. "Good luck with thinking you can use her as a witness. She thinks I did it."

"Seriously?" Cyrus shook his head. "I don't know who is more of a nutcase. Lyle said he has no idea who Sheila is, that you must have known where she was buried because of visions you had in a dream."

"Yeah, he's kinda mad at me right now."

"That's a real shocker. Hundreds and hundreds of women went missing in Georgia between 1980 and 1998."

"And you're trying to pin them all on him?"

"No, smarty pants. But I'm having a real hard time connecting the dots and trying to figure out which ones he did murder. Seven women had been found before his arrest for the prostitute, but I never believed him when he said there were no more. And now look. We have Melanie and Sheila. How many more?"

Joni picked up a stack of eight-by-ten photos on Cyrus's desk because the first image of a tiny blue birdhouse looked familiar to her. "What are these?"

"I showed you those items years ago. I asked you if they were yours."

"Oh." Joni flipped through the stack. Each one had a photograph of a knickknack ranging from a ballerina snow globe to fuzzy dice to a shot glass. "I was twelve then." Joni set the photos down.

Cyrus thought for a moment. "What if there are other things that you don't remember?"

"Like my father molesting me?"

Cyrus came forward from his chair so fast that if the desk hadn't been in the way, he'd have lunged right into her. "What?"

"I wasn't. It's just that someone from the police told that to Amanda Flockhart and she wrote that in her book."

"Doesn't surprise me," Cyrus said. "I have to admit though, I didn't read the whole book, just the parts about me."

Joni rolled her eyes. "I seem to have one of those memory banks that has to be triggered. I don't remember right off the bat, but I remember these knickknacks now. Not in the garage, just from when you showed them to me last."

"I never knew if you and your mother were protecting him or if you really had no idea about what he was doing." Joni gave him a look. "I'm sorry. I don't mean to bring up your mother. It's just that she was a part of this."

"Until she killed herself."

"I am sorry about that, too."

"You were the first person to apologize to me after she died."

"And I meant it then, as I do now," he said. "No one should have to go through what you've been through. I'm glad your mother had enough sense to get herself off the streets after she was arrested the first time."

"Arrested?" Joni was taken aback. She knew Cyrus Kenner and his old partner had treated her mother like shit back then, not believing she was innocent and all, but to arrest her? "You think maybe that's why she killed herself? You arrested her because you thought she had something to do with this?" Joni threw her hands up and felt her blood rage.

"Hold on a second—"

"All these years, I thought she couldn't handle what my father did."

"Joni, your mother was a prostitute." Those words knocked the wind out of her and didn't make sense. "I thought you knew."

Joni shook her head. "I don't believe you." Her voice began to crack. Was a person locked so deep in the dark that they had no idea who their family really was? Aunt Lacey didn't like her mother, and after the suicide, surely Joni would have been told about this. Surely it would have come up.

"That's why we were so hard on her. She'd been arrested twice for solicitation when she got into a car with an undercover cop. Prostitution has always been bad in Atlanta. I'd never heard of her until I picked up the Chaskey case. I was a brand-new detective back then." Cyrus grabbed a box on the floor and dropped it on his desk. He rummaged through it for a moment, then handed Joni a yellow folder. "For the record, your mother was clean after she married."

Inside was a report on Roslyn Pancoast, along with a mug shot that showed a woman Joni hardly recognized. Thick blue eyeliner accented her eyes, and thin straps of a shirt hung off her shoulder. Sharp collar bones protruded beneath the skin and gave her such an unhealthy look. The photo shocked her, and Joni pressed her hand to her mouth to stop the breakdown that was about to come.

"I just—"

"Shit," Cyrus said, and sat her down in a chair. He took the folder away and went down on one knee to look her in the eye.

165

"I'm sorry, I thought you knew. I thought that's why you didn't want to talk about her. I thought you knew all this because when you went to live with your aunt, she ordered a DNA test."

"I know who my father is." Deep in her soul, she knew without a doubt. You didn't fake something like that.

The day of the DNA test, she sat in a cold room with that bitch of a psychiatrist who kept asking over and over again, "Show me where your father touched you." Not, "*Did* your father ever touch you," but, "*Show me.*" Another doctor had come in and swabbed the inside of her cheek. Aunt Lacey told her it was because she'd been so upset lately that they wanted to make sure she wasn't getting sick.

"I know he's my father." Joni reflexively touched the tiny mole on the left side of her jaw, the same mole that matched the one under his left eye.

Cyrus nodded. "Yes, he is."

Joni wiped away the tears that slid down her face, and cleared her throat, and said, "I really hated you back then. I thought all of this was your fault. Even my mother's death. I wanted to hate you, but you were so damn nice to me. You gave me Coke and peppermints one day. I even remember that when you opened the Coke, it exploded all over your tie, and I laughed at you."

Cyrus nodded, said, "You remember a lot."

"I think I get that from my dad. He remembers these women like they were a part of him. Details about them, their lives. When he took each one, and what he did to them."

"We never found a single thing to link him to anything. Do you remember a lot about your childhood?"

"Yes. And I have my diaries. Oh—" She reached into her back pocket and pulled out a list of all the places she and her dad visited. "I made this for you."

"Thanks. Maybe one day we can go check out these places together."

She considered the idea for a moment and thought it would be nice. "Are you still mad at me?"

Cyrus stood and leaned against his desk. "Every time I look at you, all I see is that scared little girl asking to be with her daddy because he didn't do anything bad. You have the face of an angel and the determination of a pissed off hornet. No, I'm not mad at you, but don't put me in that situation again. I don't want anyone to think for a second that you ever had anything to do with this mess."

"I was a little girl."

"People have done worse to their kids."

That reminded her of the knickknack photos. "I wonder which ones belong to whom."

"None of them. Not a single one of those had any fingerprints except Lyle's, and after he was arrested, we asked the women's families about them. None of those things belonged to any of the seven victims."

Joni looked up at Cyrus, and for the first time thought he was dumb. "They didn't belong to the women."

"I just said that."

"What I mean," Joni said, trying to spell it out for him. "Is that these were his sorry gifts to them."

"Sorry gifts?" Cyrus picked up the stack of photos.

"They each represented a woman. Maybe I *should* let you read my diaries. My dad liked to give me gifts. My mom too when she was mad at him. These weren't his victims' possessions, but something he bought to remind him of each woman." A little research into each woman and Joni could have it figured out in no time.

"There were thirty-four on the shelf in the garage."

Joni said the one thing she didn't want to believe. "Then we have more bodies to find."

***

A prostitute, Joni thought when she got back into her car and drove to Kennesaw. No matter how long she'd been away, her hometown came flooding into her brain like a picture. Some things had changed since she was a little girl, but the cemetery was still the same.

At least now Joni knew why her mother never had any family. No one came to her funeral either, except the people she worked with and a few of Joni's friend's parents. No one was there to console her except Aunt Lacey, and the most she did was pat her on the back and tell her the pain would go away.

Aunt Lacey was wrong. The pain never went away.

Joni put fresh flowers in the vase and sat in the grass and looked down at the plaque. It only had her mother's first and last name. Date of birth and death. No one could afford a better headstone.

A prostitute?

Warm tears fell, and she didn't bother to stop them, had been holding those tears in for too many years. She and her mother didn't get along well when her dad was around, mostly because Joni always wanted to be with him and her mom was jealous. Mom would say, "You don't love me like you love him," and Joni knew exactly how to hurt her mother because she'd say things like, "I don't love you as much as Daddy or, Daddy loves me more than you."

How could she say those mean things? She ran her fingers over Roslyn's name. "I never meant it," Joni said. "I'd give up everything to have you back."

For a long time, she sat there thinking about her mother. Her soft skin, the way she smelled of powdery perfume. Sometimes the old ladies would walk into Clemmie's smelling like that, and the scent would hit her hard. Her mother cooked the best food. Everything was homemade, and she always went overboard on the variety. She wouldn't only have a pot roast with potatoes, she'd also make several vegetables and dinner rolls. Gravy. Dessert.

She was thinking about all that food because she was hungry. She'd been on the road all day. How did her mother go from being a prostitute to being her dad's wife? Did he sleep with prostitutes? Maybe that's how they met. She'd hear her parents argue early in the morning about where he'd been, and in her mind, Joni would defend her dad.

Life wasn't supposed to be like this.

It wasn't her father being arrested that changed everything. It was the sound of that gunshot ringing out in the middle of the night. It was so loud and out of place that Joni wet the bed. Everything was completely silent until she'd gotten up enough nerve to walk down the hall. She'd called for her mother, but heard nothing. When she saw what her mother had done, and all that blood on the wall, Joni screamed and ran for the neighbors where she called 911.

Even in the middle of the day, the cemetery was spooky. Joni had to get out of there, said goodbye to her mother, never knowing when she'd take the time to visit again, and drove away.

There was a restaurant down the road. As she ate, she thought about her old house, and wondered about the people who lived there now. Did they know about its history? About what Lyle Chaskey had done? Did they park their car in the detached garage? Did they know a woman committed suicide in the master bedroom?

As she swallowed down the last of her salad, she got to her feet before she lost her nerve. All she wanted to do was see the house. It's not like she would knock on the front door and ask to see her old bedroom. Although she wondered what it looked like all these years later. Was it still a little girl's pink bedroom with the butterfly border? Or maybe an office? How many families have lived in that house since the Chaskeys?

169

Instinct brought her exactly where she needed to go. Kennesaw State University was on her left. Could she ever come back here and go to college? What would that be like? She'd have to change her name, should have done that the day she turned eighteen. Joni continued until she hit Shiloh Road, took a right. A few turns later and she was there. There weren't many houses down this road, most of them were a few acres apart. When Joni pulled up in front of her old house, she was shocked. Not only did the house look smaller than she remembered, it was closer to the road. But more than anything, it was abandoned. A tree had fallen through the detached garage, and part of it hit the house. The cracks in the driveway looked like a road map.

Joni pulled into the driveway and parked. Waist-high weeds covered the whole yard. Her dad was really good at keeping the grass cut and the flowers planted. The large oak tree had crushed the whole back side of the garage. There was no need to even attempt trying to get inside.

Shutters hung from their hinges, and rust covered the wrought iron rails on the front porch. Black spray paint covered the front door in nothing other than a gang symbol. The locked door knob was hot beneath her palm.

Joni walked around to a dust covered window and peeked inside. Nothing had changed. Ivy wallpaper covered the foyer. The old brown couch was still in the middle of the living room. She had to get in there.

All the windows on the left side were locked, including the French doors that led out to a rear side entrance. Would this be breaking and entering? Her eyes followed the fallen tree straight into an extra bedroom. Easy way in, she thought, then decided against it. Didn't want to risk breaking her neck. Instead, she picked up a rock from the nearby flower bed and broke the window on the French door. Definitely breaking and entering.

An assortment of scents hit her at once. Heat and mold and dirt. The smell of old, burnt cooking oil. What struck her the

170

most was that no one had ever moved into this house. What happened? Who let it go to waste?

Joni walked through the house, getting caught up in the memories of what she remembered of her first twelve years. Of course, her bedroom was still pink with the butterfly border peeling away all over. She stood in the doorway and took an absorbing look around the empty room as the memories came flooding back to her. Her father's sleepless nights when he'd sit by her bedside and hold her hand while she slept.

Upstairs smelled like rotten eggs in a heat box. Joni covered her nose with her shirt. The hardest to look at was her parent's bedroom. Someone did a piss-poor job of cleaning up the blood spatter on the wall above the headboard. All the bedding was gone, along with the mattress. The only thing that remained was the bed frame.

For a long time, Joni had been angry with her mother for killing herself. That anger turned into hate. None of the answers back then made sense except Joni's own conclusion that her mother didn't love her. Why would Roslyn *not* kill herself? Her husband was in prison for heinous crimes, her daughter didn't love her.

Now Joni understood when the psychiatrist said her mother had felt guilty and embarrassed. Now she understood.

I'm so sorry, Mom, Joni thought and turned out of the foul-smelling bedroom, and froze when she heard a noise coming from downstairs. Her pulse kicked in as her heart slammed into her chest. Was it just an animal? A raccoon or a squirrel? No, the footsteps were too heavy. Could someone have followed her? Joni tiptoed to the edge of the stairs, listened for a moment, then pulled her cell phone from her back pocket as she backed away. It's funny how she hadn't lived in the house for fifteen years, but instinctively remembered where the creaky part of the hallway floor was. She'd just hit the number nine button on her phone when she heard the voice from downstairs.

171

She paused, and heard another, "Hello?" and the voice was all too familiar. Hitting the stairs hard, she nearly collided with him at the bottom. It was Sam, and she wasn't happy to see him.

"What are you doing here? Are you following me again?" Joni shoved Sam back against the wall and let her emotions get the best of her. "Don't tell me you just happen to show up here when, of all times in my life, I'm here."

"Calm down." Sam shoved her off and reached around to his back pocket. After he fetched a thin piece of newspaper, he smacked her on the forehead with it. "I was only curious, that's all."

The newspaper had a black-and-white photo of the house and detached garage from years ago, and next to that was a more recent photo of the house all run down and the tree through the garage. The article was about the recent bodies discovered. Women murdered before the *Cotton Mouth Killer* ever created his garage of horrors.

"This wasn't the place your mother died."

"I know," Sam said, and took a deep breath.

Taking a step closer to him, she said, "You followed me here, didn't you?" He was caught. She had no idea he'd stoop so low again.

"Joni."

She shoved him against the wall again. "Leave me alone, Sam." But he was expecting it, and changed the game. He shoved his hand to her throat with just enough pressure to scare her, and he smiled. Joni stepped back and slapped his hand away. "Leave me alone. And stop following me."

As she walked away, he said, "Come on, Joni. I was only playing. Don't be like that," and Joni now knew that Sam was too dumb to see the difference between the night at the motel and now.

***

That night Joni paced her living room and knew she couldn't let good resources go to waste, not when Amanda Flockhart was *saved by a serial killer*, and felt it her duty to highlight every detail on those women's deaths.

She uncrumpled the business card and dialed Amanda's number. Her voice was drowned out by all the background noise.

"Hello?"

"Joni?"

"Yeah, it's me. Where are you?"

"Duh, the crime scene."

Joni hesitated, then said, "I won't keep you. I know you spoke with Darla Doolan's family. I want to know if she had a son."

"You help me, I'll help you," Amanda said, all jazzed up. "Does this mean you agree to a formal interview?"

Of course, it would come to this. "No, Amanda, just answer the question. I need to know."

Amanda laughed. "Why, you writin' a book?"

Joni hung up. She wasn't in the mood for this. Not Amanda. Not Sam. Why did she not believe him? Because her dad taught her to be cautious. Sam was the kind of guy to punish her for, not Brian the ice cream boy.

The phone rang. Amanda was calling back. The noise wasn't as loud this time. "Darla quit her first year of college because she was addicted to coke."

"But did she have a son? Specifically, a four-year-old when she died?"

"No way."

So who did Joni believe? "Are you sure?"

The background noise got loud again. Sounded like a helicopter. "I spoke with one of her high school friends. They were cheerleaders. Took gymnastics after school. They went to National Championship their senior year. That's the year she bottomed out from using. So if Darla had a kid, he was born brain

173

dead because he was flip-flopped into a cheerleader's milkshake or brain dead from drugs. Cheerleaders don't get pregnant and no one notices, Joni. Why are you asking?"

"No reason."

"Bullshit."

"I gotta go."

"Turn on your TV."

"I don't care about a crime scene."

"Turn on your TV," she said, slower this time. "They found something in Jackson."

***

A ticker flashed about skeletal remains found near High Falls lake in Jackson, and Joni turned up the volume. A helicopter flew overhead. Police were everywhere, with lights set up down the bank from the bridge. Blue police lights flashed. Cameras. Then a close-up of Cyrus himself. He had on a blue jacket with GBI written in yellow on the back, and was walking across the embankment with an older man.

The strawberry blonde reporter had a microphone to her mouth. "We're continuing with our live coverage about human remains found in Jackson, where divers had been searching for days after the GBI received an anonymous tip. What the divers found... is a bit daunting."

The reporter had on a black suit, probably the only suit she owned, and her hair was down in waves. The screen went to earlier footage of a diver climbing out of the water. The view was distant due to all the trees. While footage continued, the reporter said, "On Sunday, GBI officials found a concrete weight and a frayed rope, which prompted divers to expand their search for the missing body. When I spoke to GBI director, Remy Ormond, this is what he had to say."

Remy Ormond's tight face left him with a frustrated look. He was a tall man in a suit, but also wore a GBI cap. This was the same man walking with Cyrus earlier. He began speaking mid-sentence. "—evidence that was taken from the river on Sunday is still being processed. We're thankful for the time the volunteer divers offered. Without them, this discovery would never have been made."

"Can you tell us exactly what was found?"

Remy Ormond hesitated a moment, then said, "It's evident these remains have been submerged for years. The body was caught in a tiny alcove where it continued to decompose and intertwine with the root system of a fallen tree."

The camera went back to the reporter, who was now talking about the GBI being asked to take over the case because of its sensitivity. The screen split, and a male reporter appeared.

"Callie, can you tell us anything else about what's going on?"

"At this time, the GBI and local police are offering very little, but we have reason to believe this discovery is connected to the two latest bodies found."

"Are there any leads about the identity?"

Joni groaned. The media was all over this and making connections, like every morsel of detail, was gold. The two reporters continued to bounce questions and answers, and speculated that this could be a victim of the *Cotton Mouth Killer.*

Callie turned to catch Cyrus as he rushed to a crime scene van, and two other reporters were on him as well. "Agent Kenner," Callie called out. "Has Lyle Chaskey given up locations of more victims?"

"I cannot comment on that as of now."

"My source told me it's Rachel Ikenbor. Is that true?"

Cyrus worked his jaw, and his eyes went dark. The last time Joni saw that look was the day he shoved a paper in her face at the Graninches. "It's too early to confirm that. Once we get the remains to our lab, the techs can analyze it." Cyrus held up his hand to deter questions and continued behind the yellow tape to the van.

The camera went back to Callie, and Joni muted the TV. She called Cyrus, and it took him forever to answer his damn phone. "I'm busy right now."

"Why didn't you tell me?"

"I didn't want you anywhere near this. I gotta go."

"What's going on? I deserve to know."

Cyrus paused a moment and sighed. "They found the skull and upper torso with only one arm, but the rope tangled with it seems to match the one attached to the cinderblock. Do me a favor and don't talk to any reporters."

"They're not here."

"Good," he said, and at the last second, "Joni?"

"Yeah?"

"Are you okay?" Joni thought for a second. Life could be a helluva lot better. "I threw a lot on you today and that's the reason I didn't call. I think it's too much."

"Thanks, but I'm okay."

"Goodnight," he said, and hesitated a moment before he hung up.

Joni turned off the television and stood in the middle of the living room, absorbing it all. She'd done it. Found Rachel and Sheila. And with Melanie Pavroy, that's three bodies discovered in less than a month. So why wasn't the guilt gone? Because he lied to her. Lied to everyone and would never be punished for it.

Not every punishment fits the crime.

She went for the biggest elephant first. Her favorite. Threw it against the wall where it made a huge crater, but fell to the floor with barely any damage. Did her father think she was stupid? He didn't buy her the elephants to remind her how strong they were. He did it to remind her of their fear. Beat them until they listened. Until the fear was nestled tightly in the hands of the master.

Joni grabbed the elephant snow globe. Threw that one on the tile floor in the kitchen where it shattered into a thousand pieces, water and glitter splashing everywhere. One by one, the rampage continued. What she couldn't destroy by throwing, she took a hammer to. Banged everything up until nothing was recognizable, until each gift was destroyed.

What would she say to her mother if she were here right now? Did she know? Did she know about the fucking monster? What was she trying to hide by taking her own life? Tiny pieces of ceramic flew in several directions. Did she cover for him? Was *she* just a cover up? Was Joni just a cover up? Her father didn't love her. He only pretended to love her.

Joni smashed the rest of the elephants, wanting everything vile in her life to die along with them. The dogs were barking, and before she could tell them to shut up, the hammer was snatched from her hand.

Joni spun around, breathing hard, and Teddy stood there next to a police officer. Bubba ran up to her and licked her face, and she tried to push him away from the broken pieces.

"What the hell are you doing?"

She dropped to her knees and looked at the elephant massacre. "I don't know."

"The police have been knocking on your door."

"I didn't hear them."

"The dogs were barking."

"I didn't hear them, either." Had she zoned out or something?

"Joni?"

"What?" she snapped, but realized it was the officer. A guy named Pete who dined at Clemmie's. "I'm fine. I just got some bad news, that's all."

Teddy said, "The reporters came to Clemmie's looking for you and when I sent them away, I realized I sent them right to you."

And Pete said, "One of them called 911, said there was a ruckus. I was about to bust the door down when Teddy here showed up. Do we need to report anything?"

"No. I did this. I'm just— Everything's fine."

"I'll get the reporters to back off."

When Pete was gone, Teddy took a deep breath. "You loved those elephants."

"No. I thought I did but realized how much pain they caused," she said, and looked down and saw blood on her hands.

Chapter Fifteen

Mary wouldn't answer the door. Joni knocked and knocked, and tried to peek in through the windows, but the shades were pulled down and she'd taped newspaper to the glass. Around back, the grass was to her ankles, but she went up on her tiptoes to peek in through one of the bedroom windows and inside it looked like a salvage store. Where Mary got all this junk, Joni had no idea. Four toasters sat on the dresser with piles of other appliances. Old magazines covered the floor. Breaking into the house was out of the question. Joni would call the police for assistance if she had to. Except she didn't have to because the back door was unlocked.

Inside it smelled of mothballs and wet paint. Was Mary on another one of her paint kicks? The wall to the right had brown brush strokes in a horizontal pattern and the wall to the left was, well, there was no pattern. It looked like something a child would do.

"Mary?"

She didn't answer, and Joni hoped she was okay. Mary sat in the middle of the crusty, painted sofa with her legs beneath her, rocking back and forth. In her arms was a baby blanket.

"Mary, are you okay?"

She continued rocking and looked down at whatever was wrapped in the blanket—the cat, perhaps—and hummed. As Joni got closer, she saw what was in the blanket. A doll with red and brown paint on its face and brown matted hair sticking straight up.

"Didn't you hear me knocking?"

"Shhh. Baby's sleeping."

Joni took a deep breath. If she argued with Mary, the woman would get agitated, and the last thing Joni wanted to do was upset her. Instead, she said quietly, "Whose baby is it?"

"Mine, silly." Mary stroked the bundle. "I love him. He looks just like his dad. Don't you think?"

"He's beautiful." Beautiful for a doll that belonged in a haunted house. "Have you seen the news?" Mary rocked again and looked more like a little girl than a fifty-five-year-old woman. Her hair hung loose on her shoulders. Today she had on a long cotton skirt and a Winnie the Pooh t-shirt. Her eyes were fixated on that damn doll, and Joni wanted to yank it away and tell her to snap out of it. This was serious. What if one of those reporters got word about Mary and Mary couldn't help herself from them?

"The police found Sheila and Rachel—"

Mary snapped her eyes to Joni. "I told you to leave them alone."

"No. You wanted me to find them so you'd know they really died."

"Why did you do this?"

Joni sat on the coffee table in front of Mary. "So you wouldn't suffer anymore with worrying about them."

"They died because of you." Mary cried. "They were hiding, and you found them. And you killed them."

"No." Joni touched her hand to Mary's knee and in a flash, the woman grabbed her hand and squeezed. She tried to pull her hand free, but Mary was crushing her bones. "You're hurting me."

"Not like you hurt them."

This was ridiculous. Joni used her other hand to make Mary let go. "You're upset."

Mary started crying, "My baby, my baby," and reached for the doll. "You can't take him away."

"I don't want him."

180

"He doesn't love you."

"I don't love him either."

"He went to prison because of you."

Tiny hairs tickled the back of Joni's neck. Here she was thinking Mary was talking about that stupid doll. Joni went into the kitchen to get Mary a glass of water. As the glass filled, a tiny mouse ran across the countertop. Joni jumped back and looked around the kitchen. Not being a total idiot, she went back into the living room.

"Mary, how long have you had mice?"

"I don't."

"I just saw one in the kitchen. What are you using to kill them?"

"You killed my friends."

"Mary, did you poison my dogs?" Mary threw the cat brush at her, and Joni asked again, "Did you poison my dogs?"

"Get out!" Joni took a step forward, and this time Mary banged the baby doll's head on the coffee table. "Getoutgetoutgetout!"

***

That night at work, Joni had way too much on her mind to focus on any diners and she knew she wasn't doing a good job of serving people, but what was she going to do? Take another day off? She needed money. Every month she deposited the maximum amount that she could into her dad's jail pay account. He couldn't have much, but it was something she'd done since she'd been working at Clemmie's. Plus, the vet bill for Clyde came in the mail. Joni barely made enough money to get by every month.

The best thing about working here was the flexibility. But considering Joni had no real life outside of Clemmie's, she worked nearly fifty hours a week.

Teddy was on the grill, finishing up with one of the last burger orders for the night. He had one eye on the grill, the other on the sink filling with water. "I really hate it," Joni said, "when they walk in ten minutes to closing."

Teddy only grunted his agreement. He hadn't talked to her all night, which wasn't unusual, but he was looking at her differently since she'd taken out her rage on the elephants.

In the walk-in fridge, Joni grabbed all the ingredients she needed for the milkshakes the teens wanted. They were specially blended to perfection, and Joni could go for a milkshake herself. No, scratch that. She needed some flat-out hard liquor.

By the time the teens left, so did Val and the other kitchen guy. Teddy had a head start on his cleaning, and Joni wasn't surprised when she walked into the kitchen and found him sitting at the island eating what remained of the peach pie.

"Are you going to share?"

"No," he said, around a bite.

Joni pulled up another wooden stool next to him, grabbed a spoon, and dug in. "You make the best peach pie." The pie was homemade from fresh sliced peaches, and cooked with cinnamon and brown sugar. Best when served warm, this pie had been in the fridge, but it was still tasty. Took the edge off.

"Of course, I've had my fair share, and I think yours is the best." Joni watched him take that in. She took another bite, then said, "But if I would have known I'd be missing out on this,"— she raised her spoon— "by sampling someone else's pie, I never would have done it."

Teddy snorted out a laugh, then he sat there for a moment, shaking his head. "So, who was the guy?"

"What guy?"

"The one you were with on TV."

182

He was talking about the day they found the cinderblock under the bridge. Teddy wouldn't like her hanging around with Sam Doolan if he knew who he was. "Just a guy."

"With great pie."

"I wouldn't know," she lied, and wasn't interested in talking about Sam because she'd probably never see him again, and that was okay. Trying to turn the subject back to them, she said, "I'm sorry." Joni leaned in closer to him, felt the warmth coming from his body.

He turned to look at her and Joni kissed him, and she could tell he was caught off guard, but he leaned into her and deepened the kiss. A second later, she was in his lap and his mouth covered hers as he pulled her closer. She fumbled with the zipper of his jeans, and Teddy pulled back, said, "We can't do this here."

"The office is too small."

"I mean, *not here.*"

"My place is closest." Joni looked toward the dining room. "I still have a few things to finish up."

"I'll come back and do them after."

"I didn't walk today." She softly kissed his lips.

"Go," he said. "I'll meet you there." He smiled at her, then kissed her one last time.

When Joni got home, it was like a rush job of what she wanted to do. First she set candles on the coffee table, lit them, then realized how stupid that was and blew them out. She sent the dogs outside, but that was stupid too. Why was she a bundle of nerves?

She kept looking out the picture window waiting for Teddy, but he was taking his time getting there, and anticipation rose inside her. All she ever wanted was for Teddy to forgive her. Maybe they could work things out and be together again.

Don't think too far ahead, she told herself.

Another twenty minutes passed and Teddy still hadn't shown up. She began to worry about him. What if something happened? Joni picked up her cell phone and dialed his number. He confirmed her worst fear. "I'm not coming."

***

That Saturday, Joni had been sitting at their usual table in the visiting room, but her dad had yet to show up. She'd been waiting for twenty minutes and now wondered if something was wrong. She'd never waited this long before. Inmates were greeted by their families, while Joni kept her eyes to herself and waited another fifteen minutes.

Finally, she got up and went to Officer Simon, who was sitting on a stool waiting for more visitors to be checked, and he smiled at Joni when she walked up.

"My dad never came out."

Simon pointed to the mean officer in charge of monitoring the visiting room. His name was Milton. "The guy you need to talk to."

"I'll bring you a pie next time I visit if you don't make me have to talk to him."

Simon leaned in close. "I'll bring you a pie if you switch jobs with me and I don't have to work with him no more."

Officer Milton looked like Steve Urkel in Rambo's body. Joni walked over to him, tried not to hesitate or sound like a little girl. "Sir," she said. "My dad never came out."

Officer Milton adjusted his glasses, looked down at her, then at his clipboard. "Chaskey? I did a roll call for inmates. I'll check on my next round to see if he's in his cell."

"Where else would he be?"

Milton shrugged. "The spa?"

That had to be code for something, but Joni didn't ask. Instead, she said, "Can you go check now?" He tilted his head at

184

her, remained silent, just stared at her as if he was hoping she'd disappear. Joni said, "I want to speak with the warden."

"The warden's busy. Go back to your table, please, and your inmate will be out soon."

My inmate?

"I said I want to speak with Warden Parrino. *Now.*" The words were loud enough that people's heads turned. For a long moment, he gave her another hard look. This jerk couldn't do anything except throw Joni out, but he had a smile that said her father would somehow pay.

Milton pressed a button on a walkie-talkie. "I have a civilian who needs assistance to the warden's office."

Almost fifteen minutes later, Joni was seated in Warden Lamar Parrino's office. He wore the same red bow tie as last time, but today he also had on a navy sweater vest. She wanted to tell the warden that Officer Milton was a jerk. He used intimidation to keep the noise level down in the visiting room. That if anyone remained out of their seats for more than five minutes, he asked them to sit back down. Even eavesdropped on conversations.

But the warden would only tell her he was doing his job, so Joni got to the reason she was there. "My dad didn't show up this morning. Something is wrong. He's always one of the first ones out."

"Chaskey's been acting a little strange lately."

"How?"

Parrino rubbed the side of his face with the palm of his hand. "Some trouble's been coming his way these past few days. No one's been hurt, but he's looking for trouble."

"Oh," Joni said, and bit her lip. "What's going to happen to him?"

"Keeps picking fights and he'll end up in lockdown." Parrino warden nodded, said, "I'll look into him," and gestured her out of his office, where she waited on a cold plastic chair for nearly twenty minutes. The prison offices weren't as quiet as she expected. The phone didn't stop ringing, and three times the secretary had to place someone on hold. An officer waited with her, and he stood with his back to the wall in a military stance and nodded to everyone that walked by.

What was taking the warden so long? Did something happen to her dad? After Lyle had first been arrested, Aunt Lacey only brought her here twice a year. The first time she visited, her dad had bruises on his face, said he'd run into the bars of his cell the night before. Now Joni wondered if someone hurt him again, and he didn't want to see her.

"Miss Chaskey?" the warden said, as he walked down the hall. "Your father said he doesn't want to see you today."

"That's impossible. Is he hurt?"

"He is absolutely fine. Said he's taking an extra workload in the kitchen this morning to keep his mind off of things."

"But." Joni thought she was going to cry. Her dad had never denied her anything. "Are you sure he knows it's me?"

"He sure does." Warden Parrino shrugged. "Better luck next time?" Parrino gave a nod to the officer who'd been waiting patiently, said, "See to it Miss Chaskey finds her way out."

This didn't seem right. "Warden," Joni said. "Are you being honest with me? How do I know you're not covering up something?"

Those words didn't sit well with the man who stood in front of her. He pressed his lips together so tight they turned white. Finally, he said, "I am an honest man." A second went by then: "Come, have a seat." Joni followed him back into his office and sat again in the armchair. "There's been a lot going on surrounding your father lately."

"He's not allowed visitors?"

"This was his own choice. I spoke with him directly. You can try again next weekend."

"This isn't fair. I drive three hours to get here just for him. Why is he being so inconsiderate?"

"Have you ever thought that maybe he's not ready to deal with his past with you? Maybe he needed a break? I know he did some god-awful things and sometimes when remorse sets in, inmates become ashamed of who they are. Give it some time, Miss Chaskey. He'll come around."

***

The drive back to Fayetteville was a lot quicker considering Joni drove twenty miles over the speed limit, all the while angry that her dad would out of the blue not see her. She was the only person he had. The only person who gave him money. Money was a valuable source in prison. Sure, it remained in an account and wasn't actual cash, but he could buy things to make his life easier. Joni gave that to him.

And that's when it hit her. She'd forgotten to send him a care package with all the things he'd asked for in his letter about Marshmallow. Was he seriously being a damn cry-baby about that? *Fine,* Joni thought to herself. *I'll mail you a fucking package if it makes you feel better.* He was a grown man in prison, but sometimes he acted like a spoiled child when he didn't get what he wanted, and the first thing he'd do was punish the person who took something away from him.

Anger enveloped her the whole three hours back home as she felt sorry for herself. No one ever worried about making Joni's life easier. This made her think about Teddy Glencoe. Joni did a U-turn on Highway 92 and took a right on West McIntosh. His work schedule matched Joni's, and she knew he'd be home right now because he was supposed to work the night shift tonight at Clemmie's.

Brooks was a lot brighter during the day. The last time Joni had been out here was that night she'd thrown Amanda Flockhart's book at him. Now she was shocked at what she saw.

Behind Teddy's trailer stood the wooden frame of a house he was building. He always talked about building a house, but she didn't think he'd ever get around to it.

The sound of a saw echoed, and Joni walked through the grass around the side of the trailer until the massive house came into full view. Teddy was leaning over a saw horse inside the framed house.

"When did you start this?" Joni said, and Teddy turned to her as surprise registered on his face.

"About six months ago." He picked up another smaller board and rested it vertically against another. He was framing out windows. "I don't get to work on it every day. What are you doing here?"

"You know, Teddy. You really pissed me off the other night."

"It happens."

"Are we ever going to talk about this or just keep tap dancing around it?" She wanted so badly for him to open up and tell her how he felt. "Either you forgive me or you don't, but when are you going to get over it?"

Teddy's answer was the sound of the nail gun hitting wood. Minutes later, he said, "It's really hard to get over anything when I have to look at you every day."

"You make the schedule. Put me on another shift."

"I'd still know you were there. I don't think you really know how to love anyone."

Tears welled in her eyes. "That's not true."

"Well, I'm not going to ask you to prove it to me because you already did."

"I know you're angry with me, but look me in the eye and tell me you don't still love me."

Teddy lowered his head. "I can't."

"Then what's the problem?"

"The problem?" He surprised her when he threw the nail gun across the room, where it bounced off of the table saw and knocked over a bucket of tools. "You're the fucking problem. You want me to get over it? Your dad's a serial killer and your mom committed suicide. *So fucking what?* When are *you* going to get over that?"

"That's not fair." This time, a tool belt went flying past her head. "What the hell, Teddy?"

"You think I don't know what you do? Does your new fuck buddy know how much you like the strip club? You almost had me last night, but then I had to remind myself how manipulative you are."

She stood there, stung. He had it all wrong. "It's not like that."

"I could smell the cigarettes on you that night you broke all the elephants. And I'm supposed to act like it's okay? You kiss me and the pain starts all over again. What do you want from me, Joni?"

"I don't know. You're this safe place for me—"

"Safe place?"

Joni choked back a sob she could no longer hold in. "No, you know you were more than that. I loved you."

"You can't do this to me. Not anymore. Go home. Find another safe place because it's not me."

Chapter Sixteen

The following morning, she handed Archie the resignation and thought she was going to throw up. "I know I'm supposed to give a two-weeks but I can't do this anymore."

"Don't do it then. Take some time. Come back when you need to." The disappointment was all over his face.

"I can't."

"As much time as you need." They were in his office, and he wheeled his chair closer to her. "I know you're going through some rough stuff, but this is your home. Your stability. You need Clemmie's as much as Clemmie's needs you. You can't just quit."

He was such an honest man. Joni said, "Please don't make this harder than it is."

"You sure this is what you want to do?"

"I'm sure."

"You know what, Joni. I don't pretend to like you; I really do like you. And if this is what you want, then I support you all the way." Then he shrugged. "And no matter what, you always got a home here, so go figure out what you need to do."

That simple understanding meant more to her than anything, but she had to let it all go.

***

The tension escaped her as soon as she walked through her front door. A long walk with the dogs, and a hot shower made a world of a difference until she checked her answering machine. "Hi, Joni. It's Amanda. I was wondering if you could confirm some dates for me, back when your dad lived in Decatur—"

Joni hit the delete button and cursed Amanda. There was another message. "Um, hi," came a rough, male voice. "I wanted to say that I'm real sorry about my sister and I'm real sorry about the way I treated you. I don't usually act like that. Well, yes I do, but it was only because of the beer. I quit drinking. Ten days sober. Anyway, I'm calling because I was wondering if you'd like to talk. Over drinks. Coffee. Or water. Water's good."

Joni hit the delete button. *No thanks, Henry*, she thought, because she couldn't take on another victim project. She sat at the kitchen table and wrote her father a letter. Not the nicest letter. Reminded him she was the only person he had, and his stunt on Saturday was childish. She mailed his package today, and he'd probably receive it about the same time as this letter. She wasn't making that long trip again until he wrote back, saying it wouldn't be for nothing.

Quitting a job before securing another one was bonkers, but that's what she'd done. And for two weeks she contemplated moving back to Kennesaw to go to school, but it was too expensive. She could barely pay for a parking permit. When it came down to it, she was stuck with the "replaceables." Jobs where the turnaround was inevitable. Cash register work seemed the likely way to go, so she returned home with three applications to grocery stores, plus she was going to check the local ads again.

When she got home, a package sat on her doorstep, along with her regular mail. She understood the package being left where it was, but why did the mail man leave the envelopes here like this? She wasn't expecting a package, and had to hold her anger when she saw the *Return to Sender* stamped on the box she'd sent her father. Inside the stack of mail was a letter. It had already been opened. This set her blood on fire. Had Amanda really stooped this low? But then she read the letter and knew she had bigger problems.

Knock knock.
Who's there?
Joni.

191

Joni who?
Joni who's been a bad girl.

Then another:

Knock knock.
Who's there?
Daddy.
Daddy who?
Daddy who's been watching you.

She balled up the letter and threw it across the kitchen to get it out of her hands. What the hell was he talking about? She looked out the window, but no one else was there. Was he talking about watching the news? That had to be it. Through her own actions, she was bringing him closer and closer to the needle.

But he said she was being a bad girl. How would he know about anything she'd done?

And why would he care? Is that why Amanda was so interested suddenly? Had she been watching? Joni dialed Amanda's phone number, but was interrupted by a knock on the door. She wasn't expecting Sam Doolan to show up, and asked how he knew where she lived, but that would be a stupid question.

He smiled and said, "Are they friendly?"

"No," she said, but he stuck his hand down to the dogs and let them lick him. Bubba backed up and eyed the situation cautiously. *Good boy,* Joni thought, and figured Sam wouldn't be stupid in front of two German shepherds, so she invited him in and stood between her dogs.

"Cute place," he said, looking around.

I know the truth about you, Joni thought, and said, "What are you doing here?"

He rubbed his palms on his jeans and said, "I came to apologize. I shouldn't have been following you."

"I think that's the least of what you should apologize for."

He offered her a weak smile and said, "I didn't mean to scare the crap out of you. I thought you were cool like that."

"Cool with you grabbing my throat?" Bubba and Clyde moved closer when her voice went up. "You've been lying to me this whole time. Why?"

"About what?" he said, like he was really confused.

"Cut the crap, Sam. Is that even your real name?"

"Is yours Joni?"

She took a deep breath and let a moment pass. "I know you're not Darla's son."

Sam bit his lip and looked at Clyde. When the dog barked at him, Sam jumped. "Why would you say something like that to me?" Okay, so he was sticking with his story. Gotta give him that. "Do you know how hard this is for me? There's no difference between you and me."

"How's that?"

"We want back what we lost," Sam said, and looked around again.

"Considering I don't know who you are or what you've lost, no, I don't believe we are the same."

"You," he said, "are full of shit," and the dogs barked at him, so Joni rubbed their ears to calm them down. He waved his arms and said, "You owe me a lot, and I don't even believe you were ever interested in helping me. You only care about yourself."

This was when the guilt set in, but being pissed off about him lying took priority, so screw guilt. She grabbed the dogs by their collars and said, "Who the fuck are you, Sam?"

His face went cold, and he took a step back, reached for the door. "I just wanted to be your friend. See if what she said about you was true."

"Who?" Joni said, but he was out the door, and she yelled at him about answering, but he'd only lie anyway, so she went back inside and cuddled her dogs for being such good boys.

Then the phone rang, and she answered before she meant to.

"Is this Joni Chaskey?" the woman on the other end said.

"Yes."

"Listen," she said. "I'm not supposed to be callin', but Mary Rancotti was admitted to the hospital here again—"

"Who is this?"

"You don't remember me? Ophelia from psych?"

"Of course. I'm sorry. What's going on?" Joni pet Bubba on the head.

"Mary tried to kill herself again this morning. She askin' for you, but her sister is not going to let her call you. You hear me?"

"Is Mary okay?"

"Right now, yeah. She sleepin' off her shot they gave her. But I know when she wakes up she gonna be all pissed off again."

"What did she do?" Joni said. "How did she try to kill herself?"

"Stabbed herself in the arm. Can't really kill herself that way, but she inflicted harm to herself. Her sister said she found her with the knife sticking out of her arm this morning. Around seven. Brought her straight to the emergency room. Now we got her. You didn't hear this from me, though, okay?"

"Thank you."

***

Joni had only been to the psychiatric hospital once. If Mary's sister, Nina, didn't want Mary talking to Joni, then surely Joni wouldn't be on any visitor's list. And sure enough, she wasn't.

"I didn't think you'd drive down here," Ophelia said, her ample breasts bouncing as she came around one of the desks.

"Then why did you call me?"

"To let you know."

"Is Nina still here?"

"No, she just left." Ophelia pulled Joni away from the desk where another nurse was looking through a file.

"Then let me see her for five minutes."

"Girl, I can't do that."

"But you called me." Joni grabbed Ophelia's arm when she tried to walk away. "Give me something."

"Fine," Ophelia said. "I know we not friends and all, but you gotta do something for me." She turned and began walking down a hallway. "Like when you leave here, you can go get me supper. Like something good. I'ma be here all night."

They took the elevator to the third floor, and didn't have to go far to Mary's room. "Girl, you got five minutes."

Mary was sitting in a rocker by the window. The room was small. Smaller than a normal hospital room. Everything was white and clean and smelled of disinfectant. "Mary?"

No acknowledgement, just kept staring at the wall. Joni knelt down in front of her. Her left arm was wrapped in a white bandage from her wrist to her elbow, and hung carefully in a sling. A white cotton blanket was carefully placed on Mary's lap.

"I'm so sorry," Joni said.

Mary's face and lips were pale. Her eyes blank. She'd been trapped her entire life. Lived with mental disorders and visions of what happened to her with Lyle. If Joni could reach inside of Mary's head and take it all away, she would. Was it better to be like this... or for Lyle to have killed her?

It wasn't fair.

"Mary, I'm here. I can't stay, but I wanted you to know that I at least came to see you."

Still, Mary ignored her words, but she used her right hand to pull the blanket into her lap. Pulled it up into a big ball. Then she cupped her arm around it and rocked back and forth. Stared at the wall like Joni wasn't even there.

"I'll try to come see you again. Another night when no one is around, okay? I don't know when you'll get to go home." Joni stood and walked toward the door.

"He doesn't love you, Joni."

She turned, only to see Mary sitting there rocking her blanket like a baby.

***

Joni drove to Mary's house after she'd bought Ophelia some tacos. She wondered what Mary was doing before she tried to stab herself in the arm. What set her off? The newspaper? News on the television? Memories of her dead friends?

What Joni hadn't considered were all the doors being locked. Even the back door, which usually wasn't. When she went back to the front to look into a window, all she saw was the messy house. The cat sat on the table licking up something, and suddenly she felt sorry for the animal.

A car engine startled her, and she turned to see a silver sedan next to the Pilot.

"What the hell are you doing here?" It was Nina.

"I just—" Joni remembered she wasn't supposed to know about Mary. "I just stopped by to see Mary, but she's not answering the door."

Nina marched up the front steps and stood in front of her. The woman had to be a little older than Mary. Where Mary was thin and gaunt, this woman made up for it.

"That's because she tried to kill herself again," Nina said, and yanked a key out of her purse. "This is *all* your fault." Joni followed her into the house, and Nina turned on her. "Get the hell out of here. You don't belong here. You cause enough damage for my sister."

"I've only tried to help her."

"After what your father did?" Nina shook her head.

"Mary's the one who contacted me. She's the one who wanted to talk to me."

Nina's lips went tight, and she turned to the kitchen. "Jesus, look at this mess." She yanked the cat from the table and dropped him on the floor. He meowed his protest and jumped back up.

"He's hungry," Joni said.

"I *know* that." When Nina tried to remove the cat again, he hissed at her, so she left him there and poured food for him on the table.

Joni felt awkward, and didn't know what to say.

"How the hell does this house get so disgusting?" Nina shoved a stack of newspaper out of the way.

"I think it's a safety thing."

When Nina moved a bag full of plastic bags out of the way, a little mouse ran across the floor. Joni screeched and jumped out of the way. Nina grabbed the broom. The mouse went under the fridge, and Nina kept trying to get it from the side. It ran across the floor again, and Joni pointed it out to the cat, but the stupid cat looked at Joni, then the mouse, licked his lips and went back to his dry food.

"Damn mice," Nina said. "I set out some traps a few months ago."

Joni argued with herself that Mary couldn't have poisoned her dogs because Mary didn't drive. How could she get all the way to Fayetteville? A bus? Even so, she said, "Do you think Mary would poison my dogs?"

"What the hell are you talking about?"

"Someone tried to poison my dogs with rat poison last month. I don't know who did it."

"Well, it sure as shit wasn't my sister. I think it's time for you to go," Nina said, and tossed the broom back into the corner.

Must be a coincidence. Joni looked around one more time at Mary's house. "How long is she supposed to be in the psychiatric ward?"

"I never said she was in the psychiatric ward."

Joni rolled her eyes. "Well, I know about it, okay? And I'm concerned about her. No one talks to her. No one visits her—"

"Wait a damn second," Nina said, and shoved her palm to Joni's face to shut her up. "I'm here every day. Twice a day. Three times a day. The only reason I let you visit with my sister is because, believe it or not, it keeps her calm. She talks about you like you're her best friend. She opens up and tells you things."

No, she doesn't. "How do you know this?"

Nina sighed a big, heavy breath. "When she talks to you, she stays Mary. When she can't talk to you, her brain turns into someone else. After you visit her, she's all chatty like that." That statement wasn't clear to Joni, and she was about to ask, but Nina put her fingers to her forehead, and shook her head, said, "If only I'd have gotten here earlier."

"I'm sorry." Joni felt like she'd been saying that a lot lately.

"The suffering will never end for her." Nina choked out the last words. "This dissociative disorder is getting worse and worse."

"What can we do?"

"We?" Nina said. "I don't like you. I really want you to stay out of my sister's life."

"But you just said she's okay when I visit her."

"I don't care. You put things in her head. And now that these bodies have been found—Do you know what that's been like for her?" Nina grabbed a white pet carrier box out of the living room. She tried to catch the cat, but he kept hissing at her and ran away. "Come here now," she said to the cat.

"What are you doing?"

"What does it look like?"

Couldn't she tell the cat didn't want to go with her? Joni walked over and scooped up the orange cat. He was fat and purred as she let him nuzzle her chin. "Time to go, buddy," she said, and pushed him into the carrier box. Then she handed it to Nina. "What are you going to do with him?"

"Take him to my house until Mary's son can take care of him."

"Make sure he knows to brush him—" Mary's baby doll sat in a shoebox on top of the television. "Mary doesn't have a son."

"Oh, I assure you she does. I raised him."

"Nina?" Joni swallowed down the bile in her throat. "Who's Mary's son?"

Chapter Seventeen

Joni was in a panic the entire ride home. She called Cyrus, and when he answered, she said, "I just got word that Mary Rancotti had a son thirty years ago. His name is Samuel Dixon. But I think he's been pretending to be Darla Doolan's son. That's what he said to me anyway—"

"Joni, slow down," Cyrus said. "There's a guy pretending to be Mary's and Darla's son?"

"No. He's really Mary's son, but when I met him, he told me he was Darla's son."

"Darla doesn't have a son."

"That's what my dad said."

"You talked to him about this?"

"Kind of. I just need to know if you can get any information about this guy. I think he may have been the one to poison my dogs." Fear swept over her. "I just saw him this morning."

"You hang out with this guy? Come on, Joni, you know better than that. Why didn't you tell me about him?"

"I'm telling you now. You met him when I went to Jackson."

"Oh, that guy. Looked a little shady to me."

"You're just saying that to make me feel bad."

"I hope it works."

Armed with this new information, Sam's words before he left today made sense. He was talking about Mary. If he knew Joni was visiting her, then why hadn't he come to her as himself in the first place? The game was back on, and Joni didn't want to play. Sam didn't mean enough to her to put the puzzle pieces together. But Mary did. Why hadn't she said anything about a son?

No, Joni told herself. Forget about all of this. When Mary gets out of the hospital, they'll have a long talk and everything will work itself out.

Bubba and Clyde were happy to see her. "I'm so sorry I left you again," she said and gave them kisses. "Give me a minute and we'll go for a walk."

When Joni walked into the kitchen, she was startled at what she found on the table. First, the knock-knock letter her dad had written her was smoothed out and folded neatly back into the envelope. *Daddy's watching you.* Was it Sam? Shit, she was so stupid. Second, all three of the job applications had been completely filled out. Name, address, phone number, Clemmie's. Everything was accurate. Then at the bottom, Teddy Glencoe was listed as the reference, with his name and correct address.

Joni picked up the phone and called Teddy. "Are you okay?" she asked.

"Yeah, I'm fine. What's wrong?"

"Nothing. I was just wondering."

"Are you okay?"

She hesitated a moment, then said, "I'm fine."

"You don't sound fine," he said, like he hadn't told her off two weeks ago.

"It's been a long day."

"It's been a long everything." A minute went by, then he said, "Mom printed your last check. You can pick it up whenever you want."

"Thanks."

"Okay," he said, and hung up.

Joni eyed Bubba and Clyde, and they seemed to be perfectly fine. She whispered to them, "Was Sam here while I was gone?" How did he get past them? Bubba's bark startled her, but he was only expecting attention. With her heart pounding, her instinct told her to get out of the house, but the house seemed so quiet.

Joni took the dogs with her as she did a quick search in all the closets and under the bed. No monsters there.

That's when she saw the cover panel of the doggy door had been removed. "Son of a bitch." So, that's how he got in, but how did the dogs not eat his face? "What did he feed you?" she said to them and searched until she found the quarter pounder boxes. When she held them up, they thought they were getting more. "You let a stranger inside for burgers? Shame on you." They were so sorry, they gave her their sad eyes and whined. She wasn't buying it.

She slid the panel back in place and thought about calling the police. Why did he break in? What did he want? She looked at the letter on the table. Did he find the others? All the letters her father had ever written her were stored in a large photo box she kept in a kitchen cabinet. The box was empty. Every last one of the letters was missing.

***

"Someone broke in?" Cyrus said when she called him in a panic for the second time today.

"They came in through the doggy door."

"You're going to have to call the police. I can't do anything about this." The words sounded rude, but she knew what he meant. "Is there anything in the letters about the murders?"

"Not specifically. They're mostly about his ailments and shitty prison jobs." There was nothing of importance in the letters except her father's personal thoughts.

She explained to him that the applications were filled out in blocky hand writing. "Which makes me think it's Sam, but Amanda Flockhart would gain from the letters as well. I won't know for sure until I speak with them."

"Stay away from both of them," he said, his voice going up. "Let the cops handle this."

"I want the letters back, Cyrus."

"I know," he said. "Do you know how much letters like that are worth to the media? Actual letters from *The Cotton Mouth Killer*? I think if anyone gets to read those letters, it should be me. Call the police."

He would say something like that. Before Sheila and Rachel were found, before Joni knew Mary had a son, she would have guarded those letters with her life. Now? Did she even care about her father's innermost thoughts? Yes, she told herself. Of course, she did. Just like Sam did.

"I think Sam did it," she said, "and I think I know why. What if we share the same father?" The line was silent for a moment and Joni thought she'd lost the connection. "Cyrus?"

"What makes you think this?"

"Scooby-sense."

"You mean Spidey-sense," he said, throwing back Sam's words.

"I didn't get specifics from Nina Dixon, but the timeline seems right. She has to know the truth. She said she raised him." God, this was such a strange feeling, like everything she knew wasn't real, and this wasn't even her life.

"Why'd he lie to you in the first place?"

"Because he needed to appear vulnerable. He seemed genuinely interested in knowing about my dad. He would have been the first member of a victim's family that treated me like a human being."

"Are you sure Mary was the person to contact you all those years ago?" That question really had Joni thinking. She grabbed the job applications and one of Mary's letters to compare the handwriting. They looked different. Sam's letters were blocky, and Mary's writing was that of a preteen.

"Maybe he prompted her to contact me and told her what to write. I wonder if Sam had been planning this all along." She wondered if this was part of his scheme to get closer to Lyle. "Is there any way you can check to see if Sam Dixon contacted my father?"

Cyrus hesitated. "Parrino is by the book. I'd have to wipe his ass to get that kind of information for no reason. You think your father knows Sam might be his son?"

"I don't know. I don't know anything anymore."

***

Joni promised herself she'd report the break-in as soon as she got home. Bubba and Clyde had fallen asleep before she got on the highway. Atlanta was less than thirty miles from Fayetteville, but because of the amount of traffic, it seemed to take damn near forever. This was such a stupid time to drive here, but she needed to speak with Sam. She needed to know the truth, and why he lied to her.

He didn't need to steal her letters. She would have let him read them.

No, Joni thought. *I wouldn't have. Those are my personal possessions. My father's deepest thoughts are only for me.*

But Sam wasn't the only one interested in those letters. Amanda had envious eyes the day she stopped by. Was she capable of breaking into her house? She's a liar too, Joni thought. She's capable of anything.

Joni took the Turner Field exit, then navigated her way to Cherokee, and parallel parked in front of Sam's house. Joni knew right away he wasn't home. The house was dark. He must have driven back to Macon to get Mary's cat, but she went up to the front porch with the intentions of knocking but came to a halt when she saw the *For Rent* sign in the empty window.

Looking inside confirmed the sign. Sam's house was dead empty. She thought back to when she'd last been there. At least three weeks.

Joni grabbed her cell phone out of her pocket and dialed the number on the sign. When a man answered, Joni said, "I'm inquiring about your house for rent on—"

"The rent's eighteen hundred a month. Completely remodeled with hardwood and top-notch appliances..." Joni knew all this; she'd been inside before but listened as the man went on.

"How long has it been for rent?"

"Two weeks. I'll need two months' rent up front. Last guy skipped out on me."

Joni looked back at her dogs who sat patiently waiting for her. "What was the guy's name?"

"What?"

"What was—"

"Why do you want to know that?"

She thought about telling the man she was a special agent with the GBI, but that was highly illegal, so she said, "He jumped bail, and my boss is looking for him. Really pissed him off."

"Name's Sam Doolan. When you find him, you let him know I filed a report. He owes me two grand."

Yeah, good luck with that, Mister.

Bubba and Clyde went crazy from the car, and Joni saw a man jogging down the sidewalk with a tiny poodle. The dogs couldn't seem to figure out why the man would tease them with a walking squeaky toy. Joni tried to call Amanda, but got voicemail instead.

***

She went to Clemmie's for her last paycheck, and was surprised at all the festive decorations and balloons. All the Glencoes were there and took up the left part of the diner, and Teddy stood near some booths holding his one-year-old niece.

"You here for the birthday party?" Archie said. "Mama's eighty-fifth and Katie's first."

Joni hugged Granny Glencoe, her frail bones like a bird in Joni's arms.

"You're just as pretty as I remember," Granny said.

"And look at you." Granny had on a purple sweat suit and a pearl necklace that hung down to her belly. Joni turned to Archie, "Sorry to interrupt. I just came to get my last check."

"If we don't give you your check, you can't leave," Archie said.

Teddy walked over. "I'll get your check," he said, and nodded for her to follow. The kitchen staff all gave a rowdy hello as she walked behind Teddy, who was still holding Katie.

Enrique said, "You come back?"

"Just for my money," she answered, and they all laughed.

He opened the office door, said, "Here," and handed Katie to her.

The baby said, "Oohh," and smiled.

"You didn't have to do this," Teddy said.

"Were you going to deliver my check to my front door?"

"I meant quit. You didn't have to." But she did. Joni needed to move on and find her place in this world. Teddy handed her an envelope with her name on it. Joni handed him the baby.

"She misses you," Teddy said.

Joni looked at Katie's sweet little face and doubted it. Then she turned out of the office and took one last smell of onion rings and pickles before she went back toward the crowd. Not wanting to be rude, she said goodbye to everyone.

"Don't be a stranger," Archie called out.

Something tugged at her heart as her shoes crunched the shell parking lot. How many times had she crossed this parking lot? The Glencoes were the kind of family Joni always wanted. When she was younger, she kept thinking that things would be so much better when she was a grownup. That she'd feel normal. Life was filled with little inconsistencies that she could adapt to. But nothing was the way she thought it would be.

"Joni," Teddy called, and she turned to face him. "You don't have to go."

"It's already done."

"I mean—" Teddy looked her in the eyes. "I mean now. You should stay for the party. I know you don't have anything else to do. You shouldn't be alone all the time."

The dogs were still in the car, and Teddy gave them some love. She thought about going back into her empty house and knew it was dumb to be alone, especially after Sam snuck inside to steal her letters.

"I'm not family. I don't belong here."

"That's not true. I'm sorry about the way I went off on you. I shouldn't have said those things to you."

"No. You're right. I can't keep doing this to you. My life's shit and I don't have a positive outlet and I don't know how to function in a normal society."

"I never said you were a psychopath."

"No, I figured that part out for myself."

"What's wrong?" Didn't she just tell him? "You get this spaced-out look when you're so focused on your dad you can't see straight."

"It's not him."

"It's always him."

Joni sighed. "I just found out that Mary Rancotti has a son." She watched his face as the words hit him. "I never thought a person like her could have a baby, but then again, there's nothing wrong with her female parts, so why not?" Joni thought about telling him it was Sam—

"That's the guy, huh? The one on TV?"

"Yes."

"Are you sleeping with him?"

"I told you no."

Teddy leaned against the Pilot and folded his arms. "So why did he just now tell you he's Mary's son?"

"I found out through Mary's sister. She's the one who raised him, but he knew who his mother was."

"And his father?"

"I don't know."

Teddy's voice was still rough. "Could be yours."

Joni didn't want to think about that. She hadn't gotten that far into the conversation with Nina to ask such a personal question because Nina kept rattling on about Sam stealing her finest china. Lyle couldn't be Sam's father though, because if Sam knew that, then why did he—why did he? She couldn't think about that night in the motel.

"What are you doing, Joni?"

"I'm not doing anything."

"Why are you even involved with any of this stuff? Mary Rancotti. These bodies that were just found. The GBI guy who thinks he's helping. This new best friend of yours."

Joni heard a tinge of jealousy in his voice and tried to defuse his unnecessary thoughts. "He lied to me. I'm not even talking to him anymore, so stop acting like an asshole." Her words surprised him. "What did you think, that I was going to work here for the rest of my life and die a single old lady? We will never understand each other. This conversation is pointless." Joni got inside the Pilot and drove away.

Chapter Eighteen

Southern hospitality has many faces. No one knows a stranger because they are all connected by something or someone bigger than themselves, but when there is a new girl in town, a new girl who may or may not teach their children about the real horrors in life, the southern hospitality becomes a way of keeping an enemy close.

Peachtree City, with all the southern charm a city can muster, treated Joni no differently, and it wasn't home to her.

But it was home to Aunt Lacey, where she was well known for her contributions to the schools and local non-profit organizations. She lived on the north side, in Willow Point Estates, a gated, golf-cart community with its own private lake, and Joni could get inside the gate with no problem using her old code which was the street number and last four digits of Aunt Lacey's telephone number. The entrance was lined with streetlights and Bradford pear trees.

With two-hundred homes in the community, they were exquisitely built on over twelve-hundred acres of land, with each house being no less than four-thousand square feet. Aunt Lacey's palatial colonial was nearly eight-thousand square feet with a gorgeous flagstone driveway and weeping willow in the middle of the circular driveway. The three-story house was on five acres of lakefront property, but that was nothing considering she had her own private pool in the backyard.

Joni begged the dogs not to poop in the yard and hoped Aunt Lacey would at least let them roam the backyard. They made their way up the large stone steps and when Joni knocked on the door, both her dogs barked.

"Y'all are so stupid," she said to them. "I'm the one knocking."

Surprise filled Aunt Lacey's face when she opened the door, and Joni had to pull back on the leashes to keep the dogs from going inside. "Sit," she said to them.

"You're more than welcome inside, but those beasts are not." Joni tied their leashes to the iron bench on the porch. "You can't tie them there."

Frustrated, Joni said, "I can't leave them at home alone right now, and I really want to speak with Grandmother."

"Is that so?" Aunt Lacey folded her arms over her chest. She had on a beige velour pant suit and still had her makeup on. "Your grandmother is asleep already."

Should she be rude and tell Aunt Lacey that was bullshit? "You said she wasn't sleeping well. I'm sure she'll wake up again soon."

As if on cue, a bell tingled from down the hall. Aunt Lacey sighed. "Fine, but come in through the garage and leave the dogs in there."

Joni did as she was told and left the dogs in the three-car garage where they would be safe. Aunt Lacey had gotten her money by graduating from Georgia Tech with an MBA in engineering and eventually making her way to director of the Aerospace Program for the Atlanta International Airport. Now it was Hartsfield-Jackson. Getting that job was no easy mountain to climb. She'd given up her dream to work for NASA, and stayed in Georgia to be with her mother. The job was stressful, Joni remembered the hours she used to work and having a live-in nanny for four years, but it was the kind of stress Aunt Lacey thrived in. She retired a few years after Joni moved in, but she'd kept that nanny on hand instead of giving Joni the proper time of day.

From the garage, she entered a large mudroom where she pulled off her shoes. Heaven forbid she got dirt on the marble floor. Through the kitchen, she made her way toward the center of the house, where she almost died at the sight of who sat on the living room sofa.

"What the hell are you doing here?"

Amanda Flockhart sat curled on the leather sofa like a cat. "Just verifying some last-minute things." Amanda stretched as though she'd been sitting there all day, and considering the time, she probably had been. She had on lounge pants and a tight-fitting shirt. What kind of interview was this?

"I tried calling you," Joni said.

"Oh. My phone died, sorry."

Joni breathed hard, and said, "I'm going to ask you one question and don't lie to me. Did you break into my house and steal the letters from my dad?"

"Steal letters? No."

"I swear to God Amanda if you're lying to me—"

Amanda was on her feet now. "I've been up your aunt's ass for over a week. You can ask her."

"I don't care if you did. I just want them back."

Amanda's jaw dropped. "I didn't do it, but if you're asking, it means someone did. What happened?" She picked up a notepad. "How many letters was it?"

"Shut up, Amanda." Joni turned and nearly ran smack into Aunt Lacey.

"Grandmother is ready to see you."

Joni followed her down the hall and was surprised when she said, "I understand why you feel the way you do, but you don't need to be rude to my guest."

Do you? Do you really understand how I feel? "I'm confused as to why you let her do this. You could get a spotlight with Diane Sawyer if you wanted to. Why her?"

"She's a sweet girl," was all she said.

Aunt Lacey had converted the master suite to fit Grandmother's needs, had remodeled the bathroom and sitting area for her. She'd put in beautiful carpet over the hardwood floor to keep her from slipping. Nurses cared for her for eighteen hours a day so that Aunt Lacey could come and go as she pleased. A hospital-like bed was against one wall and a table was filled to the max with medical supplies.

Grandmother coughed, and it sounded like her lung was coming up. She was frail, and her thin hair stuck up like tiny corkscrews over her head. A fuzzy rose-colored blanket was pulled up to her chest. A black-and-white photo showed a beautiful young woman sitting side-saddle on a black horse. For a moment, Joni thought this was Aunt Lacey, but she realized it was Grandmother as a teenager. Joni looked just like her.

Grandmother smiled as Joni stepped closer.

Pleasantries didn't come easy for her toward the old woman. She wasn't rude or disrespectful. Just cold, so she didn't even bother to return the smile. "You've grown so beautiful," Grandmother said. If it bothered her that her only granddaughter never came to visit, she didn't show it. "Pull up a chair."

Joni sat in an armchair closest to the bed. The old woman wasn't bed ridden by any means but in the last year she'd grown extremely tired and spent a lot of time in bed. Coughing, Joni could see, as the woman went into another spell. She used to like to sit outside under the porch and try to feed the squirrels when she'd first moved in, and Joni could get a view of her from her own bedroom window, couldn't take her eyes off the woman. But it was too much, living in a house with the woman who'd caused her father so much grief. Joni had moved out a year later, and Aunt Lacey hadn't stopped her.

Not wasting time, Joni said, "Did you beat him?"

The question caught Grandmother off guard, and her smile faded. "Is that what he told you?"

"He never told me anything except to stay away from you."

"I'm an old woman." Joni thought about Henry Graninch saying a person didn't need a weapon when they had their hands, and she didn't let Grandmother's words fool her.

"I just have to know what a woman does to her child that makes him hate her so much. To make him hurt other women. He wasn't born that way. I want to know the truth. Was it sexual abuse?"

Grandmother's eyes were tearful and her gnarled hands gripped the thick blanket as her eyes drifted away.

"You can tell me," Joni said. "I need to know before you die."

"How dare you?" Aunt Lacey's words echoed from the doorway as she bolted her way to the bed. "You will not speak to my mother this way." Aunt Lacey pressed her hand to Grandmother's cheek, looked closely at her face as though Joni had slapped her. "First Amanda, and now this? Do you have vengeance on everyone now?" That was an understatement. "Get out," she said. "Right now. I want you out."

"I didn't mean to upset her."

"You will not come into my home—"

"Lacey, dear," Grandmother said, and patted her daughter's hand. "I'm fine. Let Joni be. She has a right to know."

"Not now, Mother. You need rest."

"She's right, dammit. I'm old, and she needs to know before I die."

"Don't talk like that." There was a weakness in her voice that Joni hadn't heard before. The woman of steel cracks.

Grandmother looked at Aunt Lacey, said, "She needs to hear this from me."

Whatever Grandmother had done, Aunt Lacey had forgiven her long ago. But according to Aunt Lacey, her brother was the liar.

"Mother."

"I am a grown woman. You let me be. Now go tend to your guest."

Aunt Lacey gave Joni a stern look. "I'm right outside this door."

When Aunt Lacey was gone, Grandmother said, "She's so bossy," and sighed. "Sometimes I just pretend my hearing's gone."

This made Joni smile, and when she caught herself, she stopped.

"I know you haven't noticed this," Grandmother said with a smile, "but I'm an old woman. An old, old woman. I have no reason to lie to you or make up cockamamie stories about your father, so don't call me a liar when you hear something you don't want to. Understood?"

Joni nodded.

"Sit down, you're making me nervous."

Now, who was being bossy? Joni got comfortable and so did Grandmother. She wasn't playing around when the first words she spoke were, "He had a strange fascination with his penis since he could walk. Always rubbing himself with toys until he was raw and bloody." She looked Joni in the eyes. "He was born with a desire to pleasure himself. This one time when he was five, I remember it so well. I was bathing him and he wanted me to touch him. Kept begging me to do it, and then pitched a fit when I told him I wouldn't. I thought, how absurd that little Lyle would think this was okay." Joni's heart picked up and her face blushed as Grandmother spoke. "I took him to the doctor, and they worried that someone was doing something inappropriate to him. But who? Lyle told the doctor no one that he just enjoyed doing it. He wasn't the least bit embarrassed about his admission. By this time, Lacey was off to college and it was only he and I in the house. I dated little, although I blame myself for being involved with a man who would never marry me. I don't think Lyle's father would have made a difference in his life.

"He was such a needy child. He'd cling to me sometimes like he was afraid to be apart. I feel bad now about all the times I

214

pushed him away. I should have held him more and cuddled him more, but I was so tired. I had two jobs just to put food on the table."

"Was he a good kid?"

Grandmother smiled. "He was such a handsome boy. He liked to make me laugh. Hardly ever caused trouble at school. He was shy, but nobody bothered him."

"So what happened?" Joni couldn't figure out what the problem was if he had such a normal childhood. For being raised by the same woman, Aunt Lacey turned out okay.

A tear slid down Grandmother's cheek, and Joni grabbed a tissue. "I think he loved me too much. I mean, I know he loved me too much. He thought he was the man of the house. I knew something was wrong with him because by the time he was fourteen, his—his... sexual advances were becoming worse."

"What do you mean?" Joni asked, and leaned forward.

Grandmother sighed. "I didn't understand what was going on. I'd wake up in the middle of the night to him trying to do things to me. I tried to find him a girlfriend here or there but he said to me he'd been with girls before; he wanted a woman." A sob caught in her throat. "When he was sixteen—" The words caught again, and she coughed. Finally, she said, "He raped me."

Grandmother waited to be called a liar. Instead, Joni took the woman's hand. Something she'd never done before.

"Something was really wrong with him. I saw the pleasure of it in his eyes the next morning and he went on as though nothing had happened."

"Didn't you tell anyone?"

Grandmother nodded. "I told my pastor."

"Why not the police?"

"Because he was my son. Lyle was such a good boy. He used to pick up trash in the community on Saturdays. Fetch milk for people who couldn't drive. No one would believe me."

"So, what did you do?"

215

"I got a better lock for my bedroom door." She swallowed hard and took a deep breath, as though the hard part was over. "I lived in fear of my own son. He was quiet, and I never knew what he was thinking."

The words were true. Now that it was brought to her attention, that's how she remembered her dad. He'd zone out and get quiet for weeks or months at a time. That's when her parents fought the worse.

"Did it happen again?" Joni asked.

"He managed to get into my bedroom one night, and I thought that's what he was going to do, but all he did was—" Grandmother waved her hands as though she was waving away the memory. "I shut my eyes tight and waited for him to finish what he was doing. Two days later, he was gone. Packed all his stuff and left."

"You didn't hear from him again?"

"Oh, I heard from him all right." Tears fell from her eyes as she wept. "Called me about six months later to tell me he'd raped a woman. That he was going to rape many more, as many as it took to fulfill his needs."

Grandmother's voice was full of emotions. Sadness. Anger. Fear. Hurt. But Joni felt her own emotions and thought how all those women could have been saved if the old woman would have come forward.

"Did he call you about the murders?"

"No. The last time I spoke with him was in 1982. Never spoke to him again."

"He's led me to believe that you sexually and mentally abused him as a child." Even if Joni would have heard this story years ago, she never would have believed it. Never would have gone against what her father implied.

"I never could have done that to my own child." Grandmother waggled her finger at Joni. "I should have cut off his penis when he was five. I never spanked that boy or touched him in a wrong way. When your Aunt Lacey told me he was going to have a baby, I tried to call him, but he refused to talk to me, and suddenly everything was my fault. He returned my letters; said he'd kill me if I didn't leave him alone. So I left him alone," she said and swept her hands against each other. "He shut Aunt Lacey out of his life. What were we going to do? We had no idea what he'd been doing. I never met you until you came to live here. I don't like what Lyle chose to do, but it was a blessing you ended up here."

If Aunt Lacey hadn't taken her in, would she have ended up with her grandmother? "For what it's worth, I had a good life before all this. I think you and I know two very different people."

"Oh, Joni." Grandmother opened her arms, and Joni felt awkward as she gave in to the woman's hug. "I was a horrible mother. I turned my son into a monster. He only wants us to see the person he wants us to believe he is."

One thing was for sure. Lyle shut his mother out of his life because she didn't give him what he wanted. Thirty plus women suffered, then there were all the women he raped. Joni couldn't help but wonder if her father was shutting her out as well and how many inmates would suffer the wrath of Lyle Chaskey.

"You sure are beautiful."

"I must get it from you." Joni picked up the black-and-white photo. "Look at you."

"I used to compete in equestrian events when I was younger. I would have finalized for the 1944 Summer Olympics, but they cancelled because of the war."

Joni was so surprised. "You were almost in the Olympics?"

"Well, not quite. The rules back then didn't even allow women in the event until 1952, and by then I was too busy with two kids. Grab that box over there on my dresser."

***

217

Joni woke with a start in an unfamiliar quiet room. She was in an armchair, slumped over with her head resting on a plush blanket. Pain shot through her neck and it all came back to her when she saw the smooth wrinkles of her grandmother's hand.

Joni sat up and rolled her neck as photos scattered to the floor. She'd been up for hours looking at photos while Grandmother went in and out of sleep.

Aunt Lacey was right. Old people were like newborns. Up every two hours for something. Grandmother's eyes were partly open, her mouth with an odd gape. Did the woman bare her soul then kick the bucket? Joni touched her hand to Grandmother's neck. The old woman didn't move. She was warm. A second later, her eyes popped open, and Joni jumped. Grandmother patted Joni's arm, turned her head, and drifted off to sleep again.

Joni gathered up all the photos and mementos Grandmother kept and put them back in the box. Lots of photos of Lyle as a kid were in there too, and Joni tucked one of him as a little boy in her back pocket. She was sure Grandmother wouldn't miss it.

The enormous numbers on the bedside clock read 7:15. Joni took another look at the woman in the bed and was convinced she wasn't a bad person. Last night Joni promised she'd spend more time with her, a promise that would be easy to keep.

Guilt hit her when she remembered the dogs were in the garage all night. She made her way down a maze of halls until she came to a set of French doors that lead to the backyard. Through a side door, she went into the garage, but the dogs were not there. Aunt Lacey's BMW was parked in the middle, but no dogs.

Outside, she called for them. Nothing. What the hell? Did they cause a problem after Joni fell asleep? No, Aunt Lacey would have woken her and told her to go home. There was no way for them to have escaped. Joni went back through the house and made her way to the kitchen and there, being obedient dogs while doing tricks for food, were Bubba and Clyde all happy as can be with Amanda Flockhart.

Joni wanted to tell them to get away from her. She was the enemy. Amanda was still in the same clothes as yesterday. Joni looked down at herself and knew she wasn't any better.

Bubba balanced something on his snout and didn't eat it until Amanda said, "Okay."

"Is there anything you two won't do for food?" Their greeting was short-lived, and they went back to the hand with the food.

"Did you sleep here?" Joni said.

"Did you?" Amanda had on no makeup and her scars were more prominent, and Joni wondered if the smooth skin on her face had been grafted from her ass. Joni let out a laugh.

"What?"

"Nothing. So why are you sleeping here?"

"Because it's a long drive back home and Lacey said I could."

Lacey? "Do you have tea parties and try on each other's clothes?"

"No, but I do feel like the daughter she never had."

Such a cheap shot. "Well, too bad looks don't run in the family." Amanda was clearly hurt, but Joni wouldn't apologize.

She went back to dipping tiny pieces of Pop Tart into peanut butter for the dogs. That wasn't something Aunt Lacey would have normally stocked. Did Amanda bring her own food?

"Watch this." Amanda coaxed the dogs to stand on their hind legs.

"I thought you were afraid of dogs."

"You can never be too careful."

"You feed them now instead of throwing acorns?"

Ignoring her, Amanda said, "I've been visiting all the dump sites."

Did she have to talk about this right now? "Why are you so obsessed with this?"

"How many people can say they grew up knowing a serial killer?"

"You didn't grow up with him."

"You and I had enough sleepovers to call it that. I think we could be friends again if you tried."

"You bailed on me, Amanda, and then you wrote lies about me. I don't think we could ever be friends again."

"Did you even read the book?"

With the look on Amanda's face, Joni froze, and tiny hairs stood up. "It was you," she said, barely above a whisper. "You did break into my house."

"I didn't steal your letters."

Joni eyed her two precious dogs that meant more to her than anything, and she swallowed hard. "You put the book on my shelf." Amanda didn't respond, and Joni wanted to wring her neck. "You poisoned them to get in. You didn't have to do that."

"That's not what happened."

"Don't lie! I'm so tired of people lying to me." Joni grabbed the Pop Tarts and peanut butter and threw them in the trash. "What did you want?"

"I just wanted to read them, but I didn't steal them. I swear."

Joni took a step closer, and backed Amanda into the refrigerator, until their faces were inches apart. Strange how she was so mad, yet so calm. "You just threw your last acorn."

"What?"

"You better run this time, Amanda, because there's no one to save you. You're not writing a book anymore. You're going to go work at the animal shelter cleaning shit all day."

"You can't threaten me."

Joni grabbed Amanda's jaw. "Am I threatening you now?" Tears fell down Amanda's face, and Joni saw the fear. Felt the empowerment she held in her hands, squeezed just a little harder as the power surged through her veins, then she let go and breathed hard. Amanda choked back a sob and ran out of the kitchen. She deserved that.

The clicking of heels on marble had Joni in a panic. She grabbed the dogs by the collar as Aunt Lacey walked into the kitchen. "What did you say to her?"

"I think you should ask her."

For a moment Joni thought she'd argue, but Aunt Lacey seemed to accept that and made a pot of coffee, grinding her own beans and all. Joni said, "Is she living here?"

"I temporarily gave her a job to assist the nurses with Mother's scheduling and appointments." *Just let the Trojan horse into the castle.* "Do you want the job?"

"Well," Joni said, "I quit Clemmie's, and I believe Grandmother has taken a liking to me."

"What is with you kids today who don't know how to hold down a job?" She shook her head as she filled the carafe with water. "Will you want coffee?"

"No, thank you."

Aunt Lacey set out two cups. Probably one for Amanda. "I think you need to be careful around Amanda." This made Aunt Lacey laugh, but Joni didn't see what was so funny. "I'm serious."

Aunt Lacey took a breath and said, "Thank you. Your warning is noted."

"I should go," Joni said, not wanting to stay in the same house as Amanda.

"Sit," Aunt Lacey said, her voice stern, as she pointed to an island stool. Joni sat, and so did Bubba and Clyde. "Did you get the answers you were looking for?"

"I've spent so much time defending my father that I've never stopped to consider the people he's hurt the most."

"Put yourself first on that list, dear." Aunt Lacey grabbed a fruit tray out of the fridge and spooned some onto a small plate. "He knows how to manipulate you and he wanted you away from us because he knew you'd eventually learn the truth."

"Even with the knowledge, that doesn't change the fact that he's my father. And you know that firsthand, you paid for the DNA test."

"I had to know."

"I don't know what's more insulting, that you didn't believe him or my mother."

Aunt Lacey's lips went tight. Whatever she wanted to say, she kept to herself.

"Why didn't you tell me about my mother?"

As though she knew exactly what Joni referred to, she said, "Would you have believed me?" She was right. Joni wouldn't have. A moment went by before she said, "I'm not sorry to admit that's the reason I didn't care for her. I don't know what kind of woman—" Aunt Lacey bit her tongue and looked away.

"I don't know anything about her. Do you?"

Aunt Lacey shook her head. "I don't, but I'm sure if we dig deep enough, we can find the answers you need."

The fact that she said *we* meant a lot. "Aunt Lacey, I'm sorry I didn't turn out the way you wanted, but I had to figure out who I was on my own."

"And who are you?" The words were sincere, but Joni got the point, and couldn't answer the question.

Giving up, she said, "I don't know what I'm doing. You were right. I'm on a path to nowhere."

The coffee finished brewing, and she made the two cups, set one down in front of Joni, along with the plate of fruit.

"Thank you for letting me speak with her. You could have made me leave."

"This has been on her chest for a long time." Aunt Lacey reached over and touched Joni's arm. "I think it's something I should have told you years ago."

If she would have known ten years ago what her father had done, she would have still looked at him as a victim. Joni bit into a piece of cantaloupe. Everything's changed.

"You can visit anytime, you know that."

"Can Bubba and Clyde come?"

Looking over the island, she said, "What are they doing in my kitchen? Get out!" Both dogs tucked their tails between their legs and took off back into the mudroom.

***

When Joni got home, she took the dogs on a quick walk while she thought about a lot of things as the morning sun poured down on her. She realized that while life changed; she was still herself and, no matter what, Joni would always love her father. That would never change. When she was angry with him, all she had to do was remember back to when she was a little girl and he used to hold her hand as they visited those beautiful places.

Her little hand fit so perfectly in his, could still feel the warmth of his palm cupped around hers. She was the one true person who he ever loved, and buried somewhere deep down was the real Lyle Chaskey.

Or was the real Lyle Chaskey the monster buried so deep into his blood? That what Joni knew her father to be was only a shadow of his real identity? Could her father pretend to be two different people?

Joni was feeling good after talking with her grandmother, like maybe things were looking up, but then when she got home and saw where she'd scribbled down the contact name of the officer she was supposed to call, things got real again.

Joni put down water for the dogs and filtered out the facts from her feelings when the dogs began to bark. Joni turned to see what the problem was, and there, in the middle of her kitchen, stood Mary Rancotti.

She had on white hospital clothes and white sneakers. Her hair was a mess, and she looked even more fragile than Joni had ever seen her. Joni was so startled by the sight of her, she couldn't find words.

Mary reached into the front pocket of the shirt, pulled out something small, and lowered her hand to Clyde.

"No!" Joni tried to stop him from eating it, but it was too late. "Why did you do that?" She tried to pull the dogs away, but they got loose and both of them were sticking their nose close to Mary. It was something the dogs would do when they wanted more treats.

"How did you get here?"

Joni had never been afraid of Mary before, but she looked different this time. Her eyes were shifty and mean. Joni took a few steps and reached for the phone. The first person she thought to call was Cyrus. He'd know what to do. But Mary needed to go back to the hospital. Everything happened really fast. The dogs barking. Mary slamming her into someone. Bubba's teeth. Blood. The large rock in Mary's hand.

Part Three

Chapter Nineteen

The sight of a German shepherd at the stop sign barely registered into Teddy's mind. He saw the dog and thought it was Clyde, realized, in fact, that it was Clyde, and wondered what the hell the dog was doing out by himself at such a busy time in the afternoon.

Teddy turned the truck into the neighborhood and said, "Come here, boy," and the dog pranced his way to the driver's door. "What are you doing?" Teddy got out and lowered the tailgate, and Clyde needed help to jump inside. He panted heavily and swung his head like he was dizzy from the heat.

Joni's house was about a half a mile down the street in the back. The Honda Pilot was parked in the carport. Bubba was on the front steps and went on alert when Teddy got out of the truck. The lights were on inside the house. Joni never let her dogs out alone. She was too protective.

He knocked on the door and she didn't answer, so he went inside. "Joni!" As he stepped through the living room, he called for her a few more times but didn't get an answer. Her purse sat on the arm of the sofa. That wasn't its usual place. The dogs were looking for her, too. "Where'd she go?" he asked Bubba.

In the kitchen, next to the table, Clyde was lying on his belly waiting for Teddy to notice the blood on the floor.

***

Cyrus Kenner looked at a picture of Miranda McBean. Had he been wasting his life on this? Three were just discovered, would Miranda ever be found? The question hung over his head like a wrecking ball. Four years before Miranda, Bonnie Hesledge was reported missing, and never found. Six months before that, Janelle Ross went missing from Sandy Springs. None of them ever heard from again. Cyrus hadn't worked those cases. He was too new back then and nothing had been connected. He'd only heard of Lyle Chaskey the day he and his old partner went out to question him about Miranda.

When the Fayette County Sheriff called him per Teddy Glencoe's request, Cyrus almost hit the roof when he'd heard the words, "Joni Chaskey is missing."

Because Joni had become one of their own, Sheriff VanBuckle was taking this seriously, and Cyrus couldn't agree more. The GBI had a team that dealt specifically with sensitive missing person's cases and came to the aid of any law enforcements that needed their help. Cyrus had been a part of this team since the day he'd joined the GBI.

Teddy Glencoe reported her missing two hours ago and Lacey Chaskey signed release forms so the media could run the report with her photo. VanBuckle had established a timeline, and according to the aunt, Joni spent the night at her home in Peachtree City and left around eight that morning. Teddy Glencoe arrived at Clemmie's Diner at five a.m., and left work at two p.m. which was the time he'd spotted one of her dogs on the street.

They were looking at somewhere between eight and two. Six hours was a lot of time for someone like Joni to be missing.

Cyrus dropped everything to drive down to Fayette County. He arrived at Joni's house where two squad cars were parked on the street, and VanBuckle said he'd meet him there. He was a tall man, practically bald, and Cyrus knew this was the man's sixth term with the county. He must have been doing something right.

Cyrus walked over, said, "Special Agent Kenner," and shook the Sheriff's hand.

VanBuckle said, "I've got two of my deputies going door to door now. No one's seen or heard anything."

"How's Teddy Glencoe look on this?"

Every person in law enforcement knew that when a woman went missing and foul play was involved, the husband or boyfriend was usually the suspect. Cyrus wasn't surprised that the Sheriff had checked into him. "Archie Glencoe, the boy's father, is a good friend of mine, and I trust his word. Said his boy clocked out at exactly 2:02, and our records show he called 911 at 2:10. That gave him eight minutes to get into his truck, drive down Grady, spot the dog, go inside the house, see the blood, and call."

Cyrus nodded. He'd accept that for now. Because he was working with the county, he had to share what information he knew and brought to the Sheriff's attention that a guy named Samuel Dixon had broken into Joni's house yesterday to steal her letters. To the Sheriff's knowledge, Joni had never reported it, and that pissed Cyrus off.

"Sam Dixon is at the top of my list," Cyrus said. "I have someone checking into him now. Have you been in the house?"

"We did a visual and confirmed that she's not in there."

"What about this blood?"

VanBuckle looked down, and his voice was slow. "I'm in a bit of a pickle here. I don't know whose blood that is, could be Joni's from a cut for all we know. The house has been cleaned from top to bottom with bleach. The blood is on the floor, some smears on the wall. Doesn't look like a struggle to me. I don't know if we have a crime scene here or not."

Cyrus understood what he meant. That if Joni was in the wrong and a crime had been committed here, going in and collecting evidence with no permission or warrant would only get them laughed at by a judge. But if Joni had been in danger, and defended herself to the point of causing harm to another person, Joni would have called the police, not run off without an explanation. Taking in the history, Cyrus didn't have time for any of this.

"Joni's safety comes first at all costs. You want my help with this? I'll make the calls and take the responsibility for all actions. You know, all evidence goes through our lab. I can get a tech down here to collect, or you can use your own. All I need is your word." *Let me handle this,* Cyrus thought. *If something happens to her, I'll never forgive myself.*

"Now, wait a minute," VanBuckle said, his feathers all puffed out. "I'm only saying that I don't want this to come back and bite me on the ass."

Cyrus looked down the street as the two deputies who'd gone house to house were standing in the street talking. "If I'm not mistaken, Joni told me that her aunt co-signed on this house for her. Is her permission enough for you?"

"Lacey Chaskey may still be at the station. I'll check."

"Time is not on our side, Sheriff."

"Don't patronize me, son," he said, and pressed the phone to his ear.

Teddy pulled up, got out of his truck, and looked as rough as a bear whose den had been disturbed. "They put her into some system," he said, and looked around at VanBuckle on the phone, the house, squad cars on the street, Cyrus in the middle of the driveway. "Why aren't y'all doing anything?"

"We need permission to enter the house."

"Joni is too habitual to leave on foot like this," Teddy said. "Something is very wrong."

Just then, a car pulled up. A big guy in a Clemmie's apron stepped out, and he looked like an older version of Teddy, and just as pissed off. "Anything?" he said. Teddy shook his head, and the man said, "What the hell is going on 'round here?"

"We got it," VanBuckle called, just in time to save Cyrus from an argument he didn't want to have. "The aunt's getting us paperwork. I've got my crime scene tech on the way."

"Archie," VanBuckle said, and gave the man a nod.

"Where the hell is Joni?"

Cyrus stepped up and said, "We're trying to figure that out, sir," and introduced himself, but it didn't seem to help anything.

Archie threw his hands up in the air and looked back at the Sheriff. "I want her found, Ed. At least tell me you have a plan here. Why isn't your entire station out here looking for her?"

If it were only that easy, Cyrus thought, but wished they could shake the entire country until Joni tumbled out, safe and sound.

"Calm down, Dad," Teddy said. "It's not going to help anything."

"Listen to your son, Archie." VanBuckle gave him a hard stare. In a way that meant they had history.

Archie backed off, and said, "If y'all need anything to eat, just stop by."

Joni's house was a yellow cottage style ranch, set up like a box with the living room and kitchen separated by a pony wall. A hallway stretched down the middle with two bedrooms on the left and the master bedroom on the right. She had her own bathroom, but there was a guest bathroom just past her bedroom. A back door led to outside and Cyrus looked at the doggy door. The panel Joni told him about was back in place.

The entire house smelled of nothing but bleach.

Thankfully, Teddy put the dogs in the bedroom because they'd already walked through the blood and destroyed evidence. The lab tech was talking about the blood pattern and wounds from different people. "The smear on the floor may be from the same person who touched the wall, but all this," he said, and circled his finger above dime-sized drops. "This is from someone standing, and the blood dripped straight down."

"Someone's hurt," Cyrus said, and the tech guy nodded.

The dogs were going crazy from the bedroom, and when they were released in order to photograph the room, they both ran throughout the house as though they were looking for their owner.

"Put those dogs outside," VanBuckle snapped.

"I'm trying," Teddy said, but the German shepherds were being rascals.

They smelled everything and barked at the officers, and acted completely opposite to the dogs Cyrus had seen at High Falls. German shepherds were highly intelligent animals, being used most often as police dogs for their abilities to sniff out numerous things and take down bad guys. Some people underestimated the German shepherd as pets, which was why they were on the list as one of the most aggressive dogs. These dogs were faithful to their owners and would give their own lives to protect them. Which was why Cyrus realized they'd missed something huge. These dogs wouldn't let Joni go without a fight.

The dogs were riled up and barking, and Cyrus said, "Everybody stop moving." A nervous dog was not good. There were only five people in the house. Cyrus, Teddy, VanBuckle, the tech guy, and an officer. The dogs were looking for Joni. They barked again and began smelling each of the strangers. "This one has blood by its mouth." He wasn't sure if it was the dog's own or from the floor.

Cyrus didn't move, left his hands down at his sides, said, "Good boy," as the darker one's warm nose touched his hand. "Give them a minute to calm down. They know we're the good guys."

"This isn't *Turner and Hooch*," VanBuckle said.

Cyrus let his mind wonder through different scenarios. If Joni had done something wrong, it was like Teddy said. She wouldn't have left on foot and left her dogs outside, so they had to conclude that Joni was in trouble. Sam Dixon broke into her house yesterday. He could have done it again.

"This blood has to be from dog bites," Cyrus said, and everyone agreed. But why wasn't the guy dead on the floor? "We need to send an alert to every hospital in the state to report any dog bites or suspicious wounds."

As soon as the dogs were done smelling them, one of them ran to Teddy and jammed his snout into his legs. "What is it, Bubba?" The dog looked nervous, spun in a circle, then touched his nose to Teddy's leg again. The other dog barked, put his front paws on the counter, barked at a basket of fruit, then sat down on his haunches.

"Look," the deputy said with a laugh. "He's just hungry."

Then the dogs switched places, and it started all over again, as they realized they had the men's attention. Clyde ran up to Cyrus and nearly knocked him on his ass when he jumped up, barely touched his paws to Cyrus's shoulders, then obediently sat down right at his feet. Cyrus went down on one knee. "What do you want to tell me?"

Carefully, the dog walked back into the kitchen and jumped up to place his paws on the counter, and whined.

The cordless phone had been placed on the cradle the wrong way. Was that what the dog wanted him to see? The dog barked and pawed at the fruit basket.

When Cyrus picked up an apple, he saw something white with sharp edges sticking out. It was a rock with blood on it. "I'll be damned," Cyrus said, and looked down at the dog.

***

Cyrus was back in his SUV when Special Agent Rick Deavers called. "I got the address you wanted. It's a rental in Grant Park, but get this—" Cyrus had been working with Deavers for over eight years, trusted him like a brother. "He rented under the name Sam Doolan, so I called the landlord to get specifics. Landlord asks me if I'm the bounty hunter. I'm like, what, the bounty hunter? Apparently, a young woman called the landlord last night to inquire about his property for rent, said Sam Doolan jumped bail, blah blah blah, so yeah, I tell him I'm the bounty hunter and want this asshole and the old man, he was such a grouch, said Doolan packed up and left a few weeks ago, and to get his rent for him before we turn him over."

Had to be Joni. "Did he say what time she called?"

"Around six. But I got more news for you." Cyrus couldn't wait to hear this. "Mary Rancotti escaped out of the psycho ward," Deavers said.

"Escaped? I thought she was there voluntarily."

"Yeah, but she walked out around eight last night without telling anyone. The nurses thought she was in bed, and didn't notice she was gone until this morning when she never showed up for breakfast."

"What about any visitors?"

"Her sister Nina had been there yesterday morning, and a guy with a baseball cap and an AC/DC t-shirt stopped by at the end of visiting hours. Brown hair, blue eyes, medium build. Nurse said he was in and out like *Flash Gordon*. Her words, not mine."

Cyrus would need a warrant to check any of their video cameras to confirm whether it was Sam. "Do me another favor," Cyrus said. "See if you can track down Nina Dixon. Give her my number and let her know that Joni Chaskey is missing. I need anything she can tell me."

Cyrus hung up and tossed his cell phone on the passenger seat as he did a U-turn. Georgia State Prison was three hours away. He was sure he could get there in two.

***

The windows were bare and the evening sunlight poured through and touched down on her skin as though she were under a magnifying glass. Chains held her down, spread eagle, to a piece of plywood on a bed frame. Was she in her mother's bedroom? Above her head was blood spatter. Her vision blurred. Stale air and fresh paint filled her lungs. Where was

234

she? Across from the plywood bed was the beautiful pie safe with its delicate carving at the top. The chains clinked as she tried to move. Throbbing pain pulsed through her head as it all came back to her.

Mary.

Sam's voice.

Saliva filled her mouth as her stomach clenched to vomit, but nothing came out. Why were they doing this to her? She'd been nothing but nice to them.

Was this Sam's plan the whole time?

Or Mary's?

Tears filled her eyes, and she told herself to be strong. They wouldn't hurt her. The weight of the chains was heavy. She thought about the rock coming at her head.

Why did she feel so sleepy?

The clouds moved in front of the sun, offering her a bit of relief from the heat, and shadows played on the wall, but then the cloud was gone and it was back to burning up again. At first, she thought she was in her old house in Kennesaw, but she wasn't. This house felt different, even though it smelled of old wood and mold. Maybe it was the plywood.

Joni tried to pull her feet up, but the chains were too tight. Every time she moved her right arm, her left would pull. Same with her feet. Somehow, the chains were connected under the board. The chain looped through a bolt anchored into the wood, and secured each of her hands and feet in the chains with a padlock. Joni wasn't going anywhere.

Sticky blood stuck to the side of her neck, and sweat dripped down her forehead. Joni closed her eyes for a moment, then jerked awake. She tried to stay awake as fear settled in, but she kept dozing off.

She was so tired.

When were they coming back?

Were they ever?

***

Under no circumstances was Warden Parrino going to let Cyrus have a chat with one of his inmates at such a late hour. A corrections officer called him at his home and Cyrus waited until he showed up, and show up he did. All pissed off and bent out of shape.

"I don't care what the hell is going on, *Agent Kenner with the GBI*. I will not disrupt my prison so you can have a go at your job. It's down time around here. You know what it's like when you disturb a hornet's nest?"

"It's important, Warden," Cyrus said. His back was tight, and he stood his ground. "I'll go above your head and get you for obstruction."

The warden laughed. "What do you want me to do? Knock lightly on Chaskey's cell door and tell him you want to talk?"

"It's about his daughter. She's missing. And so is another woman."

It took Cyrus ten more minutes to convince Parrino that Lyle could handle a disruption in his schedule. Parrino said, "Consider this your wild card because this will never happen again."

Lyle Chaskey wasn't too happy to see Cyrus either. Red eyes stared at him as he sat down, and he said, "Who'd you find this time?"

"That's the problem," Cyrus said. "Your daughter's missing and I think you may know who's involved."

Cyrus loved the way all the blood drained from Chaskey's face, wanted to tell him that's how all the other parents felt when their little girls went missing. No crimes ever went unpunished. Whether through God or Karma, a person eventually paid for what they'd done.

Lyle had said nothing, kept looking Cyrus dead in the eye and waited for him to explain. Cyrus offered nothing. Lyle Chaskey was a sociopath with control problems. Being in prison hadn't changed that. In fact, Cyrus was sure that for a man like Chaskey, being locked up only made it worse. This was what Lyle Chaskey got, which was a lot better than what he deserved.

Chaskey wasn't the worst serial killer on the block. He didn't strangle women with their own intestines or cut off their breasts and make them eat the flesh. He didn't leave riddles for the police and make a game out of it. Lyle Chaskey was a decent-looking man who manipulated women to gain their trust so he could brutally rape them. He never wanted to get caught, and it was the quiet ones that were the hardest to catch. How many more women would have died if not for his simple mistake with the prostitute?

"Who's Sam Dixon?" Cyrus said. The bastard smiled. He actually fucking smiled. He said on a hunch, "You knew this guy was your son and you never told her."

"I got a letter from him about eight years ago telling me who he was. I never believed he was my son. I wrote to him a few times to humor him." Lyle shrugged.

"He could have gotten a DNA test."

"And what would that matter? It wasn't like I'd have to pay child support."

"It would have confirmed what Mary told the police."

Lyle smiled again. "Oh, no, Mr. GBI man. Mary and I were in love. We had a relationship. I couldn't help it I had to break up with her because she was a little screwy." Lyle tapped his forehead with his finger. If Cyrus didn't care about Joni, he'd tell Lyle to go fuck himself and that he hoped he went through the same hell he'd put other parents through.

Cyrus looked through his notes even though he knew the information. "Mary left the psychiatric hospital after eight last night. Last visitor was a man who matched Sam's description. Your daughter is missing, and we found blood in her house. You want to come forth with any information, now would be the time to do it."

Lyle clenched his jaw and gave Cyrus a hard look. "I'm not saying anything to you."

Cyrus slammed his fist on the table. "Your daughter is in trouble. I need to know what you did to that woman thirty years ago, because I think they went after Joni."

Lyle looked down at his hands. He said, "I tried to make her leave but she wouldn't, and I knew she was bad news when she told me she loved me. Do you know how long it had been since I'd heard those words?"

Cyrus arched his brows.

"Never. My own mother didn't even love me. Eventually, I dropped Mary off in Macon. After I was in prison, Mary wrote to me, and she told me how much her son looked like me. I never even bothered to write back." Lyle gave Cyrus a sly look. "You have to stop and ask yourself; Am I doing the right things to find this girl?"

The words sunk in, but Cyrus held his composure. *This girl.* He was toying with him. "Maybe someday soon you and I can have another chat about Miranda McBean."

"Miranda who?"

Typical response. Back to Joni, he said, "What I have to ask myself is whether you really love your daughter."

Lyle Chaskey ran his index finger up his arm, said, "Joni's the one that needs to get a lesson on love. And respect."

Not wanting to play psychiatrist, Cyrus said, "Has Sam Dixon contacted you lately?"

"Why would he want to hurt Joni?"

"Because I think it's their turn to fuck with you, Mr. Chaskey."

Chapter Twenty

Mary sat under the window, rocking back and forth, humming out of tune, the sound stirring Joni enough to fully awaken her. The sun had gone down, but the heat was trapped inside the room, and there was nothing to be done about the discomfort as sweat pooled down her neck. Strangely, Mary's humming was better than silence.

Sam was in the doorway watching her, enveloped in the dark shadows. His face came into view every time the clouds moved away from the moon. His hand was wrapped in a shirt soaked in blood. What was he thinking, just standing there with his mother on the floor humming like a child and his prisoner chained to the bed?

Fear had her enraged, and her nerves shook. Joni jerked on the chain, the sound silencing Mary and echoing through the empty room. "Sam, that looks bad. You need to see a doctor."

"The bleeding will stop soon. I stitched it up myself. You wanna see what those fucking dogs did to me?" Sam walked over and showed her their handy work. The top of his hand had been torn, and his fingers were covered in puncture wounds.

"They were only trying to protect me."

"Well, they're dead now," Sam said, and those words ripped Joni's heart out. "Stabbed them both in the hearts. Once you kill your first, the next ones are easy."

Tears slid down her face. Might as well stab her in the heart, too. "You didn't have to do that."

"They can't protect you now," Sam said.

Mary was still rocking herself under the window while she hummed, as though she was oblivious to what was going on.

"You lied to me. You knew who I was since the first time Mary wrote to me."

"Who do you think's been putting all these ideas in her head? Like father, like son." Sam knelt down next to the make-shift bed and used his bloody shirt to wipe her tears away. "You are weak," he said, and a sob escaped her. How strong was she supposed to be? "And you're a whore."

Joni wanted to make it all go away. To go back and change things. She wished she'd never have met Sam, and if she had the chance, she'd never go to the Fantasy Club again. She wasn't sure why Sam was so mad at her. She had done nothing wrong to him. But this was the real Sam, she told herself. Everything she knew about him was a lie.

"It doesn't have to be like this. Just tell me what you want."

Mary said, "He doesn't love you."

Stop crying, she told herself. *You are not weak; you are strong.*

Sam slapped her face. So much for not crying. "Are you listening to me?" She had no idea what he said. He stood up and slammed his foot down on the plywood. "Cry!" he shouted. "You're a little fucking baby."

*　*　*

"Yes," Cyrus said, to answer Lyle's question. "Everything you say can be used against you."

"It's strange how I can take someone's life without a second thought," Lyle said.

"Do you want your daughter to die?"

"I only wanted what was best for her."

"Then answer my question. Where was the house that you held Mary captive?" Lyle closed his eyes as though he had to think about it. "Do you even remember?"

"She had a dog named... Rothbart."

Cyrus took a deep breath to stay focused. "Mary or Joni?"

"You'll figure it out."

Lyle Chaskey was trying to tell him something. Was Rothbart a town? A name of a person? A street? This was going nowhere. "Are you or are you not concerned about your daughter?"

Lyle nodded. "The house was three miles west of Hogansville. A farmhouse off of Highway 54. It's off of a dirt road. You'll never find it. The place is probably rotted out by now."

"You found it," Cyrus said, and stood. "I'll find it."

Except they couldn't.

He'd called the Troup County Sheriff's department on his way there, which would take him three and a half hours. How was it they couldn't find a dirt road in their own county? At least they were checking, Cyrus told himself. They were checking for any kind of old farmhouse within a three-mile radius of the area.

His phone rang.

"I found no open records on Mary Rancotti," Rick Deavers said.

"What about on Sam Dixon?"

"He was arrested once when he was a teenager for fighting at school. Nina Dixon just called. Said she'd do what she can to help, and that Mary gave birth to a baby boy three months after she was found."

"Three months?" Lyle must have had Mary longer than she first thought.

"That's what the sister said. Mary had been giving Nina so much conflicting information, she didn't know what to believe. Mary tried to kill herself while she was pregnant, so Nina took the baby when he was born and raised him as her own. She has no idea how Sam figured out the truth."

"Maybe Mary told him."

"Nina said Sam is overly protective of Mary."

Overprotective my ass, Cyrus thought when he hung up.

***

"They're going to find me," Joni said to Sam as he dragged another plywood board toward the window. When he boarded up the window, she said, "Why are you making it so dark?"

"I thought you liked the dark."

Tired muscles could no longer jerk the chain, and she lay there limp on her makeshift bed. "What are you going to do? You can't keep me like this."

Sam took a drill, made pilot holes in the wood, and screwed it to the windowsill. He ignored her while she asked more questions. The room became darker. The only light came from a flashlight secured to Sam's head.

They must have been in a house without electricity. But why was he boarding up the windows? "Where is this place?"

"It's a secret." Sam set the drill down when he finished.

"Why did you take my letters?"

"They are just as much mine as they are yours."

"He wouldn't write you back," Joni said. Sam was a worthless loser. She tried a different tactic. "Sam, I can get him to open up to you—"

He walked to her with such swiftness, and Joni closed her eyes as he grabbed her face. "I don't need you to do anything for me. He writes to me all the time. I took the letters because I wanted to know if you were lying to me."

"About what?"

"About whether he wrote about my mother."

"Which one? Darla or Mary?" Sam slapped her face. "He doesn't have time for you." For a second, Joni thought he was going to hit her again. Instead, he flicked her forehead. "Knock knock?" He flicked her forehead again. "I said knock knock."

"Fuck you."

Sam punched her in the stomach, nearly knocking her breath out. She gasped, and he laughed. "That's for kicking me at the motel." He walked backwards out of the room and locked the door behind him.

Now it made sense. The one watching her. He told her dad something, and that was why he wouldn't see her. How much did he know?

A minute later, she heard an engine start, and within seconds it was gone. Where were they going? Were they going to come back? But it wasn't both of them in the car. She heard a noise at the door. Someone trying to unlock it. Joni couldn't see a thing when the door swung open, but she could tell it was Mary. Unruly hair stuck up on her head, and she had on a long khaki skirt and a cotton t-shirt tucked into the waistband.

"He told me to watch you," Mary said.

Joni's heart pounded in her chest. A second later, Mary lit an oil lamp and placed it on top of the pie safe.

"Mary, help me." Mary had a knife in her hand. A skinny one with a bent tip. She must have used it to open the door. "Why didn't he give you the key?"

"What key?" Mary walked over and picked up the drill. She smiled like it was a new toy.

"Do you know where the key is for these chains?"

"What chains?"

"These chains, goddammit!" Joni pulled hard on the chains around her arms. "What is wrong with you? I was your friend."

As she squeezed the trigger of the drill, the sound came alive in the quiet room, and a dark look came over her face. "My friends are dead. You killed them." Mary walked over and put her right knee on the board and touched the drill to Joni's arm.

"What are you doing?"

The pain shot in all directions of her arm as Mary shoved the drill bit deep and squeezed the trigger. The screams were deafening to her own ears and nothing she did eased the pain.

***

243

"Are you sure you believe this guy? He's a serial killer," one of the Sheriff's deputies said. His name was Billy, and he had a thin mustache above his lip.

It was after eleven p.m. when Cyrus met them at the intersection in Hogansville. "Unfortunately, yes. I believe him."

"He the one who dumped that body in the Towaliga?"

"Yes, sir," Cyrus said.

"Shucks," the older deputy said. "I used to go to school with that girl. Such a sad story."

"That house has to be around here," Cyrus said.

Billy handed him a map. "We've been up and down this highway for an hour. Went down Hammett both ways. Back and forth down all the other roads."

"Are there any old farmhouses in the area?"

"A few, but they're lived in. Maybe someone bought the place?"

Which gave Cyrus the idea that Sam Dixon may have bought a house lately if he was not renting anymore.

"This farmhouse was run down thirty years ago. Chaskey said the dirt road had a small opening. There weren't many houses on this highway back then." Cyrus had already driven down the highway himself.

"You think these people have Joni Chaskey held hostage in this house?"

"I don't know," Cyrus said, but had to rule out the place. He'd have to call for backup at some point, but he couldn't do that without a location. "I have to start somewhere."

He got back into his SUV and checked his odometer. When he hit the three-mile mark, he grabbed his heavy flashlight and began walking. Billy did the same, but the other deputy put on his spotlight and slowly drove alongside them.

On the left side of the highway was a bigger gap in the pine trees. Cyrus stopped and took a hard look at it before he walked through it. Woods surrounded him, but when he got further in, he realized there was in fact a small path big enough for a car to fit. Everything was overgrown.

"You think there's a house back here?" Billy said.

"Right there." Cyrus pointed his flashlight at the creepy house.

It looked like something out of a horror movie. The front porch had fallen in. The left side was covered in kudzu, which grew up and over half the roof. The front windows had been boarded up. The top of the left chimney's bricks had toppled to the ground.

"Doesn't look like anybody is here," Billy said.

"Yeah," Cyrus agreed. But he didn't know for sure and he couldn't be too careful. He pulled his gun out of the holster, and Billy did the same. "I'll go in through the back. You cover the front."

"Shouldn't we call for backup?"

"Yes, but I'm not. You can wait here if you like."

"No," Billy said. "I'll cover the front."

Cyrus slowly made his way around. Something smelled like death and the whole place gave him the creeps, just knowing what Lyle Chaskey did to those women here. The back porch didn't look any better than the front. The only noise was from the insects. He was thinking Billy was right. No one was here, but this could have been the perfect place to dump a body.

Don't think like that, he told himself.

Slowly making his way up the back porch, he was careful where he stepped. The back door was broken off its hinges, and the inside was a mess. He was going to have to stop watching scary movies because he was frozen in place with shadows on the wall. *Move it,* he told himself. The floor was worn, and the walls were covered in old wood paneling. He flashed his light and made his way through the dirty rooms. With the layers of dust on the stairs, he knew no one had been to the second level in years.

245

The house was empty.

Cyrus wasn't sure this made him happy or disappointed. Was he really hoping to find Joni here? A minute later, Cyrus called out from the front door, "Empty," and Billy gave a nod. Beams of lights shone through the house as the other deputy arrived on scene. Dried blood was on the back door near the knob.

This was a crime scene, he reminded himself. Would they be able to get anything after all these years? And for what? Lyle practically admitted he murdered Sheila and Rachel. That monster was never getting out of prison.

A loud crash came from down the hall and Cyrus took off. The younger deputy had fallen through the wall. "The door was stuck and when I pulled, I fell."

Billy got a laugh out of that.

Cyrus flashed his light through the doorway, which had stairs. This must have been the basement. He tested his weight on the first step, then slowly made his way down. Trapped air surrounded him at the bottom. Cyrus gagged at the smell of old urine and feces. Billy and the other deputy came behind him.

"Jesus," Billy said, and covered his mouth.

The basement had no windows. A tiny mattress lay in the corner with rusted aluminum cans. Dried blood covered the floor. Two pipes ran along the back wall.

"Is this blood?" Billy flashed his light on the wall above the mattress. "This is sick."

The wall looked like a child's finger painting, stretching from the floor to halfway up the wall. There were long rectangles, a circle with lines coming out, weird triangles. Cyrus realized it was supposed to be buildings and a tree with the sun behind it.

Thick pieces of bloody glass covered the floor. Eye bolts had been anchored into the concrete wall. It looked like one of the women had chipped away at the concrete. A broken oil lamp sat next to a dirty old blanket. This must have been before Lyle was getting rid of everything.

Cyrus called Deavers, said, "You think you can get the geeks down here to collect on a thirty-year-old crime scene?"

***

The drill bit Mary used wasn't doing a good enough job for her, so she took it out of the drill and replaced it with the slender one used to make pilot holes. Then that drill bit slipped out of the drill and stuck half-way out of Joni's arm, and every twitch of her fingers was agonizing. Blood oozed out of her nose, blood from a blow which Mary caused using the electric drill. Joni's vision went fuzzy, and her cheek ached when she as much as blinked.

Sam stood in the doorway as Mary went on a rant. "She made me do this to her," Mary said. "The pain is inside of her body and she needs to get it out. You can't sleep when you have pain in your body."

Sam had been gone for a very long time while Mary tried to get the pain out of Joni's body, and he did nothing to save her when he'd returned. Mary was so focused on her own words and her own voice that when she pulled out a blade and cut Joni's clothes off, she hadn't realized she'd cut her own finger.

"You're bleeding," Joni said, trying to distract her, but all Mary did was wipe the blood on Joni's stomach. She hadn't realized until now how serious Mary's condition was. It was like someone else controlling her brain. As Mary tossed away Joni's clothes, the photo of her father fell out of her pocket.

Mary picked it up, then held the knife to Joni. "Where did you get this?"

Sam walked over and reached for the knife. "Give it to me."

"It's mine," Mary said. "You gave it to me, so it means it's mine. I want to keep it."

"Let me borrow it," Sam said. "I'll give it back. I promise." When Mary handed over the blade, he looked her in the eye and said, "Don't kill her."

"We should throw her outside." Mary pressed the photo to her chest.

"We're going to keep her right here. If you throw her outside, she'll get away. Then we'll have to start all over."

"I won't run away," Joni said. "Just take off these chains." Pain shot through her useless left arm, and now she was half naked and exposed. "Sam, why are you doing this?"

In a flash, Sam was inches from her face, and he touched the blade to her cheek. "You did this to yourself, little sister. You never deserved that good life you had. You're a waste of a good life. You don't deserve to live. Do you think you deserve to live?" Hot breath covered her face and Joni closed her eyes.

Sam's words went through her mind like a fog with nowhere left to go. Tormenting her, he said, "Are you ready for me to start reading?"

"What?"

He smacked the side of her head. "Pay attention. I got the letters you don't believe exist. Are you ready for me to start reading?"

"I don't want to hear anything you have to say."

She underestimated him. Sam twisted the drill bit in her arm, said, "You ready to listen now?" Joni nodded. "How bad do you want me to read these letters?"

"Very bad," she said, and tried not to cry.

"Make her beg more," Mary said, and Sam pinched the soft flesh above Joni's hip, took a better grip and twisted. The strength of his finger and thumb felt like a vise, like something was biting her side and there was nothing she could do to stop the pain. She screamed out and wanted so badly to hurt them. Eight years of trying to console Mary, and this was what she'd turned into.

Although the pain was sharp, it was in an isolated area near her hip, and Joni concentrated on the pain in her arm instead. When Sam let go, she said, "Just kill me now," and figured the maggots could feast.

"No." Sam moved his mouth above hers. "My mother gets to decide when you die."

Chapter Twenty-one

At one o'clock in the morning, Teddy turned on Joni's computer. It was killing him that he didn't know what happened in this house. Bubba and Clyde protected her the best they could. The bottom line was that Sam took her. Teddy couldn't see past his own anger to realize Joni had been in trouble. He was her safe place and he let her down. Why did he do that?

Nothing in his life compared to this helpless feeling of wanting to find someone so bad and there wasn't anything he could do to bring her back this second. Sam was Mary's son, and they wanted to hurt her.

The headlines about Lyle flashed in his mind. Pictures in the newspaper. The recent article about that garage of horrors. What the hell was happening to Joni?

Teddy opened up a new document, and it felt so wrong using her computer to make a missing person flyer with Joni's name on it.

***

"Acceptance does not come from me," Sam read. *"It must come from yourself. What we want most in our lives is already there. You only have to figure out how to see past the chaos to get it. Focus on now, and in time things will come. Beware of the man who receives gifts without merit, for he shall be the one tempted to a life of indulgence."* Sam smiled, then said, "Do you know what that means?"

The room was dark, and he was using light from the oil lamp to read letter after boring letter. Okay, so her father lied to her again. He wrote to Sam and knew who he was. Who cares? Sam and Mary, that's who. Does every victim go through life looking for revenge in some way?

"Pay attention," Sam said, and began again. *"Nothing is free, my son. I believe I can confide so much in a son. You have to know how to feign a smile and blend in with the enemy before you can be understood. I believe we are beginning to understand one other—"*

"Sam, I have to pee," Joni said.

"I don't care."

"I'm serious." Joni squeezed her knees together.

"The bathroom doesn't work. Pee right there."

"I can't!"

"Yes, you can."

"I have to pee, and you can't keep me like this. It's fucking ridiculous. Let me out now, you asshole—" *Go ahead and piss him off again.* He dumped out the rest of the letters and walked to her with the plastic bag. "I'm not peeing in that."

He smashed the bag over Joni's face and held it there as she struggled to breathe. In a split-second, fear washed over her. The last bit of breath escaped her mouth, and that was it. She had no reserve and struggled against Sam and the bag.

Then she pissed herself.

Sam pulled the bag away, and Joni gasped for air.

"Don't interrupt me again." Sam sat back down and picked up the letter. "Now listen carefully, because this is important."

***

Clemmie's had become the command post for everyone involved in the search. Coffee and biscuits were handed out generously. Seventeen hours missing, and the community pulled together, donating time and resources, connecting in a way communities do when a tragedy happens.

"Turn on the TV," someone yelled, and Teddy did.

251

Clemmie's was packed full, but everyone quieted down long enough to hear the seven a.m. news. The GBI director was making a statement. Said that at this time they believe Joni to be alive, but in danger, and her safe return was their top priority. They were following up on all leads, and if anyone had any information, to call the number at the bottom of the screen.

Joni's photo popped up, along with Sam's and Mary's, and Teddy turned away to make more coffee. When the news was done, Teddy turned down the volume and said to everyone, "Listen up." All eyes were on him, and Teddy pointed to the thousands of flyers on the tables that the office supply store opened early to make. "Tyler, you take a group and go west to Peachtree City. Mike, you go east. We need to spread out and not waste time. Communicate with each other so we'll know where we hit. Talk to anyone you know and get the word out."

Within five minutes, the place was cleared.

"You Teddy Glencoe?"

Teddy turned. An older man with a beard down to his chest stood near the door. "Yes."

The man held out his hand. "Henry Graninch."

"Graninch?"

Henry smiled and held his hands out to show he wasn't hostile. "Only here to help. Was told to find you."

"Yeah." Why would Henry Graninch want to help find Joni? Teddy poured the man a cup of coffee. "Seems strange you being here."

"Well," he said. "I know what it feels like. I'm sober now and I owe that girl a favor."

Teddy nodded. "Cream and sugar?"

"Nah," Henry said, and took the cup. "Just tell me what I can do to help."

***

"What does Lyle Chaskey have to say about his daughter's disappearance?"

"Did he have anything to do with this?"

"Do you think this is a publicity stunt to get attention?"

"Did Lyle Chaskey's daughter have anything to do with the bodies found?"

Cyrus knew all too well how the media could help or hinder any case, and when Remy Ormond opened up for questions, the man was peppered with ones that wouldn't help find Joni.

Every Sheriff and Chief of police from every county in the state of Georgia had been sent specific descriptions of Joni Chaskey, Sam Dixon, and Mary Rancotti, and to be on the lookout for a blue Toyota Corolla registered under Sam Dixon's name.

Cyrus was still waiting on the lab to match fingerprints and blood samples. After Remy Ormond's statement, he caught Cyrus in the hallway. "You're too close to this," Remy said. "Do you have any idea what kind of circus this has turned into?"

"Sir," Cyrus said, and suddenly felt deflated. No one ever wanted their efforts to go unnoticed.

"Did you get any sleep at all?" Remy said.

Ignoring the question, Cyrus said, "I need phone records. Bank statements. And I want a copy of Lyle Chaskey's visitor log and phone recordings. Is there any way to get a warrant for his mail?"

Remy shook his head. "I'll see what I can do. What else do you need?"

"Joni Chaskey alive."

Remy shoved his finger into Cyrus's chest. "You better find her," he said, and held his gaze too long.

When he was gone, Rick Deavers walked over and said, "He's just pissed because we look better in front of the camera." Cyrus turned toward the elevator. He didn't have time for jokes right now. Rick pulled a granola bar out of his pocket, said, "You hungry?"

"No." The truth came from his growling stomach, but when Cyrus didn't take the granola bar, Rick ripped open the wrapper. The elevator doors opened, and they both stepped in. "How the hell did this happen?" Cyrus said.

"Is it worse when you know the person?"

"I can do my job," Cyrus snapped.

"Then do it," Rick said, clearly not taking his shit. "You haven't had a case like this in a long time. I just want to make sure you're okay." Rick finished eating the granola bar and shoved the wrapper into his pocket.

"I'm fine," Cyrus said. Murder cases and crime scenes can get the best of anyone. Missing women and children's cases were like trying to make the world stand still, but nothing ever stopped. The elevator door slid open, and they stepped out.

"You need help with Nina Dixon?" Deavers said and pulled another granola bar from his pocket.

"No. Let me know if Remy gets any reports back." Cyrus took the granola bar out of Rick's hand. "Thanks," he said, and headed to go interview Nina Dixon.

"Thank you for your patience." Cyrus set down two fresh cups of coffee. Nina was a plump woman, nicely dressed in slacks. Her hair was cut short and hung loosely on her shoulders. Cyrus shook her hand and sat down across from her. They were in a small conference room because he wanted to make her comfortable.

She'd brought some photos of Sam. Cyrus had paid little attention to the guy when he'd first met him near High Falls. Now he looked closely at his face. His cheek bones were high on his face, bright blue eyes, dark brown hair. He was a good-looking kid with a mischievous smile.

Usually, when someone was being interviewed, the idea was to take it slow and keep them talking, but Cyrus didn't have time for it. He said, "I hate to get right to it, but why didn't anyone ever get a DNA test done?"

"You have to understand that Mary has schizophrenia, but we didn't know that when she was growing up. She was misdiagnosed. She was very promiscuous from the time she was thirteen, and would disappear for days sometimes. Her life revolved around these crazy stories, and she'd paint them out and we were expected to know what she was talking about. So when she claimed to be held captive by this man, no one thought much of it, especially when she claimed to love him. We didn't understand what was going on." Nina took a deep breath, then continued. "When Sam was born, we had no one to test his DNA with. When Lyle Chaskey was arrested in 1998, Sam was sixteen years old by then. He knew Mary was his mother, and I raised him because she was sick. I didn't push the issue because I wanted to protect him. I just wanted him to be okay."

"How long was Mary gone?"

"We're not sure. She was visiting a cousin in Atlanta for a few weeks, then said she wanted to go home, and that's when she disappeared, but my cousin never called to tell my parents." Nina sounded mad. "Never bothered to say that Mary had left to come home. I think a month had passed by then."

"You told Agent Deavers that you didn't know Sam had figured out who his father was."

Tears filled Nina's eyes, and Cyrus grabbed a tissue. "He never let on that he knew or was bothered by it if he did. I do so much," Nina said. "I'm the only one to help the two of them. So much of my time has been taken away from me and devoted to my sister and nephew. I'm the one who took her to all her doctor appointments. I'm the one who makes sure she takes all her medicine."

Cyrus patted the woman's hand. "I appreciate you driving all this way to speak with me, and I'd like to learn as much as possible about your family. Do you mind telling me what Sam was like as a kid?"

"He cried a lot as a baby. Nothing I did soothed him. I had two older kids at the time and Sam became over stimulated by their noise. I was constantly telling my kids to quiet down. When Sam was a boy, he got his feelings hurt easily, and always said no one liked him. He liked to be by himself a lot. His imagination was over the top, you know what I mean? But he seemed normal to me, considering I grew up with Mary, who suffered from crazy mood swings." She took a sip of coffee.

"Has Sam ever been diagnosed with anything?"

"Like Mary? No. I urged him to see a doctor at one point because by the time he graduated high school he'd become aggressive toward other boys."

"Is this when he was arrested?"

Nina looked embarrassed. "It was just that one time, but he got into fights for no reason. I asked him why he'd grown so angry over those last few years and he said it was social pressure."

"And this was around the time Lyle Chaskey had been arrested?"

Nina slowly nodded. "It was right after, yes, I believe so. Then, after he went off to college, he pulled away from us. I saw him maybe a few times a year. And then he moved to Atlanta, and I only saw him during Christmas, if that. I was going to put Mary in a home, but Sam wouldn't let me." Nina took another deep breath. "Mary's dissociative disorder has gotten worse. She hasn't been diagnosed with dissociative *identity* disorder, but I know she has it."

"Multi-personality disorder?"

Nina nodded. "She's on medication. I can make you a list."

"That's unnecessary."

"I do not know what will happen if Mary doesn't take her medicine. I don't think Sam has any idea, either."

"That's why we need to find them." Cyrus pulled the conversation back to Sam. "He's had six residences in the last ten years. The last house, he skipped out on rent and didn't leave a forwarding address. Your sister is missing, and so is Joni."

"Why do you believe Sam had anything to do with this? What if Joni is the one who wants to cause harm?"

Cyrus had to connect the dots. If Nina was correct about who Sam's father was, then Joni and Sam were brother and sister. He looked again at the photo and didn't see a resemblance between the two. Sam could favor Lyle if Cyrus stared at the photo long enough, but the similarities weren't dead on.

"People hide what they don't want you to see," Nina pointed out.

"Tell me, Nina. What's Sam hiding?" Cyrus said and told Nina how Sam rented a house under the last name of one of Lyle Chaskey's victims.

Chapter Twenty-two

Sam was hard to read. One minute he was calm and the next explosive with anger, but she didn't know what was setting him off. If she could hold out longer than Sam expected, maybe he'd let her go. If she was nice to him and did what he wanted, maybe he would stop hitting her. It appeared all he wanted was for Joni to confirm everything he said.

The room was still dark, but tiny flecks of sunlight peeked out of the cracks between the wood and the windows.

Sam sat in a creaky wooden chair near the door. Kept staring at her. He spoke no words, answered no questions. Just watched her. In the semi-light, Sam looked a lot like her dad. Now that she knew the truth, she could see it. He had Mary's blue eyes and dark brown hair. Mary's craziness mixed with Lyle's desire to hurt people made for one screwed up guy.

"Sam? Please take these off." The chains were digging into her wrists and ankles because they were too tight. "We can forget about all of this and go back to being friends and joking about Japanese food." Tears slid down her face. "Remember?"

His voice was low when he finally spoke. "We were never friends. You only felt sorry for me. I don't need you or your holier than thou shit." His voice mocked her. "*Fuck me but not too hard. Fuck me but don't kiss me. Fuck me but let's pretend it never happened.*" His voice went back to his. "You're pathetic."

"You went to that motel room with me and you knew who I was. You're the one who's pathetic." Sam's face went tight, so she chose her words carefully because she didn't want to get raped. "Why didn't you just tell me? What are you going to do, keep me

258

chained to the bed for the rest of my life? What do you want from me?"

He came over to her, and she thought she was getting through to him. Surprise hit her when he wrapped his hands around her throat and squeezed. Joni arched her back, but no air could enter her lungs. Her face grew hot as blood was cut off and her eyes felt like they would pop out of their sockets. Sam smiled at her, then let go.

Air burned her lungs as she sucked in gulps.

She began to cry again. That was the second time Sam choked her.

"I can be just like him," Sam said, and adjusted the bandage on his hand. "My mother was his first victim. You'll be mine."

***

She was exhausted but scared to sleep. She'd dozed in and out through the morning, and now she was fighting with herself. Maybe if she weren't in chains, she wouldn't feel so vulnerable.

Her stomach growled for food, but more than anything, she wanted water. Her mouth felt full of cotton. She made the mistake of thinking about her dogs. Tears turned to sobs, but she made herself stop crying.

Don't be weak.

She had to get out of here. But how? Even if she got the eye bolts out of the wood, the chain itself went under the plywood and was locked with padlocks. Each ankle and wrist had a chain wrapped around it, secured with a padlock. Four padlocks. Four keys. She tried again to free her right wrist, but it was wrapped too tight.

Joni's hands and feet were practically blue from the shortage of blood supply, and her left arm was shot to shit. She'd give anything right now to get the broken drill bit out. She'd stab Mary in the heart with it.

When Mary entered the bedroom, Joni laughed. Really laughed. Was she delirious? It was like God saying, "Here she is. Go ahead and kill her."

"What's so funny?" Mary had a bucket of paint and a paintbrush with a long wooden handle.

"Doesn't this bother you, Mary? That this happened to you and now you can see it happen to someone else. Doesn't this *bother* you?"

Mary took the paint lid off and dipped the brush in. "Sam said that you're the reason Lyle won't talk to me."

No, he won't talk to you because you're batshit crazy.

All the times Joni talked with Mary, she tried to reason with her and work through why she thought the way she did. She wanted to help Mary be reasonable about the facts and what was in her imagination.

But not anymore.

Mary slapped the wet paintbrush to Joni's leg and smeared the red paint on.

"What are you doing?"

"Painting you dead."

This made Joni laugh. Delirious. That's what was happening to her.

Mary responded by painting Joni's face. The paint was cold and thick against her skin. She closed her eyes to keep the paint out. "Where's Sam?"

"At the store. Things are happening sooner than he thought. The house wasn't ready for you."

Which meant that Sam had no plan yet and was figuring it out as he went. Mary continued painting Joni, paying extra attention to her ribs and neck. When she touched the brush to the drill bit, Joni winced in pain.

"Where are we?"

"Right here, silly," Mary said, sounding as silly as a kid herself.

"What's he going to do?"

"I don't know." With the paintbrush in her hand, Mary moved over to where the antique pie safe was against the wall and painted it. When the paint brush went dry, she walked over to the can, dipped in the brush, then walked back to the pie safe as paint dripped in globs to the hardwood floor.

"Mary, don't you see what Sam's doing? He's the one keeping you from Lyle. Look what he's doing to me. I'm the only one that can get you to Lyle and Sam's locked me up so I can't help you."

"Sam said when we're done, we'll get to be with Lyle." The front of the pie safe was now covered in red paint.

"He's lying to you. I'm the only one who can see Lyle. You know that." Mary stopped painting. Joni said, "Listen to me carefully. When I found Sheila and Rachel, they were scared of Sam. They told me to protect you from him. I can't protect you from him like this. Get the keys. Where are the keys, Mary?"

A moment passed where Mary thought about what Joni said. She stared past Joni in a daze.

"Mary?"

"I don't know why he let me go."

"You escaped."

Mary shook her head. "He let me go. I know he loves me."

Feeling hopeful, Joni said, "Do you want to go ask him? I can take you to him, but you have to get the keys."

Mary dropped the paintbrush to the floor.

Joni breathed a sigh of relief. As long as she kept Mary believing that she could see Lyle, Joni had the crazy woman on her side. "Mary!" Joni called because she was taking too long. How long would Sam be at the store? Shit. What if Sam had taken the keys with him? No wonder Mary couldn't find them. What else could she use? Bobby pins to pick the lock? A bolt cutter? What were the chances of having one of those lying around?

"Mary?" Joni gave up on the idea of the keys and wanted Mary to find something else. "Mary, get back in here. Mar-ry!"

261

But when Mary returned, she had the keys in her hand, and Joni's heart rate picked up with urgency. "Thank God. Hurry, we have to catch Lyle before he leaves us."

Mary got on her hands and knees to unlock the chain under the plywood. Next came her feet. Joni could feel her freedom, could feel the weight of the chains already coming off her. She was going to knock Mary out as soon as she was free. Joni did not know where she was, but she'd figure out what to do as soon as she was out of this house.

"Hurry up," Joni said.

Mary chewed her tongue as she stuck the key in the lock on her right arm, and when the chain came off, the breath Joni had been holding felt like such a relief. Next was the left arm. Pain shot from her wrist to her elbow and she wanted to scream, but didn't dare. Keeping a calm, happy voice, Joni said, "Almost there. Lyle's gonna be so proud of you." The chains rattled as Mary worked the lock, and she wasn't being careful with the arm, but Joni swallowed down the pain as she turned the key.

"What the fuck are you doing?"

All the blood drained from Joni's body. And apparently Sam thought so too, with the shocked look on his face. Then he realized the red stuff was paint, not blood. What confused Joni was that Sam was in a pair of boxer shorts and a dirty t-shirt. His hair stuck up on the side of his head. He'd been sleeping. Not at the store. And Joni screaming for Mary probably woke him up.

Good going, Genius.

Joni scrambled off the board, but the long chain was still attached to her left arm. Sam moved fast, and shoved Mary against the wall, shoved her hard enough to make her head bounce, then she fell to the floor and cried. Sam came at Joni. She tried to fight him off, but she'd only managed to push him away. He grabbed her by the hair and pulled her across the room. The chain dragged as he pulled her down the stairs.

All of the antiques Sam had were piled into the living room. The house seemed familiar to her, but it could have been some old farmhouse out of a television show. The house was bare, and that's all that registered in her mind before Sam pulled her outside. She'd done it now. He was going to kill her. Warm sun bathed her skin while he pulled her through the knee-high grass. Crows cawed in the trees. Not another soul around. To the right of the house was a big, empty pasture. The house looked to be in a big field with the long driveway disappearing into the woods that must lead to a road. Why did she know this place?

Sam dragged her to the back of the house, where a green garden hose was attached to a spigot. Cold water hit her naked skin. "Get it off," Sam yelled. "Wash it all off."

He really was just like her dad. His dad. It was in their blood.

Joni used her right hand to wipe away the paint as Sam held the hose to her. She gulped down water as it splashed over her skin.

"You're going to pay for this," he said.

"I didn't do this."

Sam hit her face hard enough to knock her sideways into the house. He continued to spray her with water.

"I don't know what you said to her to make her sneak into my room and get those keys, but if she says one fucking thing about her dead friends, I'm going to shut her up. That'll be on you."

Joni gritted her teeth and yanked the drill bit from her arm. Why did Sam care about the delusions in Mary's head?

"Get up," Sam said, and Joni did.

He never planned on killing her. He was going to hold her hostage for the rest of her life and torture her. Joni couldn't take it. This wasn't how her life was supposed to be, all because of her father. He did this, and Joni suffered the consequences.

So did Sam.

But Sam wasn't Joni's problem.

She raised her arm and slammed her fist into the left side of his chest. When she pulled her hand away, the four-inch drill bit stuck out. Sam looked down.

Run.

The chain slowed her down, but she gathered it in her arms as she ran through the field toward the woods. She didn't turn around to see if Sam followed, just ran. Sweet gum balls poked the bottom of her bare feet. Thorns scratched her thighs, and she heard her dad's voice say, *You got yourself into this, now get yourself out,* and she kept running as hard as she could. She stumbled over a log. Was he dead? Was Sam dead? No, that drill bit was too small to kill him. Breath came to her in short takes.

That's when Sam called her name. Joni froze. Then, "Oh, Jo-nee." His voice was in the distance behind her. She looked left and right and made herself move again. She couldn't stop. His voice was closer when he spoke. "I like hide and seek. It's not as fun as *Mother May I.*"

Dense woods surrounded her, and she moved farther in about fifty yards. Suddenly Sam was to her left and gaining quickly.

"Mother, may I break Joni's neck?"

The chain was heavy in her arms. As quietly as she could, she took cover behind a log and covered herself with pine needles. The thought of bugs and spiders freaked her out. And snakes. But she'd take her chances with the ground. *Please don't let him find me,* she thought as she covered her naked body.

He moved forward to the left. "Mother, may I stab Joni in the eyes?" He continued straight without stopping. He didn't have the luxury of shoes either, but he wasn't weighed down by a chain. Joni would wait him out. Wait until dark to come before she moved. She kept still, trying not to let the chain rattle as she dug her back deeper into the ground. Was she covered enough? Dirt and leaves and pine needles stuck to her damp skin.

Sam called her name again, this time in a clipped tone. He was now thirty to fifty yards ahead. His voice carried in the distance and traveled to her right. Was he circling around and going back to the house? Moments passed, and Joni heard nothing.

But she never had time to relax. By the time she heard the leaves crunching behind her, it was too late. Sam reached over the log and grabbed her hair again. Joni screamed and swung the chain at him, but he grabbed it and used it to hold her steady. She tried to pull away, but in her weakened state, she was no match for him. He dragged her out of the woods like a dog.

He hosed her down again, and that's when she gave up. "Just kill me."

Sam's grip was tight on the chain. Without a word, he shut off the water and pulled her back inside. Coming from the front door, now she knew why the house was so familiar. Joni stepped toward the stairs, but he pulled her down a hallway. "You lost your bedroom privileges." He opened a door, said, "Mother, may I? Yes, you may," and shoved her down the wooden stairs.

***

It was difficult to find people who didn't want to be found. That only posed as an obstacle, not a definite road block. The hard part was getting started and too many directions to go in. Cyrus had made calls to all the counties where the original seven bodies had been found and asked them to expand their search from a one-mile radius to a three-mile radius. He didn't know if Joni was face down in a ditch or stuffed in a hidey-hole in a detached garage somewhere.

He'd been checking Sam Dixon's phone records. He hadn't made a call from his cell phone in over forty-eight hours, which meant he probably dumped the phone. The phone records proved to be useless. He spent over an hour connecting the numbers to people and places. They were waiting on bank statements to see the last places he'd spent money.

The last place Sam Dixon was seen was North Macon Psychiatric Hospital when Mary left. Would a money trail lead to Joni? Her purse and phone were left in her house, but Cyrus couldn't be too sure that a credit card in her name wasn't used. If the judge would hurry and sign those damn warrants, Cyrus could move on.

They also checked Sam's employment record. Not only did Sam Dixon move from house to house, he also job-hopped and there was nothing consistent about his work. He went from operating a tow truck to fast food to an electronics store. He'd had over fifteen jobs in the last fifteen years, but after 2011, they had nothing on him, and now they were checking under the name Sam Doolan.

"This just came back." Deavers handed Cyrus printouts from the lab. All it showed was that the blood was O positive. Still waiting to see if it matched Joni.

Deavers unwrapped a fried pie and said, "Prints put Dixon at the scene though." He took a bite and cherry filling oozed out.

"We have print matches for Joni, Mary, Teddy, and Sam." Cyrus looked at Deavers. "Amanda Flockhart? How was she in the system?"

"Various counties when she questioned detectives about the *Cotton Mouth Killer* bodies." The fried pie was gone. "You know how it goes."

"We need to bring her in," Cyrus said.

"Already on it."

There was a commotion down the hall, and an agent went running. Cyrus and Deavers followed him. Two women were yelling at each other near the elevator. It was Nina Dixon and Lacey Chaskey.

"You should have had that woman and her offspring put to sleep like dogs," Lacey said.

"Your brother is the dog."

"Believe me," Lacey said. "I'd be more than happy to put a needle in his arm. And when his little bastard son is found, I'd be more than happy to do the same to him."

"Ladies," Cyrus said, and thought they were about to go at it in the middle of the third-floor lobby. "Now is not the time."

Turning on him, Lacey said, "Have you found my niece?" He wasn't about to get into specifics, but the answer to that question was an obvious no. "You should question every single one of her family members. She has children, doesn't she?"

Nina was appalled. "You leave my children alone; this has nothing to do with them. My sister and nephew are innocent. You Chaskeys just couldn't leave us alone, had to go dig that knife in just a little deeper."

"May I remind you," Lacey said, "that it was your sister who contacted Joni in the first place, and against my better judgment, she proceeded to form a relationship with this woman? And now I find out Mary has a son no one told Joni about. If you ask me, this whole fiasco was planned from the get-go. Is your sister really crazy or is she faking it?"

"Ladies," Cyrus said, stepping between these two cobras. "This is not helping." He looked at Nina. "I thought you were going home to make phone calls."

Nina gave Lacey a look. "My son is at my house, and my daughter is at Mary's. They said they'd call me if they heard anything. I just don't know what to do," she said, exasperated.

Lacey said, "I'll tell you what to do."

"I will sue you," Nina said, "for harassment. Slander against my nephew. The damage my sister suffered all these years." Nina stood to her full height, chest all puffed out. "Keep at it, Princess, and I'll be telling you what to do."

Cyrus nodded at the other agent. He took Nina by the arm and led her away.

Under her breath, Lacey said, "Hippopotamus."

267

"Lacey—"

Her eyebrows arched. "Don't disrespect me, Agent Kenner."

"*Ms. Chaskey*," he said, and gestured for her to follow him down the hall to his office. "Have a seat."

The space was small and covered in case files. To everyone else, it looked like a pigsty, but it was his organized mess. "Do you have anything new?"

Ms. Chaskey scowled at him, said, "I came here to ask you the same thing. This is your job, Agent Kenner, not mine." She pointed out the tiny window. "You should be out there right now trying to find my niece, not scouring over your paperwork collection."

Lacey Chaskey was a beautiful woman who looked like she took pride in herself. Although her gray skirt was past the knee, the matching jacket she wore was unbuttoned, exposing a tight, fitting royal blue blouse.

He didn't want to tell her he wasn't about to go driving down roads hoping to spot something. That's what the officers were for, plus the missing persons team was interviewing and keeping in touch with Fayette County. It was a sit and wait game until something came up.

"I have money," she said, her voice about to crack. "If that's what this young man wants, I have it. I can—" She pressed her fingers to her lips, swallowed hard. "I can get it right now. Just say the word."

"I don't think money is what this is about."

"He should pay for what he's done."

"Ms. Chaskey—"

"Please, call me Lacey."

Oh, now she wanted to be informal. "Lacey, as soon as we find them—"

Her fingers twisted the necklace she wore. "I'm speaking about my brother. The DA didn't push for the death penalty because you wanted the glory and let him become this serial killer celebrity."

"That's not what happened." They had seven murdered women, three of which were Jane Does, and the plea bargain was for their identities plus the guilty pleas. In return, Lyle Chaskey only wanted his daughter kept safe. Cyrus had seen a monster melt away to nothing that day, all for the sake of Joni. It was only through his wife's suicide that they were able to get the confession.

Cyrus said, "You know enough about what happened to understand how sensitive the case was. We had a solid case, but no jury was going to give him the death penalty for a prostitute when Lyle didn't have a previous record. He'd be out of jail by now if that's all we had on him. Since he is already in prison, it was a lot less tax money to tack on ten more to his sentence for Melanie Pavroy, but now that we have Sheila Graninch and Rachel Ikenbor, you may just be able to witness your brother's last breath."

"How does any of this help Joni?" she said. Cyrus sat down in his chair, clearly in over his head again, but he'd never admit that to a single soul. Then Lacey said, "You don't know what you're doing, do you?"

"Yes, I do."

"Have you even worked a missing person's case before?"

"It's what I do. That's what I specialize in."

"You must not have a very good track record," Lacey snapped, and tossed her tiny purse on his desk as she eyeballed all the missing women's photos he had tacked to a wall. There were over sixty.

"Listen, lady. That's all the missing women from my region in the last thirty years, and I'm slowly finding out they weren't missing at all, just moved away. I think some of these women were Chaskey's. As far as Joni, my primary suspect, is Sam Dixon,

269

so I'm trying to get into his mind and find every scrap of information that I can about him."

"Do you have any leads on anything else?"

Cyrus had to step carefully, since this was an active case. "Between you and me?" he said, and Lacey nodded. "We found Amanda Flockhart's fingerprints inside the house."

***

Sharp pain rode her spine when she tried to move her legs, but she made herself do it. The windowless basement left her blind to the surroundings. She pulled herself to a sitting position and concluded that something was wrong with her hip, but not broken. Maybe it was twisted. Or maybe her back was out of whack and caused the hip pain. After being doused with cold water and thrown into a cold concrete basement, even her bones were cold. Her vision adjusted to the dark, and her skin and scalp itched. Bugs from the woods must have gotten on her.

Could she loop the chain from the top of the basement stairs and hang herself? End her life like her mother? Like mother, like daughter; isn't that what they say?

Then something else crossed her mind. Did she have enough strength to wrap the chain around Sam's neck? Kill him dead?

The basement was maybe twenty-by-twenty feet of nothing but empty space. The house was smaller and different. Maybe this wasn't the house Joni thought it was.

If Mary was right and Sam didn't have time to prepare, then what made him make his move? He was being unreasonable. But name a crazy person who *was* reasonable. Sam made choices. Very bad choices.

Surely Sam locked the door at the top of the stairs. Why waste energy trying that?

So, how was she going to get out of here?

Just then, the door opened, and a flash light came to life above the stairs. Mary was yelling at Sam, her arms wild with anger. "Sam," Joni said, her voice raspy. When his grip was tight, Sam shoved Mary down the stairs, and like a rag doll, she flipped a few times on her way down, then landed face down at the bottom.

"Wait," Joni said, but Sam closed the door. A second later, Mary curled into a ball and cried. "Mary, it's okay." Joni carefully crawled over to her, and patted her on the back, was aware that the woman could flip out on her at any moment, blame her for the pain.

Not only was she crying, her breathing was labored and wheezy. Joni pressed her palm to Mary's chest and touched something thick and wet. Wet paint crossed her mind, but it was too warm. Mary was bleeding.

"Oh God." Joni tried to pry her hand away, but Mary stayed curled into a ball. "Let me help you."

"The baby was crying."

Joni choked back a sob; she was beyond trying to keep it all in. Mary's paintbrush was in her skirt pocket, and so was a set of keys. The keys to the padlocks. Joni tried two before she could unlock the weight around her arm.

"I want—"

"Shh." Joni pulled Mary's shirt up and saw blood oozing out. "Did you do this to yourself, or did Sam do it?"

Mary touched Joni's face. "We need to get dressed... for the party."

"Okay," Joni said, and ran her fingers through Mary's hair. "We'll go to a party."

Mary coughed and groaned in pain, and Joni didn't know what to do. Joni took Mary's hand and pressed it to her cheek. She felt so warm.

When the door opened again, Joni scooted away from Mary and pressed her back to the cold wall as Sam walked down the stairs. When Sam got to the bottom, he looked between the both of them, then walked up to Mary, leaned down and said, "You're not in charge of me. You gave me away, remember?" and Joni used the distraction to loop the chain around Sam's neck.

Chapter Twenty-three

Without raising her voice, Lacey had brought Amanda to tears in a matter of minutes. Cyrus had been trying to question Amanda about the fingerprint, which was standard procedure, but suspicious when taking into consideration they found it on the doggy door. Then Lacey barged in and hadn't let up. "I don't care that you didn't steal anything. It's morally wrong."

"And illegal," Cyrus added for good measure.

"Above all else," Lacey said. "I trusted you when my niece said I shouldn't. What would possess you to do such a thing? Did you even think about the consequences? Have you no shame?"

The room was suddenly quiet, the only noise coming from Amanda sucking in air. Cyrus studied her for a moment. The scars on her face were noticeable, but a dog attack wouldn't be a person's first guess. Cyrus thought about the blood on the kitchen floor.

"Did you have anything to do with this?" Cyrus said.

"No."

"Are you willing to give a DNA sample?"

"Yes," she said, and wiped her face on her arm.

"How'd you get past the dogs?"

Amanda blinked back tears. "I—I made a mistake, okay? They were nice dogs, but I didn't know that."

"What did you do?" Lacey said. Amanda shook her head, and Lacey put her hand on top of Amanda's, but the gesture wasn't sincere.

Cyrus took in the cold look on Lacey's face and wondered if he should get her out of here. They were getting nothing out of Amanda.

"I poisoned them," Amanda said. "I'm sorry. I'm so sorry. I won't write the book, just don't be mad at me."

"I'm not mad at you," Lacey said, then to Cyrus, "I want her arrested."

"No," Amanda said. "This is all a misunderstanding."

Cyrus stood. He'd let someone else take Amanda to jail. Right now, he had more important things to do.

"Wait," Amanda said. "I have information that may help you."

Cyrus leaned in close to Amanda. "She's been missing for almost twenty-four hours, and *now* you have information because you're in trouble?" Cyrus had to ask Lacey to leave, and she mumbled something about handcuffs on her way out. "What do you have?" Cyrus sat back down.

"Joni called me the night they pulled Rachel from the lake, asking about Darla Doolan and if she had a son."

"I know this already. We're looking into this guy." Cyrus got up.

Amanda grabbed his arm. "I couldn't let it go," she said, her red swollen eyes serious. "I kept asking myself, why would someone pretend to be Darla's son, and why Darla? So I dug further into Darla's life, but I didn't find anything."

"Do I need to remind you I don't have time for your stories?"

"All I know," Amanda said, "is that Darla Doolan graduated from Athens High, and fifteen years later, Sam Dixon was fired from there. I found that out this morning."

"What else?"

"Once his name was in the news, I referenced it to some of Lyle's victims. Sam drives the same model car as Colleen Garrish. Paige Folly was a swim instructor and the media just said Sam used to work cleaning pools. Joni is Lyle's daughter. Mary was a victim—"

Cyrus couldn't get out of the room fast enough. Amanda may have been on to something. In his office, he grabbed two boxes of files and went into the large conference room where Deavers was following up on the last places Sam spent money.

"You found something?" Deavers said.

Cyrus pulled out all the files, then grabbed the papers containing information on what they knew so far about Sam. "I'm looking for similarities between Sam and the victims' lives. What cars they drove. Where they worked. Hung out. Sam worked at Athens High where Darla graduated. That's not a coincidence." Cyrus told him everything Amanda said.

Sam tried to make his life like the victims. Closer to Lyle, like stepping into the serial killer's life. Sam's first job was in a packaging store. Colleen Garrish worked at a packaging store. She also drove a blue Corolla. They'd been so focused on the dump sites, but what about the places they lived?

"What happens when you're sixteen and you find out your father is a serial killer?"

"Either hate him or want to connect," Deavers said.

Another agent named Gavin Hallahan walked into the room. "Parrino just tossed Chaskey's cell. Found a cell phone and letters from Dixon. They're faxing them now."

"Thanks," Cyrus said.

Lyle Chaskey was a liar. He'd told Cyrus that he'd only communicated with Sam a few times when the boy had first written to him. Second, he never told his own daughter about his relationship with him. Part of Cyrus wanted to go back to GSP and beat the shit out of him, but that wasn't going to get them anywhere.

"Hey," Deavers said. "Tracy Doolan worked at a psych hospital in Macon when Darla went missing. She's the older sister. You think she knew Mary?"

"It's worth looking into," Cyrus said. "Nina said Mary has been in and out." Would it be worth dragging the Doolan's into this? Yes, he told himself. Everything mattered.

Hallahan came over when he realized what they were doing. "It's all over the place with no trail. What if he's taking on other identities? Where do we start on that? Sam Graninch? Sam Ikenbor?"

"Sam Chaskey?" Cyrus said. "Is that how he's been operating? As Lyle's son?"

"Get rid of the sister," Deavers said, and he becomes an only child. He's curious about how Lyle lived his life."

Heat prickled the back of Cyrus's neck as his heart slammed into his chest. It felt so good to have something. He grabbed the file on Lyle. "He grew up on farmland in Jefferson. That's thirty minutes northwest of Athens. Here's the address."

Cyrus ran to his computer. He pulled up the city archives search engine and typed in the address. After ten minutes, Cyrus had found that the house had been built in 1905, and had been in the Chaskey family name until it was sold in 2000. But in 2010 the house was sold again, going back to the Chaskeys. And Cyrus Kenner knew damn well Lyle Chaskey couldn't buy a house from prison.

"I got you now, you little bastard."

***

The good news was that Joni managed to twist the chain tight. The bad news was that she was running out of strength, and from this angle, with him kneeling, Joni had to press her knee into his back for leverage.

But he slipped free and when he did, he'd barely taken a full breath before he came after her. He swung the chain and caught her across the knee, swung again, and her knees buckled beneath her. With the next blow, the chain caught her at the side of her head.

"I'm going to mail tiny pieces of you to our father. I don't think he likes you best anymore."

"None of this is going to make you feel better."

"I already feel better and I haven't even done anything yet." He swung the chain and caught her bad arm as it wrapped around it.

"Mary is dying."

"I know," Sam said. "She was too fucked up to take care of me as a kid. Why should I care about her?"

"She was sick." Sam seemed to have shut off his feelings because he shrugged like he didn't care. Joni said, "What do you want?"

"I want to make him proud of me."

"By killing me? That's not going to do it. Don't you think you could have handled this better? I could have helped you connect with him."

Sam's face went cold. "You think I'm stupid?" When he came for her this time, he went for her throat, grabbed tight and slammed her head against the floor. Her vision blurred with each blow her head took and she thought her skull cracked. Joni grabbed at his hands. "This is what you wanted," Sam said. "That night in the hotel. You know this is what you wanted."

A second later, Mary was on Sam's back, and clawing at his face. He fell forward, and Joni sucked in air to catch her breath. Her head went dizzy and everything swayed, the room spinning like treetops in a storm. When Joni finally got her bearings, she heard the noise coming from a few feet away. It was Mary, and Sam was on top of her, killing her.

Joni slapped her hands over her ears, and closed her eyes, and threw up. This was not happening to her. This was not real.

For a moment she was frozen with indecision, then thought it was now or never, and took to the stairs. She slipped once in Mary's blood, and got to the first step, but it was too late. Sam grabbed her by her hair and dragged her over to Mary.

"You see what you made me do?" He shoved her face down. "Look at her."

All Joni saw were those elephants at the circus. Those beautiful, majestic creatures. Her father told her that people who could control another's fear had the power over them, and elephants were no different. But how did they make them have fear? To her horror, he'd told her they beat them for days, until their spirits were crushed because even though the elephant knew it was much bigger than the man, and all he had to do was step on him, the elephant feared the pain.

Joni tasted blood in the back of her throat and knew she was going to die. It only took one day to beat the spirit out of her. She thought back to all those times her daddy locked her in the basement as punishment. He was trying to control her fear. It was manipulation, and with that, he ventured into emotional abuse.

It started with his own mother, in this very house. Joni had been here many years ago when she came with Aunt Lacey to clean it out so it could be sold. Joni should have burned the house to the ground that day.

Was she glad Mary no longer had to suffer her own life? Yes. Was she sad Mary was dead? Joni no longer cared. She wished now she'd never laid eyes on Mary Rancotti. One way or another, we pay for our sins. That night in the motel came back to her. She caused her own pain, and she will pay for that now.

Sam said, "I'm going to visit our father on Saturday. This time I'm going to tell him *everything*. Maybe he'll tell me what I should do with you." He shoved her aside and walked up the stairs, giving her one more glance before he locked the door.

Three months, Joni thought, and looked at Mary's dead eyes. She did this for three months. Joni closed Mary's eyes and ran her hand one last time through her hair. *No more suffering, Mary.* There was no telling how long Joni would have to go through this. But she couldn't. It was time to end this right now. No way was she going to continue to be a punching bag for Sam. Joni ignored the pain throughout her body, and grabbed the chain.

She crawled her way up to the top of the stairs, found a gap where the wooden stair met the concrete wall, and dropped one end of the chain down. On the same step, she let the other end drop. Joni stopped to breathe for a moment and wondered if she could do it. Make all this pain go away. All the guilt she'd had for years.

Joni went underneath the stairs and grabbed both ends of the chain, and gave the middle a bit of slack so it would hang off the step. Then she called for Sam. Screamed his name at the top of her lungs over and over until her own head screamed with echoes.

He flung the door open and said, "What?"

"Mary's not dead. You're so stupid you didn't even do it right."

When his foot hit the third stair, Joni pulled the chain and Sam fell down the rest of the way. *How does it feel, asshole?* Joni yanked the chain free, looped some of it around her good arm and swung it at him. She hit him as hard as she could, over and over, and hit him again when he tried to get up.

She spotted the paintbrush next to him, and jumped on him, held his arms down with her legs. She pressed the handle of the paintbrush to the space between the clavicle bones. For a moment it did nothing, but the pressure had him struggling for breath. "Why won't you die?" Joni pushed down harder, let everything escape her mind, let the moment take over because she had nothing left to lose. There was a pop and warm blood filled her hands, and Sam's body jerked beneath her. He blinked a few times and Joni didn't feel one bit of remorse for what she'd done.

***

In Cyrus's opinion, there were too many damn farms in Georgia. The crows called out as though to tell them the secrets of the place. An empty pasture spread out to the right, and far in the distance, two silos stood to the sky.

A car was parked in the knee-high grass, and Rick confirmed it was Sam Dixon's Corolla. Remy Ormond asked for local SWAT along with the Critical Response Unit. The police department was on standby. With everyone in position, the place was nothing but quiet. Every person was given orders and not another word had been spoken. The house was surrounded as SWAT checked every window on the lower level for activity.

Cyrus stood a few feet away from the front porch, his eyes scanning the house. SWAT was ready to clear the house when suddenly the front door opened and Joni fell to her hands and knees. In only her underwear, she was bloody from head to toe, and screamed in confusion at the sight of the team.

Cyrus ran to her, put his hand on her back, and the team stepped inside to secure the house. She was confused and disoriented, and looked like she had been beaten to hell. "Joni," Cyrus said, but she crawled down the steps like her legs were broken. She tried to stand but fell and crawled through the tall grass as though Cyrus wasn't even there.

All the breath had been knocked out of him at the sight of her. "You're safe." He was close to her as she continued to crawl away from this house and these people who caused her so much torment. Cyrus hoped Sam would pull a gun so someone would shoot him for this. How in the world did Cyrus ever think Joni could have a safe life?

Men surrounded her, and Cyrus said, "Don't just stand there, somebody get —"

Someone shoved a blanket in his hand, and Cyrus moved closer to Joni, said, "It's okay." She slapped his hand away. "It's me. Cyrus. I'm here to help you."

Her only words were, "No. No. Nono."

"You're safe now." Cyrus wrapped the wool blanket around her.

"I want to go home," she said.

"I'm going to get you home."

Her left arm was at an odd angle, and small bubbles of pus and blood were oozing out of tiny holes in her arm.

Cyrus pulled the blanket closed and picked her up. "You're okay, Joni. I'm going to get you home." His own words caught in his throat as he carried her toward the road where he'd wait for the paramedics.

"We need an ambulance," Deavers called out from the house. "We've got a live one down here, tried to swallow a paintbrush. You should see it."

Cyrus looked down. *Good for you, Joni. Good for you.*

***

Joni opened her eyes and had no idea how long she'd been in the hospital. Sun poured through the window and landed on a small table filled with bouquets of flowers. More bouquets lined against the wall. So many flowers. Did she die?

She wasn't in any major pain, just aches throughout her body when she moved. The blanket was pulled up to her chest, and she would have sworn a blanket was on top of her head. Her arm was wrapped from wrist to shoulder in thick gauze and something kept her arm at a bent angle. Even under the blanket, she could tell her left leg was in some kind of contraption.

A nurse walked in and wasn't surprised she was awake. "Good morning," she said, and wheeled a small cart inside the room. Her name was Missy, and Missy's right arm was covered in tattoos. How could she stick needles in her arm on purpose? "Are you hungry?"

"No." Her voice was barely a whisper. "What day is it?"

"Sunday." Missy wrapped a blood pressure cuff on Joni's good arm, and she felt the IV in her vein as the cuff squeezed.

"Sunday what? How long have I been here?"

"Four days."

281

"Was I in a coma?"

Missy smiled. "No, they've kept you on some pretty strong meds after the surgery."

Joni looked at her wrist where the chain left bruises, and blood was caked underneath her fingernails. Was it her blood or the others? Missy held up a thermometer and Joni opened her mouth. These last four days had gone by without a spark of a memory.

"Are you feeling any pain?" Missy removed the thermometer. "I can get you more morphine."

Not if it would make her forget another four days. "I'm okay."

"You sure? You went through some pretty nasty stuff." Now Missy was looking closely at Joni's lips. Joni touched her face and felt bandages. "You have a lot of stitches," Missy offered. "I'll let the doctor know you're awake, and you can ask him about your injuries. I know he wants to speak with you."

"I don't want to talk to the doctor." Missy seemed surprised. Joni said, "When can I go home?"

Concerned, Missy said, "Sweetie, do you know why you're here? Do you know what happened to you?"

Joni nodded and only wished she didn't remember.

"I'll get the doctor."

As Missy walked out, Teddy walked in with a large gift bag. "Hi," he said, and stood at the foot of the bed, like he was unsure of what to say or do. His eyes were sad, but tired, as though he hadn't slept in days. "Everyone sent flowers. I brought flowers too, but I thought you'd like this," he said. He set the bag on her lap and Joni opened it. Inside were matching German shepherd stuffed animals. She didn't know if this was a cruel joke or something from his heart. "I'm glad you're awake. You've been sleeping so much. They moved you out of ICU yesterday. Joni, are you listening?"

Her eyes were focused on the dogs, but she nodded and couldn't look at him. Not knowing what to say, or what he wanted to hear, she certainly didn't want to talk about what happened.

"The nurse said I've been here for four days."

"You've been in and out, but they've done an amazing job of taking care of you. You're at one of the best hospitals. There's a guard at your door. You're safe here."

All around the room was something with Athens Regional on it. He must have been here at her bedside this whole time.

Teddy sat down on the bed, touched his hand to Joni's face. But she couldn't feel it. Putting her own hand to her face, she felt nothing because of the bandages. She pulled one of them off.

"Don't do that."

"Why is my head wrapped in this stuff?" Joni unwrapped the gauze from around her head.

"Wait for the doctor to say it's okay."

Her face felt oddly numb. And her hair? "Where's my hair?"

"They shaved your head." Teddy's face fell as he explained. "You had some fractures and gashes all over your head. I'm sure the doctor will tell you everything as soon as he gets here."

There were stitches over her face and head. "Do I look bad?" Teddy didn't answer. "Teddy, do I look like me?"

"Of course. You just have lots of injuries, and yes, they look bad, but you'll heal up just fine. You're still beautiful." Joni couldn't help but think about Amanda. He took the gauze from her hands and wrapped her head back up. "I was so worried about you. You're never leaving my sight again."

"I'm pretty sure I'm more screwed up now than I was before," Joni said, and Teddy laughed. Funny, he thought she was being sarcastic. Joni lifted the stuffed animals. "What'd you do with them?"

"They're at your house."

"You just left them there? Inside?"

"It's not like I could bring them to visit."

"What?"

283

"I promise they're safe."

Now she was confused. "Safe? As in alive?"

"Yeah," Teddy said. "My mom has been staying with them. We can call and check on them if you want. They miss you."

Joni lowered her head and cried, the pain in her head finally outweighing the pain in her heart. Her precious dogs were alive. For once, she was thankful Sam lied to her. "He told me he killed them."

"Bubba and Clyde are perfectly fine." Teddy kissed her hand.

Joni rested her head on the pillow. An ache began behind her eyes and she thought about the morphine. Maybe she needed to sleep for another four days. "I'm here," Teddy said. "Whatever you need, I'm here for you. I just want you to be okay."

"I don't think I'll be okay for a long time."

He pulled her into a hug, and she didn't have the heart to tell him how much that hurt, even though he was such a comfort right now. "Don't feel sorry for me," she said.

"None of this should have happened to you. I can't believe they actually attempted to save that fucker's life."

Cold fear hit her again. "Who?" Joni pushed Teddy back to look at him.

"Mary's dead. Sam's—"

"He's alive? He's here, isn't he?"

Teddy nodded. "He's still in critical condition. Police are all over him. Don't worry about him getting out of that bed anytime soon." His look said he wished he could make that permanent.

A doctor walked in and said hello. Teddy kissed her on the forehead and stood. He shook the doctor's hand, and Teddy said, "Thank you," then turned away. Joni didn't want him to go.

"Teddy?"

He must have heard the worry in her voice because he said, "I'm right here."

Chapter Twenty-four

It took nearly six weeks for her to recover from the injuries, and that was still putting it mildly. The nerve damage to her arm kept her from forming a complete fist, and she still couldn't fully straighten the arm. She'd spent most of that time with a physical therapist who said her arm was getting stronger every day. The head injuries healed nicely and she would have no permanent damage, which was the doctor's main concern because those were the tricky wounds.

Even with the economy gone to shit, Joni's house sold six hours after the *For Sale* sign was posted. Aunt Lacey took her in again until she could get on her feet, but this time Joni wasn't so hostile about the situation.

Bubba and Clyde stopped taking Aunt Lacey so seriously, too. She'd told them they had to live in the mudroom, but once they felt comfortable, they made their way into the kitchen. Then she said okay, but that's as far as they could go. Next was the living room, and that was okay too, but they couldn't get on the sofa. After they spent one night on the sofa, they owned the house.

Grandmother was recovering from pneumonia, and Aunt Lacey said, "You two crippled ladies are milking this for what it's worth," but she smiled and wouldn't let Joni move out if she wanted to. Not yet anyway.

Joni had to pull some major strings with Warden Parrino to get a special visitation with her father. She wanted to speak with him alone, not on a Saturday when every inmate and their grandmother were around.

Good thing Warden wouldn't let her speak with him right away because it had taken her two months to get her thoughts together. When her dad walked in, she swore he had tears in his eyes. The CO didn't give him time to hug her, brought him to his chair and sat him down.

"You look nice."

Joni had on a knitted beanie style cap to cover her fuzzy head. When she pulled it off, her father didn't flinch. "One hundred forty."

"What?"

"That's how many staples and stitches I had over my entire body. My head. My face. My lips. My arm."

Lyle looked at his hands. "I never meant—"

"To what? Be such a fucking monster that this could happen to me? You thought I was immune? I loved you more than anything, even after I knew the truth. And now, I will live with these scars for the rest of my life. Your scars."

Joni's left arm was in a sling, pins holding her bones together from Mary's drill. She barely had muscle control from her elbow to her fingers. Her right hip and left knee were fractured, and she'd just finished her last round of physical therapy and gave up the cane to walk inside here today. Her vision would never be the same, and the doctors weren't sure why, only said that head injuries were hard to determine the full extent. The doctor asked her about reconstructive surgery for the scars on her forehead, but that wasn't something she wanted to deal with right now.

According to her father, *she looked nice.*

He said, his voice almost a whisper, "Did he rape you?"

Is that what bothered him the most? Would it shame him? "Yeah, Dad, he raped me. Over and over, just the way you liked it. Too bad you couldn't watch. Sam should have recorded it for you. Is that what you wanted? Is that why you had him watching me?"

Her father snapped his eyes to hers. "You should have protected yourself."

"Like Mary? I watched her die, Dad. How was she supposed to protect herself? How was I supposed to protect myself? You blame those women for what you did to them like they deserved it."

"They weren't doing anything with their lives. Just like you aren't doing anything with yours."

If she hadn't sensed the coldness in his tone, she would have been shocked by his words. She was well aware of the CO who remained in the room because Lyle wasn't allowed to be left alone. "I hope when you die you go to hell."

"Lessons in life are complex."

"What's that supposed to mean? Doesn't it bother you that this happened to me?"

Lyle said through clenched teeth, "You are not a victim."

"I'm letting you know now that this is the last time that we'll see each other and I'm not taking any more of your lies. Your *lies*. You don't deserve me in your life."

"You have your life. Go live it. This will make you stronger. Don't let it happen again."

Was this another of his stupid life lessons? Nearly ended up dead, and it's all her fault? "You knew exactly who Sam was that day I asked you about him. You could have warned me, but instead you let this happen."

"What did he say?"

"Nothing. But I've come to the conclusion that your son was jealous and wanted me out of the picture to be closer to you. He was a snitch."

A smile came to his face, and Joni thought she'd be sick. "There isn't enough room for both of you."

"What's that supposed to mean?"

"I'd choose you over him in a heartbeat. He doesn't know what family is." Lyle tried to touch her hand, but Joni pulled away. "Come on, baby. Don't be like that. Give yourself some time to get over all of this, and you'll come visit again. I know you will."

His convoluted brain just didn't get it. Blood or not, she was done with him.

"I know what you did to your mother."

"Joni," he said, his voice getting stern. "I told you to stay away from her."

"Grandmother tells me stories." Joni cleared her throat and lowered her voice. "She tucks me in late at night. Sometimes I crawl into bed with her. I trace my fingers over her old bones and wonder where you touched her."

"Shut up, Joni."

"You raped your own mother."

"She deserved it."

"And my mother killed herself because of you."

"She was a whore."

With those words, Joni jumped across the table and grabbed at her father's face. But he was too fast. In a second, he had her flipped to her back on the table. He said, "You don't respect me. You're a whore just like her and have forgotten everything I've taught you. I didn't raise a whore." Then he spit in her face.

Even with cuffs on his wrists, her father was a violent man. The officer pulled him off and shoved him to the wall. Cold eyes stared at her. They escorted him away, same as fifteen years ago. Except this time, she didn't want to go with her daddy. In fact, she no longer wanted to be his daughter. All these years she'd compromised herself for him, but he just gave her the last piece of the puzzle to rid herself of every ounce of guilt she'd ever felt.

"I'll be there when they execute you."

Lyle turned, said, "I've got what they want. I'm not going anywhere."

Chapter Twenty-five

People grow comfortable in places where there's no threat. They breathe deep the air around them, and relax their minds and bodies. They trust their surroundings and become emotionally attached to the peace.

Prison was not a place to grow comfortable. Enemies lurked around every corner. Noises became unbearable. Sleep never.

All those sleepless nights so many years ago when Lyle would get in his car and drive for hours. He missed that. The sound of the engine. The feel of the steering wheel. Tires on the highway. It didn't matter whether he was driving on a dirt road, back road, curvy road, bridge, highway. People who never went to prison took things like driving for granted.

Lyle took a lot of things for granted, too.

He wanted his old life back.

More than anything, though, he wanted to snap Sam's neck for fucking up the plan. He was not supposed to give Joni his real name; he was not supposed to get involved. He was supposed to be a random guy, with a random name that went along with her to the motel and scare her out of being a whore.

The boy had spent some time in Diagnostic and Classification in Jackson. Same as Lyle. Then he was sent to Central State, where he wouldn't conform. Apparently, prison life wasn't for Sam. He was sent to GSP, where Lyle was shocked to see him. Who knew they'd end up like this?

For the last three months, Lyle had been playing the part of the doting father. He kept Sam safe. Told him who would ruin him, which pigs in uniform would turn their heads, and the best way to hide contraband was not up his ass.

Doting father, Lyle thought as he sat down on a bench next to Sam. The rats were let outside twice a day for an hour. This was when they usually talked. Well, Lyle talked, Sam listened. The most he did was nod and talk in a baby voice, which made him a huge target.

"You okay?"

Sam smiled. Always happy to be in his father's company.

Except Lyle knew without a doubt that Sam wasn't his son. He knew because he'd seen the swell in Mary's belly the first time he'd raped her. She was so messed up; she had no idea she was pregnant and asked Lyle to take care of her. He said sure and actually thought about it. Maybe that was why he couldn't kill her. Now he wished he had. Should have choked the life out of her and her little bastard.

Lyle could see himself now, slipping his hands around Sam's throat. Or maybe he could try something new, and shove a blade into his heart, watch his eyes scream with fear while his voice failed him.

Sam was an annoying rat who never gave up writing to him, but Lyle never replied. Not until Sam mentioned that he'd been following his daughter around and she'd been a bad girl. So Lyle wrote to him, said, sure, keep an eye on her. The more Sam told him; the madder Lyle got. How could she do those things? The thought made his skin crawl.

Sam said something, and Lyle leaned closer. "What's that?"

"Still nothing?"

"She'll come around."

It had been a year since he'd last spoken with his daughter, and it bothered him she wasn't here every other Saturday. Bothered him he didn't know if she read the letters he'd sent every week. He loved his daughter more than anyone in the world, but Joni needed to be punished for her choices. Lyle had no idea that Sam was going to take things to the extreme, but he'd thought one thing for sure. Joni would kill the little rat bastard and Lyle would never have to hear from him again.

But that's not what happened because Sam fucked up. Didn't plan. Took things too far. Lost control, and did very bad things to his little girl.

So, for now, Lyle slipped back into the duplicity that came so naturally to him and played the part of father to his son. And one day, Sam's punishment would come as well.

A note from the author:

Thank you for purchasing my book. I hope you enjoyed reading it as much as I enjoyed writing it. When I set out to write this story, my purpose was to show how an individual's choice can affect a rather large amount of people. A killer's family is also hurt by those unspeakable crimes they've committed. Joni is a special character to me, created solely through my imagination, and I hope I did her justice while bringing her to life.

Keep in touch at:

Kristyroland.com

You can also find me on Facebook:
Facebook.com/Kristy-roland

Thank you for reading!

Made in the USA
Middletown, DE
28 April 2022